In Want of a Knife

In Want of a Knife

A Little Library Mystery

Elizabeth Kane Buzzelli

CROOKED
LANE

NEW YORK

Published in the United States by Crooked Lane Books, an imprint of The Quick Brown Fox & Company LLC.

Crooked Lane Books and its logo are trademarks of The Quick Brown Fox & Company LLC.

Library of Congress Catalog-in-Publication data available upon request.

ISBN (hardcover): 978-1-68331-737-1
ISBN (ePub): 978-1-68331-738-8
ISBN (ePDF): 978-1-68331-739-5

Cover illustraton by Stephen Gardner
Book design by Jennifer Canzone

Printed in the United States.

www.crookedlanebooks.com

Crooked Lane Books
34 West 27th St., 10th Floor
New York, NY 10001

First Edition: September 2018

10 9 8 7 6 5 4 3 2 1

For Elizabeth Mae Schurig, who doesn't yet know she deserves acknowledgment just by being born. And for her sister, Hazel, of the wonderful smile; Eli for being serious; Aria for being an elf; Ollie, trilingual before the age of one; Vella, with stars in her eyes; and Scarlett Bea for scooping up all the dimples in the world.

For Shawne Benson, who got me back on the path with a couple of questions.

Josh Mullin, my techno-genius, who keeps me writing—literally.

Carolyn Hall and Patty Sumpter, women who help me through life.

Edna Mae Karpinski, because she knows all my secrets, so I have to put her in here or she'll tell.

Tony Buzzelli, my lifelong love.

Mr. Darcy to Elizabeth Bennet:

"There is, I believe, in every disposition a tendency to some particular evil, a natural defect, which not even the best education can overcome."

—Jane Austen, *Pride and Prejudice*

Prologue

One thing with Harold Roach was that he liked driving best when early dawn spread—wild and red—up the eastern sky, with Lake Michigan to the west, still hung in night, and nobody else was on the road to bother him.

Five days a week Harold drove his pickup along U.S. Route 31, heading to Traverse City to get the newspapers he'd soon be delivering to small towns along the Michigan shore.

This morning, like every morning, Harold had a lot on his mind. For one, there were the deliveries he had to do fast. Christina wanted him back soon so they could get into town and buy new carpeting for the living room. She was into spring-cleaning. "Building her nest" was the way Christina put it as if she was a robin, or another bird with expensive tastes.

Another thing about Harold was that he didn't like to let his young wife down, but he'd checked their savings three times yesterday and he was going to have to nix that carpet she wanted so badly, which could lead to some long, cold nights for him.

With all the thinking and worrying going on in his head, it was a miracle he noticed the white bundle lying beside the road ahead of him.

He slowed down because the one thing Harold always said about himself was that he was a careful man. He wasn't the kind of man who took his eye off the ball, no matter whose ball it was, nor why it needed watching. So, no matter how deep his thoughts got, he kept his eyes on the road, watching for deer. They'd be running crazy now that it was early May. Tom turkeys would be spreading their tails at the edge of the road, surrounded by a flock of hens who were more interested in new shoots of grass than a spread of pretty feathers and all that should have meant to them.

One thing Harold knew for sure was that when sex was on the table animals went crazy. He knew well enough how sex could almost ruin a man. One terrible sin and a man forever had a blot on his soul. Forever worried about somebody finding out.

One of his axioms for his sons was: keep it in your pants. A thing he'd preached to his two boys early, though only Robby'd half-listened and hurried into marrying Joyce Farmer, who had a baby six months later. He could still swear that baby—his granddaughter, who he loved by now—looked a lot like Joyce's last boyfriend, before Robby.

And then there was Ken. Twenty-two with two kids that he was already supporting. Not like it was back when Christina and Harold were brought together by their mothers and everything was on the up-and-up. Those two women were in the same church and worked together on church dinners and cleanings, and one day Christina's mother mentioned she had a daughter who didn't like to push herself forward but was in need of a husband. Harold's mother said she had a very sound son who'd lost his wife in a car accident a couple of years before, leaving two young boys who sorely needed a mother.

"My son's forty-two years old. Getting up there. About time he found himself another woman." Harold's mother had nodded, and the two women agreed that between the two of them they could better their children's lives. And that was that.

For himself, Harold was grateful for Christina and wished his boys would've listened and brought the girls home to her before they got them pregnant. But they didn't. And there they were. Stuck for life. Or maybe not stuck. Robbie seemed happy enough with his baby girl—no matter who she looked like.

The thing with the bundle lying beside the highway was that it was really noticeable, even for a man with a lot on his mind. It wasn't at all like a thrown-from-a-window bag of garbage. Too big.

He stopped the truck next to it and then, though pretty sure it was just an old white rug, he pulled ahead, parked his pickup on the verge, and got out, flashlight in hand. He ambled back to stare down at the abandoned bundle. He walked around it, checking it from one end to the other. A growing breeze picked up the edges of the dirty white cloth. No rug, that was for sure. He figured, since it was probably meant for the dump and might be hospital waste, he'd keep his hands in his pockets and toe the thing. Still could be something valuable rolled up inside, like he'd read about other people finding. Good stuff: jewels or a stash of mob money.

But this was dirty, flimsy looking material. Maybe a roll of cloth lost in transit.

He pushed at it lightly with his toe, then harder, until the whole thing moved, as if one part of it was connected to all parts of it.

Interested now, Harold squatted and poked the rags with his flashlight until the bundle gave a little more. He poked again. He hit something hard. The bundle rolled toward the ditch and the material unrolled and a young girl's pale face, surrounded by a messy swirl of blond hair stuck through with sticks and grass, stared up at him.

Startled, Harold yelled at the girl. She didn't sit up and laugh, though her blind-looking blue eyes were wide open. She did nothing but stare as he backed away, one step at a time, keeping his eyes fixed on her until he turned and ran to his pickup.

That was one more thing about Harold Roach; he wasn't a man who got fooled easily. If he didn't know another thing in the whole world, Harold Roach knew death when he saw it.

Part 1

"I am half agony, half hope."

—Jane Austen, *Persuasion*

Chapter 1

Jenny Weston turned over in her narrow, childhood bed and swore one of her favorite curses under her breath: "Hell's bells and panther tracks." She whispered the words, liking it most because no one knew what it meant.

Seven thirty. There was no reason to get out of bed. It was a Saturday and she didn't have a single need to be awake. No real job to go to, only Tony Ralenti's mail for his new construction company, Little Libraries, Inc., to take care of. Invoices and blueprints to go to the post office on Monday because she was like an office manager for him, with a salary as small as her duties. Monday was two days away. The trip to the post office would take no more than a half an hour, so that left the rest of the week to do nothing.

No real job in over a year. She laid back and put an arm over her eyes. With the weight of her arm holding her down she listened to a car go by on Elderberry Street; then she listened to the buzzing inside her head, like bees but without one solid, stinging thought.

This must be what getting old would be like, Jenny told herself, spitting strands of long black hair from her mouth. Up at the crack of dawn. Feed the chickens. Milk the cows. Dash off a letter to Keith Robbins, city manager of Bear Falls, complaining about the garbage men coming too early and clanking her cans together so she couldn't sleep.

No chickens. No cows. Not even those small needs for Jenny Weston . . . who'd lost her big life in Chicago and now settled for a very little life, in a very little town, on a very little street, in a very little house . . . to get out of bed.

She rolled over again and groaned. Was it that time of month? The time when she ticked off all she'd lost in her marriage to Ronald

Korman, Chicago attorney at law and cheating bastard who ran off to Guatemala with a big-breasted, tiny-waisted Spanish husband-stealer?

Once a month she came up with all the reasons she despised Ronald Korman and chanted her mantra: *He's out of my life. Better things are coming . . .* until now it didn't seem so much like a mantra but more like a little kid's hopeful prayer.

So okay. *This month I'll get back into a legal job. This month I'm getting my hair cut so I don't look like a guitar player in a nineties rock group. This month I'm going to help Mom around the house more.*

Or even bigger: *This month I'm going to get my resume out to law firms in Chicago.*

Or even: *This month I'm going to decide about Tony.*

She sighed, sat up, and swung her bare feet flat against the cold floor. Mom would be out in the kitchen cleaning something or baking something. Mom was always busy, and she didn't moan about her lot in life, which should have been a good example for Jenny but wasn't.

Zoe Zola, their neighbor, would be over for coffee soon but all she'd say, if Jenny dared to grouse to her little friend about her misery, would be for Jenny to put her big girl pants on and get her life moving.

No help at all, this Little Person with the big brain and big ego who had somehow taken over a big chunk of Jenny's life.

Through the slightly opened window on the backyard, Jenny heard wind whipping bare hickory branches, one against another, then pushing hard at the window glass: a breath in, a breath out. Not the way she wanted to start her Saturday: with a cold north wind; with futile worry about what she would be when she finally grew up; and not with getting up way too early.

Maybe she wouldn't get up at all. She sat with her shoulders slumped. Maybe she would fall back into bed, cover her head with the yellow blanket, and let the wind blow through the room if it wanted to, as long as everybody and everything else is the world left her alone on this, her monthly loser day.

Chapter 2

Next door, the local, almost-famous writer, Zoe Zola, slid out of bed at seven thirty with the feeling of something coming at her. The feeling trickled down to her stomach and made her queasy. A day like this—from the first pat of her feet on the floor of her bedroom—came straight from nowhere and went nowhere except she knew she was going to be unhappy. The feeling was there, and her day was shot to hell already.

She shuffled barefoot into the kitchen, followed by her very sleepy, sometimes grumpy, one-eyed dog, Fida, who always ran into the door at least once when Zoe let her out to pee.

While Fida was battling the May wind to get her bottom close to the ground so she didn't wet herself, Zoe made coffee and filled a bowl with cereal, thinking that her uneasiness came from dreaming things she didn't want to dream anymore. Or maybe she'd cried in her sleep. Or it could have been all that talk of marriage the night before as she sat on Dora and Jenny Weston's year-round front porch with flames from the little gas stove throwing moving shadows up the walls.

Dora had said how fast the days were going; she'd said June would be there before they knew it. The three of them talked about spring wedding announcements and were soon on to the spring whispers of rushed weddings to come.

Three big weddings that they knew of in town, so far. Big church weddings with white dresses and monumental receptions in a Traverse City banquet hall where maybe a dove or two might fly above the guests—always a bad idea. Then would come the surprise weddings that embarrassed parents passed off with bland faces.

She'd said last night and thought again—there was nothing like the boredom after Christmas and New Years to get kid's hormones racing. Dora said she was missing the point of love and Dora was probably right, though Jenny agreed with Zoe: hormones.

"Marriage. Who needs it? Such a big deal over a license to have sex," Jenny said. "Since when do kids care it it's legal? Just nature overruling good sense. Then they get in trouble, there's a baby on the way, and the world keeps right on spinning."

Yuck, Zoe thought now. The whole conversation started because her new literary study was called: *Caged: Jane Austen and Marriage*. Maybe it was a cultural study or could be a psychological study—whatever her New York editor, Christopher Morley, was calling her books on fairy tales and the works of famous writers. Anyway, the book would be about marriage.

That was as far as she'd gotten with Jane Austen: a title and some research. She already detested Austen's world. Hated those awful, grasping, growling mothers trying to auction their daughters off to the highest bidder because, as Austen claimed, "It is a truth universally acknowledged, that a single man in possession of a good fortune, must be in want of a wife."

These weren't the funny, nutty, carefree women she remembered from a college text. Nothing here to grab on to, not a modern note to point to and say, *See! This is who Austen was and why she's like us. This is why she wrote books like* Pride and Prejudice. *Why she celebrated simple-minded women and perfidious men too dumb to escape.*

Phooey, Zoe told herself as she ate her cereal. She should have thought this topic through better. If she yawned and fell asleep at her computer while writing, why should her readers stay awake while reading?

She crunched her cereal and thought of all the historical crap she had so far, nothing to do with Austen's life or world or mindset; nothing to illustrate the woman's need to write whole novels about marriage while she stayed single.

Marriage! Zoe laid her dish and spoon in the sink, ran water over them, then stood with her small hands holding on to the sink's edge, thinking.

Not for her—she needed nothing and nobody. She and Fida had their own home now, and winter was over. The sun was shining straight through her kitchen windows and the snow was gone from her garden. She might spend the day outside. Let the earth fall through her fingers, surprise a worm or two, and take her wonderful fairies from their winter boxes in the shed and set them into their summer homes—into their ornate castles and sturdy mills and rustic cabins.

Marriage—phooey, she thought again. She had no man around to tell her not to spend so much money on fairy statues or tell her to pay more attention to her writing. *"That's what brings in money, Zoe. Not your silly business with fairies . . ."*

Sadly, she felt at times as though she already had a husband buried deep in her brain, ordering what she could do, what she should do, and laying out her day for her—nice straight lines like metal bars.

Or maybe that was her mother's voice, from her death bed, telling her to watch out for terrible people who would try to hurt her; to keep her eyes down so she wouldn't see the startled looks when people saw her and flinched at her smallness.

"Ooh, look at the dwarf . . ."

"Stay inside, Zoe. With me. I want to keep you safe. The world is a cruel place," her mother would call out every time Zoe left the house.

So, this was sure as hell one of her shabby days, a misery day, and she was tired of it already and would have liked to go back to bed. Only, retreating never helped and the day would be with her until it wasn't any longer. Nothing she could do would change it.

She let Fida back inside, pushing hard against the door to close it against the wind. With a cup of hot coffee in her hands, Zoe went to the living room with Fida trotting ahead of her, needing a nudge through the doorway since Fida, who only saw half the world, always bumped her head.

She dug down into the sofa cushions for the TV remote and turned the set on, ignoring it at first, still caught up in her current bad day. Until it was Fida's turn to complain, interrupting Zoe's thoughts with a sharp, demanding bark because she thought the house was under attack from the wind, and she must get back out to defend the castle—and maybe poop again while she was about it, or catch a chipmunk digging up old nuts.

A newswoman on television said something about a death on U.S. Route 31, up near the road to Bear Falls. Zoe snapped to attention, hurrying to stand directly in front of the TV to listen.

"Janice Root," the woman said. "Seventeen. Lived on Shore Drive."

"Hell!" Zoe put a hand to her mouth, exciting Fida, who nipped at her bare feet. "Janice Root!" The girl who sold peaches at the family fruit stand in the fall. The girl with a shy smile. A splash of acne across her forehead. A slight limp—a small turning of her left foot putting an extra bounce into every step she took.

This was it, what she'd felt coming all morning.

"Hit-and-run. The police are looking into it."

Eight thirty. She wouldn't call next door. That wasn't the right way to deliver news this bad to her friends. She hurried to the bedroom instead, throwing on clothes and shoes, the "shabby," shadowy feeling hurrying along behind her.

"Poor kid," Zoe said aloud as she hurried out the door, bending almost double into the wind, Fida tangling in her feet, on their way next door to give Dora and Jenny the news.

Chapter 3

The news of Janice Root's death spread from the north end of town, where small houses clustered around Falls Park and neighbors gossiped above the noise of the falls thundering down a stone cliff to the river below. The news spread to the west where mansions and the rustic, old money cabins of the wealthy stood on the very edge of Lake Michigan. Then up east a few miles, to Oak Street and Myrtle's Restaurant, where people were half-blown through the door, greeted by Myrtle's warning bell, and fell at once into sharing the terrible news.

The accident that killed the Root girl was all that was talked about over coffee and a helping of Myrtle's specialty waffles with blueberry syrup and walnuts.

"Poor child," women whispered from table to table. "And poor Sally Root. Heard something happened at the birth. Baby dropped to the ground. That's why she limped."

"Never said if it was at that hospital, did she? Would only say 'dropped,' like the word was the worst thing a person could ever hear."

A woman here and a woman there shook her head and said, "I heard something. Oh, yes, I certainly heard something about that."

But they were ignored, like a very old chorus, and talk about the accident went on.

Fathers said how they wanted to get their hands on the driver who did this to the girl. They spoke of retribution.

People left. New people came in before the daytime waitress, Demeter Hopkins, got the tables bussed.

The same ground was plowed over and over, "Not that dear girl who limped? A little acne? Sweet as punch?"

Priscilla Manus, permanent president of the Bear Falls Historical

Society, turned around to remind everybody that Janice Root was to get a Rotary Scholarship upon graduation. "That's less than a month away. Wonder who they'll give the scholarship to now?"

They all chewed their waffles as they chewed the news: very slowly, mired in their own form of mourning, until the first shock passed and talk turned—table by table—to what they could do for the Root family.

"We'll all be sending sympathy cards. Somebody better warn Mr. Harrington he'll need a lot of them," Stephanie Wilder, said. She owned the gift shop but had no sympathy cards since she only sold happy things.

Pretty Elizabeth Wheatley, slim and fashionably dressed at every hour of the day and now secretary to Abigail Cane, the town's wealthiest woman, suggested they start a fund to cover the funeral expenses, and order a large bouquet of flowers from the whole town.

Angel Arlen, now thirty-six with three daughters—one already with a baby, making Angel a grandmother—wasn't having this town newcomer telling her what to do. "Rather send my own flowers," she spoke up as she moved around on her chair, showing her dislike for slim, pretty women with jobs and no children.

Priscilla Manus suggested a Cross of Remembrance be erected out at the road where Janice died.

Vera Wattles thought that was insensitive. "Why in all that's holy would the Roots want to pass a thing like that every time they go up to Petoskey?"

Chuck Spenser, owner of Chuck's Saloon, said he'd put on the wake—no cost to anybody for anything but their drinks, which people agreed was nice of him and thanked him for his generosity.

That was the moment when Demeter came out of the kitchen to say that Myrtle was getting nervous. "She wants to know if you'll all be clearing out soon so she can get ready for lunch."

Demeter leaned her order pad on one hip and said in a louder voice, "Myrtle says to tell you that today's special will be meatloaf, in case somebody's still hungry after you cleared her out of waffles already."

* * *

Minnie Moon hurried up Elderberry Street with her red hair blowing like Medusa's snakes. She was dressed in a red-flowered muumuu under a puffy purple jacket, her feet in old tennis shoes. She braced her rather large body against the wind and hurried faster on her way to Harrington's Drugstore to buy tampons for Dianna, her nineteen-year-old, whose name used to be Deanna, the perfectly good name Minnie gave her, until recently when the spelling didn't suit her.

It had been a particularly awful morning. "Dianna" refused to get out of bed because she swore she had cramps like no other woman ever suffered before, while Candace, Minnie's fourteen-year-old, laughed and taunted her sister into a full meltdown.

There'd been no time to catch the morning news because she already had a headache and didn't need news of plagues and floods making it worse.

The walk to the drugstore would have been a treat but for the wind trying to knock her over. Still, she welcomed any excuse to get out of the house for a couple of hours. Maybe more, if she could come up with an extra errand or have a long conversation with Mr. Harrington, the pharmacist. He was a widower who always found time to listen. A nice man, Clyde Harrington. A man who cared if a woman was having a bad day, and cared if that woman's husband was up in Jackson Prison on an uttering and publishing charge for counterfeiting ten-dollar bills in their basement, and cared if she was having trouble with two teenaged girls she couldn't wait to marry off.

For Dianna, the wedding thing had to come sooner rather than later. The one prayer Minnie consoled herself with day after day was that a man would drop into Dianna's lap, get her out of Minnie's house, into a life of her own, and stop the hormone wars waging on and on without end.

Dear God . . .

A good man. A decent man, Minnie prayed now, pushing along under the bare maples, the wind clanking branches above her head.

She smiled halfheartedly as she passed Dora Weston's house with her Little Library boxes standing at the curb. One for children's books painted with fairies and superheroes, and the other for adult books, with flowers and tractors. Minnie thought she might stop to see if there was a new cozy mystery to take her mind off her problems, but didn't.

She turned to look at the newly greening lawn leading to Dora's pretty house, half-hoping Dora would pop out from the screened-in porch and invite her up for a cup of tea and a plate of fresh cookies.

If ever there was a woman who understood the trials of raising girls, Dora Weston was that woman, Minnie thought as she pressed on, facing into the wind. One girl off to Lord knows where—making movies or some such thing, with no husband in sight. And the other back home with Dora after—what was said around town—a terrible divorce. The talk for a long time was that the man cheated on Jenny and then ran off to some Central American country with that woman because he thought she was very rich, which, it turned out, she wasn't.

How she prayed that wasn't going to be her fate—getting her girls back after she married them off.

Minnie turned at Maple, toward the center of town, rolling her eyes heavenward, and praying as she went. *Maybe a man with a job, if you don't mind, Lord. Or maybe a man with a whole lot of money.*

It happened to other mothers, she consoled herself.

"You hear about Janice Root?" Mr. Harrington asked the minute Minnie stepped up to the counter with the box of tampons in her hand. She immediately forgot her miserable day.

Sensing a piece of tragedy to chew on, Minnie stopped and cocked her head to one side. She leaned on the counter, looking toward

Mr. Harrington as she waited for this bit of news he was willing to share with her.

"What do you mean?" she asked finally, lowering her voice and batting her short red eyelashes at him. "Haven't heard a word. I know the girl's wild. If I told my Dianna once I told her a thousand times, 'I don't want you having anything to do with that Janice Root.'"

"Found dead last night."

"Dead!" Minnie snapped her head back. Not the kind of thing she wanted to hear. Not at all. "Never heard she was sick. Was she sick? A wild girl, like I said. But not sickly."

"Killed out on the highway last night. Left to die beside the road. Harold, the *Record-Eagle* delivery man, found her."

Minnie pursed her lips. "Dead? You sure about that? As I said, maybe a little . . . well . . . loose. No, I take that back. Not loose at all. A very nice girl." She shook her head.

"You really mean it? Dead? You said Janice Root, eh? Not the girl I was thinking about. Not that one at all. Why, poor Janice—I heard she was getting a scholarship from Rotary. Nice person, that Janice Root."

Slowly Mr. Harrington nodded, the few black hairs he had left on his head unmoving, stuck in place forever like little strokes from a paintbrush. "Hit-and-run is what they say."

Minnie's eyes grew huge. "But what was she doing out on the highway at night?"

Mr. Harrington shook his head again. "Nobody knows. Maybe she was hit earlier and nobody saw her body 'til Harold Roach drove by."

"Why this is terrible! Just terrible." Tears burned her eyes. If Minnie had one thing, it was a big heart and her big heart was throbbing.

Mr. Harrington shrugged. "It was on the morning news. Most likely everybody's heard by now."

"Not me. I don't have time to watch TV. Those girls of mine . . ." She stopped, losing interest in complaints about her daughters and instead thinking, for the first time in a long while, how lucky she was to have her girls at home where they belonged and not out gallivanting in the middle of the night. *Just see what that gets you!*

"Wonder if Ed Warner caught the driver yet. That would be a good thing . . . and . . ." She stopped to put a hand to her mouth. Tears rolled down her cheeks. "That's just terrible, Mr. Harrington. Just terrible. The poor Roots. Such a sweet girl. Imagine if it was one of my own dear girls . . ."

She was gone, the bagged box of tampons left on the counter in her hurry. She found she was desperately in need of a talk with Dora Weston, who would help her better understand the cruel ways of the world.

* * *

Over at the U.S. Post Office, Joanne Sledder rubbed at her long nose and answered: "Yes, it's true. Hit-and-run," for the umpteenth time that morning, then lowered her voice as one woman in line burst into tears. Probably thinking about her daughter, Joanne figured, and suffered her own pangs of fear. *There but for the grace of God . . .*

For those who didn't know the girl, Joanne Sledder filled in what she could as each customer reached the front window.

"Blonde girl. Curly hair. Pretty face. Limped a little. Had a bit of acne but what kid doesn't get that at one time or another . . . ? Anyway, you know the Root's Orchard—apples and peaches, out on the Shore Drive? They got that stand. Some of the best peaches anywhere around. A nice couple, Sally and Jay. Bring me fresh bread sometimes, when Sally's baking. Girl was nice, too."

Others chimed in to say pleasant things about Janice Root, which irritated Gladys Bonney, a tall woman with knots of black hair fixed in place all over her head. She'd been standing in the line—at a dead stop—for almost twenty minutes and wasn't happy about it. She was at the post office to mail a letter she'd written to the *Record-Eagle* protesting that a photo of her daughter, Tammy—who had just won the tile-painting contest put on by McMillen's Framing in Traverse City—wasn't in the paper.

Then, to make it two birds with one stone, she wanted to ask Joanne about the people who'd just moved into that new mansion on the Lake Michigan shore. She'd driven by a few times and had seen Cadillacs and sports cars that she knew had to be expensive because they were so small. All she wanted from Joanne was what their name was and if it was a couple or a single man. If the owner was a single man she didn't want to waste any time. Rich as he was, she knew the man would just love Tammy. Who wouldn't?

If he was a bachelor, she'd take over one of her coveted blueberry cobblers to break the ice. Just to be neighborly, of course, though it didn't hurt for Tammy to meet the right people.

"All I need is a stamp," the thin woman called aloud up the line, and parted the waters—so to speak—so she could make her purchase and be on her way. There wasn't an opening to ask Joanne about the new people, but there was always Myrtle's. What wasn't known at Myrtle's Restaurant, and passed around, wasn't worth knowing anyway. And at least there she could flash the photo of Tammy receiving her award and get that much satisfaction.

Once out on Oak Street, Gladys looked up and down, noticing fewer people around—a lot fewer than most Saturday mornings.

Too bad, she thought as she patted her purse, where she'd slipped Tammy's award photo in case she ran into neighbors who would want to know all about Tammy's triumph.

Chapter 4

Dora Weston, still shaken from the news of Janice Root's death, walked out to the front curb, the chilly breeze pushing at her. She wanted to straighten the Little Library boxes after a few days of neglect, while she'd been trying to keep Jenny happy. The girl had been sulking for days now though she'd said over and over again nothing was wrong.

A mother knew.

Maybe still the divorce. Maybe a general malaise. Or maybe one of a hundred things women older than Jenny knew better than to stress over.

Dora sighed and bent to open the canvas bag of books she'd brought out with her, then opened both the children's Little Library and the adult box to see if people had been visiting.

Books had been taken and that pleased her. A few books were new, left in place of others. This part of keeping her Little Libraries—both boxes built by her husband, Jim, to resemble the house behind her—was the most fun for her. This was the treasure hunt, seeing what neighbors thought fit to share, though sometimes this part was an embarrassment, like the books the porn man left. The porn man thought he was an updated Hugh Hefner, bringing sex education to the masses. All she did was throw his books into the trash, unashamedly, unabashedly—though first checking to make sure there was nothing redeeming about them, at all. A practice she wouldn't admit to, though Zoe Zola suspected and teased her unmercifully.

Looking up from the bag of books, Dora smiled toward Zoe's house. What a picture perfect little place the tiny woman had made. Red shutters, red front door, red railings around the porch. And flowerbed after flowerbed, all with fairies soon to be guarding castles, and fairies soon sitting in upper windows of those castles, and fairies soon in work clothes toiling in tiny gardens. It was a sight to behold, Zoe's garden, drawing townspeople down Elderberry Street to stop and gawk and sometimes seek gardening advice from Zoe, who never minded giving out a tip or two.

And maybe, at the same time, a few of those people took a book from Dora's Little Library.

While she was smiling toward a particular flowerbed, she caught sight of Zoe and Fida cutting through the pines between the houses, on their way over for coffee and maybe a pastry or two. A crust of toast for the little, one-eyed dog.

It was their morning ritual.

"I heard Jenny back in her room," Dora called out to the little figure hurrying, bent, across the grass. "She's up, just not 'really up,' if you know what I mean. I'll be in shortly. Coffee's on the counter. All made. Tea bags are in the tea container, if you don't want coffee. But you know all of that. Help yourself."

"You hear about Janice Root?" Zoe called from a place near one of her flowerbeds where a new fairy castle would soon be settled, as soon as the UPS man brought it.

Dora nodded yes. "Heard this morning. All over the TV. Didn't tell Jenny yet. No use making her miserable too early."

"Might as well all be miserable together."

Zoe went on around back of the house and out of Dora's sight, leaving Dora to pull her sweater around her, bend to the book bag, and think how fitting the cold wind was on this day of all sad days.

Dora put a hand above her eyes to look upward. Sun was too bright for such a day. That was only one of the wrong parts to this particular morning. Embarrassing, really. Sun shouldn't be shining the way it was when a young girl lost her life just a few hours before, only a few miles away.

And what about those poor parents? She could only imagine their suffering. Her chest felt as if it was caving in, making a deep breath hard to take.

Dora Weston was one woman who knew what a terrible day felt like; when a day put an end to life as you knew it.

Jim died on a day like this one—struck and left beside U.S. 31, too. Dora sighed and put out a hand to hold on to the book box.

Dead on the road. Death of her salesman—his territory from the Mackinaw Bridge to Saginaw.

She bent and pulled one of the books she kept for emergency days from the bag—not syrupy stuff that momentarily lifted the spirits and then slammed them down hard when reality hit—but what she loved most: a vivid mind reaching out to tell an uplifting story; a story of courage, or a story of love, or just a story of people and the havoc they survived. Good solid writing.

Bel Canto by Ann Patchett was perfect for taking the reader away then bringing them back better off that they'd been, even if this book was really kind of all-around sad.

That one went into the book box, because it was one of her favorites.

Then Annie Proulx—*The Shipping News.*

Anne Tyler. Any of her books were good for the soul. *A Spool of Blue Thread.* That went into the box.

All those Anns and Annies. Dora stopped, looking up and down Elderberry Street, thinking about a bunch of Anns and Annies writing away in little garrets, backs hunched, cartoon bubbles flying above their head, spelling out the words as they wrote. She loved to think of her favorite writers that way—always working so people would have another good novel to bless their world.

She sighed again and reached for more books. She slipped *Lucky Jim* and *Cold Comfort Farm* into the box. If her neighbors wanted a book to take their mind off this new misery, these were for them.

For the spiritual (not religious) minded, she pulled out *The God of*

Small Things, and for men, *The Last Lecture*, then she closed the adult box and opened the children's library.

One of her favorite books went in, *The Girl Who Circumnavigated Fairyland in a Ship of Her Own Making;* then two Harry Potters, rather tattered and worn, but still serviceable for developing minds needing wild places to grow.

It was good to be with her libraries—adult (in the proper use of the word) and child. She had been trained as a librarian. Got a great job at the Detroit Public Library and then met Jim Weston. They came to Bear Falls from southern Michigan to live because it was near the middle of his territory and Dora thought this growing town would soon have a library.

It never did, and so she began, in her own small way, to bring books to the town's readers.

Books, unlike some people she knew, brightened her world. Things made sense in books, or if not exactly sense, they gave her hope that there was a sane and ordered world out there somewhere.

What Dora loved most about books, she thought as she slammed closed the doors to both boxes, was that she could open the cover of one in the morning and be in ancient Greece.

In the afternoon of that same day she could be out in intergalactic space, flying from star to star.

How anyone didn't read books amazed her. It would be like living a quarter of a life—or less. A tiny life, ignoring worlds of experience, deprived of fascinating people. She found that, sometimes, she couldn't help but stare at people she knew didn't read. Sometimes she wondered what they thought about all day long. A mind empty of other voices had a desert quality to it, she thought. Little, dusty, unopened rooms inside.

Dora bent to pick up her canvas bag.

And to think how well her day had begun, with Lisa, her oldest, indie filmmaking child, calling very early to say she'd just signed a contract for a new film. Not a documentary this time but a full-length film telling the story of generations of women in an Upper Michigan town where they used to mine copper until the country didn't need that much copper anymore and the families were left behind, deserted like the mines themselves, trying to fit old lives into a new century.

"Great script, Mom. The women tell the story, and I know how you feel about telling women's lives straight. I promise you, I'll do just that. I'll make you proud." Her voice was filled with happiness—this daughter who followed not just her own drummer, but all the down-trodden drummers in the world who needed their stories told.

"You already have." Dora loved this unpredictable and sometimes—when she was little—almost unmanageable child.

"Be happy for me, Mom. And don't worry. At least I won't be wearing a burqa this time. And I'll be home on lots of weekends. You and Jenny and Zoe Zola can come up and visit the set. We'll be close again. Can't let you forget me."

Dora had to laugh, as if she'd ever forget either one of her very special children.

Dora hung up feeling happy, until she'd put the TV on and her pretty world came tumbling down around her ears.

She took a deep breath and looked again from one end of Elder-berry Street to the other and, to her dismay, caught sight of a very recognizable figure turning up the street. Minnie Moon, all ruffled in a blurry mass of red flowers, covered by a big purple jacket, her red hair blowing around her head with each blast of wind.

Minnie Moon raised her arm, wiggling her fingers, calling out, "Dora! Yoo-hoo. Dora."

Dora heard the call only faintly. She could still ignore it. She could pretend she'd been looking at the sky, not at Minnie.

She might even get into the house before . . .

A black SUV pulled in at the curb and parked. She was all about avoiding the fast-approaching Minnie Moon but when she turned to find Keith Robbins, Bear Fall's city manager, waving at her as he got out of his car, she knew her day had just gone from bad to worse.

One thing Dora had learned, since moving to Bear Falls so long ago, was that friendliness took more time here than in a big city like Detroit. It took a smile and a wave at the thin young man. She had to pretend she had nothing else in the world to do but talk to Keith, ask how he was doing, how Bernadette was doing. And the twins? All the while Minnie Moon was steaming up the sidewalk, a hand to her throat, now calling out a louder: "Dora! Dora Weston! Just the woman I want . . ."

Dora smiled wide at Keith Robbins because she liked the small man and, by now, was resigned to her fate. Keith ran Bear Falls with an iron fist. Though everybody usually got along and were happy neighbors, there were times when a question about the volunteer fire department needing a new truck or how often the snow should be plowed that roused tempers. Keith was a good man for those times. Firm, but willing to listen, Keith always formed a consensus of thought that left everybody grumbling and blaming him, though there was peace in the town again.

"Well, Keith, nice surprise. Here for a book? Got some good ones, brand new. Horizon Books donated them. You can be the first in town to read one." She smiled as he ambled up the lawn toward her. No getting around it, by the look of Keith, here was another person whose day was going downhill.

"Suppose you heard about the Root girl?" she asked. There was no mistaking depression.

"Did, Miz Weston," he said. "I did. Terrible thing."

Keith was still nodding and shaking his head as Minnie Moon drew closer. She was in front of Zoe's house now, slowing down, tennis shoes slapping the sidewalk in near slow motion. She yelled again, "Yoo-hoo" and headed straight to where Dora and Keith stood, beating at her chest as if trying to restart her heart.

"Got something I'd like to talk to you about, Miz Weston." Keith eyed Minnie and frowned. He lowered his voice. "It really has to be . . ."

"Well, well, well. Keith Robbins." Minnie smiled wide as she reached them, propelling the top of her body forward as she stopped. "Haven't seen you in ages. How ya doing? And the wife and kids? Good. Good. Good." She got her neighborly business out of the way in short order and turned to Dora. "Have to talk to you, Dora. Just awful, what I heard . . ."

"If you mean about Janice Root, I know all about it. Awful. Why don't the both of you come on in? I've got a pot of coffee on the stove." Dora smiled, offering because she had to. "We'll talk inside. Zoe's there with Jenny."

"I . . ." Keith hesitated, "I hoped to talk to you alone." He looked hard at Dora, signaling urgency.

Minnie put one hand to her back, eyes bright at the thought of sitting down and having something to drink. And pretty soon, too, she hoped, since her tongue was as dry as an old lady's . . .

"Don't mind me, Keith," she said. "I can only spare a minute, then I'll be on my way. There's nothing you can say to Dora that I'll go spreading around. Don't have to worry about that. You all know me by now."

She hurried up Dora's sidewalk ahead of the other two, talking over her shoulder. "Terrible thing, what happened to the Root girl. Just terrible. I was thinking . . . Well, you ask me, there's no question about what killed her. Right there beside the road. Could be, in the dark, the driver didn't see her. Might've thought he hit a deer."

"Awful, Miz Moon. Chief Warner's been out there all morning," Keith said to her back.

Minnie grabbed the screen door and held it for the other two, then followed through the living room and dining room out to the yellow kitchen with crisscrossed fluffy white curtains and a round maple table with yellow placemats, yellow saltshakers, and yellow crocuses in a yellow pot at the very center. They greeted Zoe and Jenny, both slouching in their chairs, looking miserable.

Minnie stripped her puffy jacket off fast, pulled out a chair, and slumped down, knees spread apart. She let them all know that she couldn't move another step without a cup of very hot coffee and maybe a piece of cake.

"You go on now." Minnie waved at Keith, who frowned over his watch. "Tell Dora what you're here for and I'll just enjoy sitting awhile."

"Shouldn't take long." Keith cleared his throat. "Thought maybe I could run this by you, Dora, and get on over to the hardware store. Need mouse traps. Found a mouse running around the kitchen this morning and now Bernadette's too scared to go anywhere near there. Said if I wanted supper, I'd better do something about the mouse."

"Boy, don't I know mice! Big as . . ." Minnie hooted.

Dora and Keith said nothing. Zoe and Jenny exchanged odd looks.

"I better get going. I've got to get groceries." Zoe slid from the pile of phone books on her chair and raised her eyebrows. "You want to come, Jenny?"

Jenny was quick to say she'd loved to go to Draper's Superette with Zoe, sweetly asking Dora if she needed anything, which brought a confused look from Dora, who'd done their weekly grocery shopping just the day before.

She wished them a good trip as they said goodbye to Keith and then to Minnie, who frowned at Zoe, warning her not to buy the ground beef at Draper's if she valued her life. "Seen how they put fresh beef all around that brown stuff. Not fooling me anymore. I'll go up to Charlevoix for meat if I have to."

Jenny and Zoe escaped.

Minnie drank her coffee—ever so slowly—as she looked out the back window at a massive hickory tree, branches tossing back and forth. She pretended not to be paying a bit of attention to the others in the room.

"Well." Keith cleared his throat and twisted his cup between his hands. "I'd come back another time, but I need an answer today. What I was hoping was that I could get you and Jenny, and maybe Miss Zola, to help me out tomorrow. Any time after church would be okay. Like one o'clock."

"Help out with what?" Dora asked. "Something about the Roots? You know me and my girls'll be happy to . . ."

Keith shook his head. "This is different. Hate to bring it up at a time like this, but the man who came to see me thought it was important. That was last night, before they found Janice Root. I was going to call him this morning and say this wasn't the right time . . . but Bernadette said she thought the town could do with a dose of good news. Anyway, you know the new mansion over on the shore?"

Dora, surprised at the change in topic, nodded. "Been building it all year. Heard Gladys Bonney asking about it yesterday. So excited. Seemed to think the owners were very, very wealthy."

Dora smiled at Keith who knew Gladys Bonney well enough. "But I don't know a thing about the place. Nor the people. Not much help, I'm afraid."

Minnie's cup was in the air. Dora got up to refill it.

"The man who came to see me is Charles Bingman," Keith went on. "His friend Fitzwilliam Dillon owns the house. Guess you could call it a mansion, you ask me. This Bingman said Fitzwilliam would like to be a good neighbor. He's thinking of having an open house closer to summer. He wants to invite everybody in town to come see the place. But first, he wants to meet a few of us. Kind of talk about the party and . . ."

Minnie looked up fast, her small eyes getting a lot smaller. "Are they single men? This Charles Bingman and—what'd you say, Fitzwilliam? I'd say that's one hell of a name."

Keith shrugged. "They're from Chicago. Looks like old money. At least that's what I picked up from Bingman's clothes and his car. Then there's the way he talks."

"Fitzwilliam Dillon." Minnie grinned from ear to ear. "Sounds like . . . what was it? That Great Gatsby. Have to have Dianna look him up. She knows how to do things like that. Now me, I don't know one end of the computer from the . . ."

"I'd like . . . to get to why I'm here," Keith interrupted her. "I'm supposed to meet both men at that house tomorrow. Anyway," he went on. "When he came in to introduce himself . . ."

"What's he look like? How old? Did he mention a wife?" Minnie's pale eyes went wide as she ticked off items on her pokey fingers.

Keith turned his back to her. "What he came to see me about is this meeting tomorrow. One o'clock. Fitzwilliam Dillon would like to have just a few of us this first time. He's got something to talk over with what Charles Bingman called the 'movers and shakers.' Something about a . . ."

He glanced at Minnie, who was already talking over him.

"Well! Me and my Dianna don't have a thing to do tomorrow." Minnie turned her head away quickly, as if she had no interest in what they were saying and hadn't been hanging on every word. Then back—her eyes so small they were almost shut. "What time did you say that was?"

Keith focused hard on Dora. "I told Charles Bingman about you and Jenny. And I told him about Miss Zola—that we've got a famous writer right here in Bear Falls. He wants to meet all of you and thinks Zoe, especially, might enjoy knowing Fitzwilliam. Bingman mentioned her more than a couple of times."

"Are we the movers and shakers, Keith? Slim pickings, if you ask me." Dora smiled to herself.

Keith, his serious face drawn longer, said, "It's something else he's got in mind, Dora. I'm not supposed to talk about it until we all meet."

"What'd you say?" Minnie leaned out from her chair.

Dora frowned at Minnie.

"If you ask me . . ." Minnie, scooting around in her chair, shook her head at them. "I think me and Dianna could come up with a list of folks to come to that party, if that's what you're asking. Young men always want to meet the available girls in town rather than the well . . . older ladies like Jenny. You understand what I mean, don't you?" She looked at Dora, then away fast.

"It's not just a list for the party." Keith bit at his lip. "At least that's only a part of it."

"Well!" Minnie sniffed and lifted her nose in the air. "If you ask me, I don't see a thing wrong with going over there to talk with those men. It's the neighborly thing to do."

"There's more." Keith looked straight at Minnie. "If you don't mind, Miz Moon, I'd like to talk the rest of this over with Dora. It's kind of a confidential thing."

Minnie waited, expectant.

"Alone," Keith said.

Minnie huffed and bent to put her sneakers back on, taking a long time to untie, then retie, the laces. "Just imagine if both those men are bachelors. Be the biggest thing to hit Bear Falls in a month of Sundays. Can't you just see that Gladys Bonney going crazy to get that poor, silly Tammy of hers married off to one of them? Whew! Now me—I don't think money's what a girl should think about when she's looking for a man."

She stood, shrugging into her jacket. She almost got to the kitchen archway before turning back again. "What time was it? Over to that mansion, I mean? I want to do my part."

Dora looked at Keith, who bit at his lip and said, "One o'clock. Don't want the whole day taken up . . . But nothing is sure yet. I'd wait for the party if I were you, Minnie."

Minnie sniffed. "Only want to help. Like I always do. Just like I always do."

She headed through the kitchen door toward the front of the house.

They waited until she was gone.

"The thing is, Dora," Keith twisted in his chair. "I know what you mean about bad timing. With the Root girl's death and all."

"Maybe you should call and tell him. Put him off awhile. And I don't like this business about asking only a few of us. Seems like snobbery to me, and you know me well enough, Keith. I'm not a snob."

"I understand, but there's this other thing."

"What other thing?" Her patience was severely tried. Even she, who set high standards for friendliness, was about done with visitors.

"The reason he wants a few of us over there is because he'd like to talk about a substantial gift to the town."

"We've had those before." Dora sniffed, unimpressed. "Look at that bronze statue of himself Joshua Cane gave to the park. Nothing but a couple of fancy bathroom signs now, and a bronze marker. Serves that terrible old man right, too. We don't want to make another mistake like that one."

"This is different," Keith said. "Charles said Fitzwilliam would like suggestions for something big the town needs."

"I could tell him without any fuss at all. Potholes all over the streets. A couple of times I thought I was going to fall out of sight when I hit one of those things."

Keith lifted a finger to his lips. He tipped his head in the direction where Minnie Moon had disappeared. "Are we certain Minnie's gone?"

She clucked toward Keith. "Of course. Do you think the woman would be hiding in my dining room?"

He looked properly embarrassed. "It's just that this is a really big thing. I wouldn't want it spread around."

"My goodness, Keith. I think you will burst if you don't come out with it."

"The man's talking a couple of million dollars, Dora."

Dora's jaw fell. Her almost misty eyes widened. "A couple of million? Well . . . then . . . A couple of million. You're sure?"

Keith nodded.

Dora wiped her hands again and again on her dishtowel as she said, "You mean enough money to build a nice library?"

"Or a football stadium at the high school." Keith gave her an odd smile.

Dora thought awhile. "In that case, I'm pretty sure all three of us can make it. Long as it doesn't take up the whole afternoon, as you said. Sunday, you know."

"One o'clock. Bernadette is coming, too. Got a babysitter for the twins. Reason is she wants to see the house, to tell the truth. So, we'll meet you there if you don't mind. Right now, I've got to get those mousetraps or I'm not eating tonight. And thanks, Miz Weston . . . er . . . Dora. You see now how important this is."

Keith got up, hesitating. "Do you think Minnie Moon will really be going with us?" he asked, looking down at his immaculate white sneakers. "I hadn't planned on so many. We don't want to jeopardize the gift."

Dora, sensing a touch of disapproval, bristled.

"I hope so," Dora brightened. "I do hope she and her girls will come. Minnie's a force of nature, you know. Be good to have her there. Show this man Bear Fallsians come in all shapes and sizes."

Her smile was smug, then slid as she realized Minnie Moon and her over-painted girl Dianna were going with them. Dianna would be wearing one of those half-dresses of hers, so short it wouldn't cover her underwear—or what Dora hoped was underwear and not a bare bottom. Not that Dora ever really looked.

And Minnie would be sporting a glamorous, fruit-printed muumuu with, maybe, black sneakers.

Dora reddened with embarrassment. "*Hoist on her own petard,*" as her father used to say. "*And more shame to ya,*" he would've added. Keith left a chastened Dora Weston behind him.

Chapter 5

Earlier that morning, Tony Ralenti was driving and thinking about Jenny and what was going on between them. Maybe it was nothing, only something sitting in his head for no reason—because he'd come to believe they could be . . . that maybe . . .

She'd been cool, even distant, for the last couple of weeks. He tried to get her to look at him, and she lifted her chin away. He suggested she come stay over—they'd gotten that far. But she was always busy. Always something else to do, and this from a woman complaining her life was going nowhere.

Maybe what they needed was a dinner out, a long drive . . . some time alone to talk. Sex wasn't always the best thing. It had taken him a long time to learn that. Sex put a Band-Aid on problems. A guy could bask in the memory and not even know the woman he was with didn't talk to him from beginning to end. He didn't want to make that mistake again.

Maybe they could go away—just for the day. Talk and drive and work things out.

He was headed into Traverse City for wood to make a couple new Little Library boxes for customers. One wanted painted oak. The other thought a birch bark covered box would be perfect since the woman lived in Milwaukee.

He was sitting at the red light in Elk Rapids when he turned on the radio and heard the news about Janice Root.

"Damn!" he thought, shocked out of thinking about ordinary things. He must have driven right by the place where she was killed when he'd turned on to U.S. 31 from Bear Falls.

A kid. A damned kid mowed down and left to die. Old instincts kicked in. Once a cop, always a cop—especially a homicide detective.

When the light turned, he whipped his pickup around and headed back to Bear falls. Chief Warner might need him. With only Ed and one deputy to cover the whole town area there were days when things got tight, and the chief was glad Tony came in to help.

Any thought of doing carpentry that day slid straight out of his head. Making things with his hands was okay when he was feeling good, when the bullet in his leg from back in Detroit didn't remind him how he'd gone after the guy who'd shot him. How he'd shot the guy in the gut and then, even with a bullet in his own body, he'd thrown his arm around the guy's throat as if it was nothing for him to break a man's neck.

He was taken to the hospital with his own blood staining the blanket laid over him. They'd put him back together—a scar down his face from being gouged, bullet in his left leg so there was a limp—but when he was released, the first thing he did was take early retirement and get the hell out of Detroit.

He hit the steering wheel with his hand. Back to that dripping thing in his head about life being cheap. Nowhere he could go to get away from unnecessary, dirty, deliberate . . . death.

Poor kid. Hit-and-run.

He had death stuck in his head the way it used to get stuck. He looked out the truck window, narrowing his eyes at the open landscape of soft hills and open fields. Sun and high white clouds. Just like that day back in Detroit. Spring, like this. Cold and sunny. But no bare fields. No bare woods. Downtown Detroit. Just picking a guy up for questioning.

Windy that day, too. Like he could remember papers blowing all over downtown. The people mover thundering overhead. He'd killed a man that day and knew too much about himself to go on living the way he'd been living. His wife was gone in a month. His house was gone. His friends stayed away. He came north like an empty man, nothing left of his life.

Tony took the steps up to the station two at a time. And then he was inside, smelling the leather and oil and heavy wax from the wood floor. He felt his old nervousness at a case to solve; he felt the urgency—as if he was going to change the world.

Ed Warner, Chief of Police, was at his desk behind the wooden railing, there to keep people back. Ed was a tall, nervous guy with a head that could slowly sink to one side while he talked to you. Now, when he saw it was Tony, he leaned on his elbows, bobbing head resting in both hands.

"You heard, eh?"

Tony nodded. "Awful. Anything on the driver yet?" He sat in the chair across from Ed, sticking his bad leg out straight.

Ed shook his head.

"You get an approximate time she was killed?" Tony asked.

Ed shook his bobbly head and stared straight into Tony's dark eyes. He looked even more mournful. "This isn't Detroit, Tony. Things don't work so fast up here."

Tony got the feeling maybe he was sticking his nose in where it wasn't wanted and pushed the chair back. "I don't like to bother you. Just thought . . . if I could help."

The answer came in a wave from Ed. "Sit down. Sit down. Trying to process a phone call I just got."

"Yeah?"

"Medical examiner."

"What'd she say?

"Well, to tell the truth I got an approximate time of death all right. But it doesn't make sense." Ed looked off over Tony's shoulder, out the big glass window with BEAR FALLS POLICE DEPARTMENT etched on it—backward. "You know, sometimes things get hard for no reason at all."

"What's that mean?"

"Wasn't a hit-and-run. The girl's been dead about two days. Rigor gone. Lividity gone."

Tony leaned back and made a face at him. "She was found out

next to the road. What else could it be? You mean she was lying there like that for two days? Nobody saw her?"

Ed examined his large, chapped hands. "There's more than that."

"What do you mean?"

"No trauma. No car killed her."

"You're kidding? What? She have a heart attack? Wasn't shot or anything, was she? Turkey season."

"Season's over and they don't hunt at night. Except way south of here. Season still on down there. But anyway, no gunshot."

"You saw the body, didn't you?"

Ed nodded. "Harold Roach, the news delivery man, called me from out on the road. He found her."

"Look like a hit-and-run to you?"

"Only saw her by flashlight. Barely light by the time I got there. Didn't touch her. You know, roll her over or anything. How the hell would I know what killed her if it wasn't a hit-and-run?"

"What'd the ME say? Cause of death?"

"Like I said, no signs of trauma, only some drag marks, probably from the gravel beside the road. The body was wrapped up pretty good. It's got to be something else. That's what she said."

"Something like what?"

"Didn't know." Ed shook his head. "Said the girl looked like she shouldn't be dead, except for blood spots on her chest and in her eyes. Petechiae, the ME called it."

Tony nodded. "Comes after death. Different causes for it."

"Might still know today. Maybe not. Could take longer. And I've got the Roots coming in about now. What the hell do I tell them? Bad enough they think she was hit by a car."

He scratched at the back of his head.

"You said she was dead two days. Why didn't the Roots report her missing?"

Ed shrugged his shoulders. "A question I'm gonna ask."

Tony slumped in the chair, trying to remember strange deaths he'd covered in Detroit. People frozen to death. Some died of starvation. Some keeled over and nobody found out why. But this was a kid. Out in the country. Found by the side of the road at night.

"ME say anything about an overdose?" he asked. "There's always that with kids."

Ed Warner shook his head. "She's kind of cautious. Doesn't like to get things wrong."

"Good for her, but tough for you. Better when you can get right on a case."

"Yeah. Broke the news to the Roots early this morning. They couldn't even talk, so broken up, but they'll be here soon. Their pastor's coming with them, I imagine. What'll I say? 'Your daughter wasn't killed by a hit-and-run driver, Mr. and Mrs. Root.' 'Nope, it wasn't a bear attack . . .'"

Tony let out a long breath that turned into a whistle. "If you had to take a guess, what do you think got her?"

"Honest to God, I couldn't say. Wasn't rape. If she wasn't hit by a car and it wasn't an overdose the only thing I can think of is maybe exposure."

"Wasn't that cold last night. She have a coat on?"

Ed shook his head then let it wobble to one side as he thought. "That's another thing."

"What's 'another thing'?"

"Something else."

Tony waited. The chief took his time.

"When we found the dead girl, she was wearing the damnedest thing for a girl her age. Not what you'd expect. The ME said she'd never seen anything like it. Some kind of long white dress with a lace collar and big pearl buttons down the back. I didn't think a thing about it at the time, but the ME says it's weird. Old looking. Like some kind of costume." He shook his head. "I saw the girl around town from time to time. Not exactly a stranger. But I never saw her, or any of the other girls for that matter, in anything like it."

"Ask her parents what she was wearing when they last saw her?"

Ed nodded. "Mother was screaming. Father said he thought it was a pink and white striped shirt, maybe black tights. A black jacket with a hood."

When he looked up at Tony, Ed's eyes were red. "Worst part of the job. Now I've got to tell those grieving folks it's even worse than they could imagine. Somebody did this to their daughter on purpose. Dumped her body after something awful happened. Sure as hell hope it wasn't kids up to something that backfired."

"Maybe it was a costume. Like she was in a school play."

"Could be. I'll call Principal Stoves soon as I know a little more."

They thought a while.

"What're you going to say?" Tony asked.

"Say to who?"

"The Roots."

Ed shrugged. "The truth. They can't plan a funeral until the ME releases their girl's body. Won't be for days, I imagine." Ed rubbed hard at his forehead as if chasing growing pain to either side. "And they want to see her. Had to argue them out of it this morning."

"Maybe they know about the dress."

"I'll ask Sally Root. You know, what Janice was wearing when they last saw her. Just to be sure. Could be Jay was wrong."

Tony got up and stretched hard. He wanted to see Jenny. Maybe for her smile. On a day like this a sweet smile could take a man a long way. Sometimes she made him laugh. Sometimes, when she got mad at him, she didn't.

It was like they'd gotten close—really close—but in the last few weeks she'd changed. Better than it was at first when she was just home from Chicago, after that bastard she was married to left the country with some rich lady. Not like that—when Jenny could stare knives through him just for opening his mouth. Now it was more like . . . being friends. Only lately, she was distant again. If there was one thing Tony thought he knew about women, it was not to push when they had something on their mind.

"If there's any way I can help, you call me, okay?"

Ed made a wry face. "Trust me, I'll be calling. Got the state boys, but this whole thing looks like something we never handled before. I'll be calling on you, Tony. And let me say up front—I appreciate it."

Tony shrugged as he slowly got up from the chair, favoring his leg. "See what the ME comes up with. I'll bet Zoe and Jenny will help out, too."

Ed made a face. "That little lady makes me laugh. About one half the size of me. Walks a little funny—kind of like a penguin. That voice—well, she sounds like a kid, to tell you the truth. Smart as hell, though. Never met anybody like her."

Tony laughed. "Nobody has."

"And don't forget, she writes books. Never knew a writer either."

"Yeah," Tony nodded a few times, holding back the urge to laugh again. "They're a really weird group, you ask me—those writers."

"You're making fun of me." Ed gave a weak, embarrassed laugh.

Tony only smiled while Ed's face went from a smile to something near being sick.

"Something else I gotta tell you, Tony." Ed leaned way back in his chair, fingers beating a tattoo on the desk. "You know Pamela Otis, from the credit union?"

"Yeah. Know her. Nice woman. Dora was saying something about her one time. That she had a rough life. Not that Dora was gossiping, just that she thought the woman looked tired and was kind of wondering, was all."

"Her life just got a lot tougher. Came to report her girl missing."

"What the hell?" Tony's face went dark. The scar along his cheek moved as if with a nervous tic all its own.

"I know the kid," Ed said. "Not from any trouble she got into. From church potlucks, things like that. Name's Camille. Mom calls her Cammy. Sixteen. She's a little slow; I guess that's what you call it. But always a smile and willing to help anybody with just about anything. Good kid."

The chief leaned back and squeezed his eyes shut a minute.

"What's going on?" Tony asked.

"Gone since yesterday. Maybe late morning. Maybe afternoon. Pamela was at work all day."

Tony made a face.

"On this one you've got to know the whole story," Ed went on. "Girl's done it before. Pamela says sometimes she wanders off like this, but always comes home. Once, it was an overnight. She stayed in somebody's barn or something. Pamela said she wasn't really worried, but she heard about Janice Root this morning and was afraid they were wrong and that it was Camille dead out there on the road. Came in here crying her head off."

"What're you going to do?"

"Miz Otis brought me a photo of the girl."

"Yeah, you don't want to wait with kids. Never know."

"Another time I might not move this fast—kids are always running off and coming home in a day or two, but with Janice Root now . . . I can't ignore it. Got an amber alert out."

"Be On the Lookout, too?"

Ed nodded. "Across the state. Every officer in the North Country will be watching for her. If it weren't for the Roots coming in this morning, I'd be out there already."

"Do you know what she was wearing when her mother last saw her?"

"Some kind of jacket with a bear on the back. A shirt with radio call numbers on it. Sneakers. There's a phone but she doesn't answer."

Tony nodded. Kid clothes, like they all wore. "Think you'll need a search party?"

"Let's wait and see. Give the girl a chance to come back. Tell the truth, I've got no idea where to start unless somebody saw her."

"I wouldn't worry too much, Ed. Probably be home before Pamela gets back there."

Tony got out of his chair and stretched. "Guess I better get moving. Call me as soon as you know what killed Janice, okay? I'll get a search started for Camille. Tomorrow morning? If she's not back by then . . ."

"Yeah." Ed shook his head. "Tomorrow morning. I'll check around town today."

Tony nodded, stopping just inside the doorway. "I'll put the word out that we need searchers."

"Yeah. Yeah," he said. "But, God, I hope Camille's okay."

Tony turned when he felt the door pushing open behind him. The Roots were on the other side, on the outside stoop, waiting for him to move. Behind them was the Reverend Everett Senise from the United Baptist Church.

Tony closed his eyes for just a minute before telling Sally and Jay Root how sorry he was about their girl. The two didn't seem to understand what he was saying. The Reverend Senise put his narrow hands on Sally's back, then prodded both confused people toward where the police chief waited.

Tony shut the door quietly behind him and hurried down the steps, thinking he'd head over to Jenny's. More than anything, now, he needed to see her. Maybe they could take in a show at the State Theatre later. Get their minds off everything else. Maybe they'd go someplace for dinner. Maybe they'd stay home and talk about nothing much at all. Maybe she'd stay with him and join the hunt in the morning. What hit him then was something he'd never had to think about in Detroit. Miles and miles of woods. Empty woods. One mile looked just like the next mile. Terrible job ahead of them—looking for the girl.

Made him want to see Jenny all the more.

Chapter 6

Pamela Otis sat in Dora Weston's kitchen. She'd come straight from the police station, something driving her, eating at her, propelling her to the house of this woman she didn't know and had only heard of. She'd tried, but there was no going home. Cammy wouldn't be there. She knew it as well as she knew a girl in town was dead and other parents were grieving over their daughter.

Sixteen years old. A little different from most girls, but her daughter wasn't dead. There was no world in which Cammy could be dead and never coming home—like Janice Root was never going home again.

She knew she was being pacified when the chief looked at her and said: "She'll be back. Bet you by tonight. Kids run away all the time, Miz Otis."

He smiled the way men do when they say, *"Don't worry your pretty little head over it."*

That was when she came looking for Zoe Zola and found her at Dora Weston's house. Zoe Zola was in the newspaper from time to time—had a knack for solving crimes people said, and here she was at Dora's table: a little woman with a troubled face and wild, curly blond hair; with blush on her cheeks, and lipstick and mascara, and a wearing a soft, purple, cotton sweater.

Pamela cleared her throat. "Cammy is . . . a special kind of girl, you see. The doctor said autistic, then something else. A little slow but independent. She's gone away before. Once she wanted to see how far she could get before it got dark. I've always been able to reach her by phone. But this time . . . I keep calling. Over and over. It rings then I get nothing."

"I wouldn't worry, Pamela." It was Dora Weston talking, a woman with a sweet face and a way of making her words sound like pleasant things let loose in the room.

"She'll be home. Bet she's there when you get back." Dora's daughter, Jenny, said. She yawned a couple of times, then wiggled her bare feet on the edge of the chair next to her, staring at her chipped, red toenails.

Jenny's hair was black with a little bit of gray in it, pulled back and tossed on top of her head, held there in a kind of fountain by a tortoiseshell clip. She didn't say much, mostly listened as Pamela explained again why she was there.

"She's my daughter. She's sixteen. Janice Root is dead. And my girl is gone . . ."

Zoe Zola eyed Pamela Otis and didn't see a nervous woman, nor a hysterical woman. More a sad woman.

"She would normally find a way to call me. You don't know, Cammy. She's a determined girl . . ."

"You said she's special. But even special girls come home." Zoe poked a short finger into her hair then removed the finger and placed it at her left temple where she bent her head against it. "No phone call doesn't mean she's not out there. And if she did this before . . . well."

"Please don't tell me what I feel is wrong." Pamela closed her eyes and took a deep breath as if she already knew nobody would help her, that she was on her own the way she'd always been on her own.

"What she was wearing?"

Pamela sighed. "When she left for school I think she had on her WTOM radio station shirt. Her black jacket is gone. She must have worn that. Probably her white sneakers. Or—dirty white. And jeans. She always wore jeans."

"Humph!" Zoe, back on her pile of phone books at Dora's kitchen table, thumped her hands together. A bit of churlishness crept into

Zoe's voice. "Most girls return. Probably be waiting for you when you get home. I don't know what else we can do . . ."

"Now, Zoe," Dora laid a hand on her small hand.

Zoe's eyes flew wide open. "I'm just being informative."

She turned back to Pamela and, this time, frowned as she tipped her head to listen ever so closely.

Pamela twisted a Kleenex between her fingers. "I think she left while I was at work yesterday. We were going shopping when I got home. She should have been there. If she'd gone anywhere she would have left me a note. If she was going out for ten minutes, there would have been a note. She would have explained."

She tore the Kleenex to bits. "I went to the police chief this morning . . ."

"Why not last night?" Jenny asked.

Pamela's red-rimmed eyes looked from Jenny to Zoe, and then back again. She didn't answer Jenny's question. "I heard about the Root girl being found dead on U.S. 31 this morning. I was sure it was Camille. Had to be."

Interrupted by a cough, Pamela stared down into her hands "One time Cammy wanted to stay in the woods and listen to the owls. She came home early the next morning. She doesn't know what the world is really like. She doesn't know how bad some people are. Everybody's wonderful, that's what she thinks. All it would take is that one evil person. I tried to tell her. Over and over."

She closed her eyes.

"But you see," Zoe made a clucking sound toward Pamela. "You're afraid this time because you heard about Janice Root. That's what it is."

The woman's shoulders lowered, her head tipped forward so her hair hung around her face.

"I'll bet you'll find her at home." Jenny's voice was soft. "Her cell's dead, is all."

As if giving up, Pamela Otis stood to leave. "Of course," she finally said. "Of course."

"We'll help if you need us . . ." Dora promised, narrowing her eyes at Zoe, who she wasn't happy with right then.

"She's only sixteen," Pamela said.

"Is there a boy in the picture?" Jenny asked.

"Kent Miller. A sweet boy with . . . some of the same limitations Camille has. He's somewhere in Southern Michigan hunting turkey with his dad right now. That's what Camille told me."

"She wouldn't try to go see him, would she? I mean, head off hitchhiking or something like that?"

Pamela shook her head.

"Kent Miller?" Jenny asked again.

Pamela nodded.

"You know where he lives?"

She nodded. "Pleasant Street. I don't have the house number."

"Telephone?"

She shook her head.

"I was thinking . . . just in case." She looked over at Zoe. "Maybe we should go see him."

"He's with his dad. He wouldn't be with Cammy." She walked toward the doorway.

"Please call us when you get home," Dora asked.

The woman nodded then left the room, her head high, her shoulders slumped. They heard the front door close softly.

* * *

Most women grieved alike, Dora knew from her sixty-four-years of living. Something so terribly familiar about the process. It was the way she'd grieved for Jim. And the way she'd grieved for her parents. As if she, along with everyone around her, were terribly fragile and might break into pieces if a voice was raised or a laugh was too loud.

She felt that way now about Pamela Otis. And felt that she'd let her down.

She recognized the smile Pamela wore. It was her smile after Jim died. She found it easier to worry about others while she walked uneven ground. She saw to Lisa and Jenny meticulously, urging them to eat, pretending that nothing had really changed in their lives. Just this little difference—no husband or father any more.

If anything, this was worse, this frozen woman holding herself together, blaming herself for not knowing the unknowable. This woman's child was gone, and the woman's body was stiff as if it could be easily broken, like an odd, glass body.

Dora got up to get the coffee pot from the stove, taking it to bend at each woman's shoulder, filling her cup, then pushing the cream and sugar forward in an old, reassuring gesture she'd learned from watching her own mother.

"She's in trouble, isn't she?" Dora asked Zoe, looking straight at the frowning woman.

Jenny waved a hand. "Camille will be there. I'll bet anything."

Zoe and Dora looked at each other. Dora said nothing more. Zoe shook her head.

"The kid's gone," she finally said. "That's two. I don't want it to be true."

Zoe slid from her chair, toeing Fida, who grumbled, to get up. "I'm going home. Call me when you hear anything."

They didn't look at each other.

Neither Jenny nor Dora spoke.

The door closed behind Zoe with the softest of sounds.

Chapter 7

When Tony left the police station, his stomach growled at him. He headed up Oak toward Myrtle's. A breakfast taco sounded good. Scrambled eggs with a sausage in the middle, all wrapped in a piece of thinly cut white toast. No matter how gross the idea of such a thing might be, it appealed to him, unless Myrtle decided it was too late for breakfast and dug her heels in, refusing to make him a breakfast taco when her board clearly said: MEATLOAF.

Demeter Hopkins went to the kitchen to see if a breakfast taco was still possible and came back with the taco double wrapped in greased paper, then wrapped in triple napkins, with a paper cup of coffee to go with it.

"Myrtle's not herself today," Demeter said. "She's got a lot on her mind. Not nearly as ornery as usual. We heard about Janice early. Then, little while ago, somebody came in and said Camille Otis is missing. Is that true?"

Tony shook his head and reached for a few more napkins to catch the grease coming from the wrapped taco. "Heard the same thing," he said.

"Myrtle is in a bad way. Doesn't seem to care what she cooks, nor when."

Demeter gave a deep sigh and looked off, out the big front windows. "Lots of people been asking about a search party."

"In the morning. Tell whoever wants to help to be at the police station by eight. If she's found before then we won't have to do a thing."

"You know everybody will be there. They all want to help." She walked away to wait on a couple that had just walked in. She stopped to look over her shoulder at Tony. "Almost forgot. Would you go out and see Myrtle for a sec? She's got something to tell you, she says. I told you she's not herself today. Hardly wants to actually talk to anybody."

"Glad to." He had to laugh. Three years in town and this was his first invitation into the mighty Myrtle's kitchen.

Myrtle wasn't a big person but she stirred a big pot at the six-burner stove in the large, half-dim, foggy kitchen. Her hairnet askew, standing on a stepstool, she stirred and stirred as she watched Tony come hesitantly across the kitchen toward her.

He stopped next to the stove—plenty of room between them left to run should she take after him with her monstrous spoon, now making swiping noises as it went round and round in the pot.

"I know things," Myrtle said, one eye closed against the steam.

"Yes, ma'am. I imagine you do."

"Are you being a smart ass?" Myrtle was quick to stop all motion and glare at him. "I don't take to smart asses."

"No, ma'am. I meant I imagine a lot of news comes through a place like this."

"What do you mean 'A place like this'? What do you think my restaurant is—some kind of hot bed of . . ."

Tony sighed, leaned against the stainless-steel table behind him, and crossed his arms. "Okay, Myrtle. You asked me to come out here. I imagine you've got something to say."

She stepped down from her stool, laid the spoon on the stove, and stood with her chin in one hand, looking off into a corner.

"I do have something to tell you. Maybe you know it already and maybe you don't."

She looked at him from the corner of her eyes. "Do you know it already?"

Tony shrugged. "How would I know if I know it unless you tell me what you're talking about?"

"What do you think I'm talking about?"

"No clue."

"Pamela Otis, that's who."

"What about her?"

"Then you don't know."

"Don't know what . . ." He turned to go, figuring he'd wasted his time. The woman had nothing to say.

"Pamela's girl, Camille, is missing. You're new here. I want to tell you about Pamela Otis's life because maybe it has a lot to do with where Cammy is now."

She pulled a chair out from the table and sat down, making a noise as she rested her feet. "Pamela's like everybody's daughter here in town. Her folks were terrible people. All tied up with some religious cult that had a campground or something or other out in the woods."

"You hear any of this?" She snapped her head up.

"No. Nothing."

"Okay. Here's the whole story. Just let me tell it and don't interrupt." Her shoulders settled, she bent her head forward, and began to talk. "You see, that man and that woman were just awful to Pamela. If anybody got a rotten pick in the parents department, it was her. That church they belonged to believed in group-beatings for kids. They'd meet out there where a bunch of 'em had this kind of camp. They'd beat the kids for so much as falling asleep during the deacon's sermons."

"Were you in the church, too?" he asked, his old habit of interrogation coming on him.

"Told you not to interrupt." Myrtle fixed him with a freezing stare.

"Pamela was a teenager when she met Gerald Hoskins, he was an older guy, managed The Falls movie house for a while. Next thing we heard Pamela was pregnant and Gerald Hoskins left town. When the baby was born, Margaret and Jeddah Otis didn't go to the hospital to see Pamela or the baby. Fact of the matter is, they went around saying the baby was wrong in the head. God's judgment on their sinful daughter, they kept telling anybody who would listen. In a couple of days those two emptied out the house, put it on the market, and moved with their church, though I heard the church broke up later. Think some of 'em went to Ohio and others went to another place here in Michigan. When Pamela and Cammy got out of the hospital there was nobody to meet 'em. Nobody to take 'em home. They're evil people, those two. Probably all the rest in that church just as evil."

She took a deep breath. By now, Tony knew better than to say a word.

"Ladies at the Baptist church heard about what happened and went into Traverse City and picked the two of 'em up from the hospital. Whole church got together and collected clothes for the baby. Patty Ann and Dorian Westlake made a home for both of 'em. You know, he's the manager at the credit union. Took care of them like their own. When Pamela turned nineteen, Dorian got her a job at the credit union, and she's been there ever since. Saved a bit and bought that house she's in. All the while she loved that little girl like nobody ever saw a little girl be loved."

Myrtle got off her chair, climbed back on her stool, and stirred her soup again.

"Is that it?" Tony pushed away from the table, taking a step back.

"Not finished yet." She stirred slower, then slower as she thought. "Everybody in town said it was God's judgment on the Otis's, that the church moved right then, and they had to go with it. I say it was judgment on the Otis's that they lost their daughter and sweet grandchild. But a couple of times lately they've been spotted around town. First I'd heard of them in years. That's what I wanted to tell you. People saw 'em and somebody got the idea maybe they wanted to steal Cammy away now that she was old enough to be taken into that church. That's what people started to say. Well," she frowned, "it was me started to say that because I don't trust either one of them."

"So, what you're telling me is maybe it was Pamela's mother and father who took Camille?"

She nodded hard and fast. "That's what I imagine happened. Wanted you or Ed to know. He hasn't been in here, so it had to be you."

Tony worked at something in his head. A little fact that might have belonged somewhere in Myrtle's story.

"Those church people ever wear funny clothes, you know like old-time dresses, anything like that?"

She shook her head. "Don't ask me. I don't belong to that church, just heard about them. And heard those awful people were back in town."

Chapter 8

Tony finished the taco, slopping sauce on his jeans as he drove. He rubbed away what he could with the handful of napkins he'd taken, then carefully drank his coffee from the feeble paper cup. He let himself think about what Myrtle told him, though he wasn't sure it was worth thinking about. Nothing about Pamela's mother and father tied them to Janice Root. Probably looking at a coincidence here. Two girls at one time: one dead, one missing. He was already coming to disbelieve—or maybe just hope—that a thing like that couldn't happen in Bear Falls.

For no reason at all he drove over by the high school. A few kids were hanging out near one corner of the fence, huddled together, sharing a cigarette. Of course kids were like that—getting in trouble, sometimes trouble bad enough to harm them. But what did a bunch of high school kids have to do with murder?

He turned up Maple toward Jenny's street, waving to one of Angel Arlen's girls. She was pushing a baby carriage. A baby herself. Eighteen. She would have known Janice and had to know Camille. But almost everybody in town would have known them, or knew them by sight. Why was Janice found dead on the road? Why was she wearing an old white cotton dress? Where were her clothes? Why was Camille Otis gone?

He braked for the Reverend Robert Senise, Bear Falls' Evangelical minister and twin brother of the Baptist minister. He was a thin man, like his twin brother, but this pastor rarely smiled and Tony understood why. The man had seven kids, a very fertile wife, and a small church.

The reverend nodded as he hurried across in front of Tony, heading to the post office.

On Elderberry, Tony slowed, turning up Dora's driveway as

Pamela Otis came out the front door of the house and stumbled down the steps. She didn't see him and hurried off until she was beyond Zoe's house, when she began to run.

Tony tapped at the screen door, then tapped again until Dora came scurrying across the porch and pushed the door wide.

"Tony. Come in. Come in. So much going on I didn't hear you."

"I saw Pamela Otis leaving."

"You heard about her girl?" Dora's eyebrows went up.

"Ed told me. I went over there to see if there was anything I could do to help with Janice Root's death. He said Pamela'd been in. Said Camille was missing."

"Then you can guess why the poor woman was here. Word about Zoe solving crimes has been all over town."

Tony followed Dora into the kitchen to stand in the doorway looking hard at Zoe Zola, seated on her phone books, small face deep in thought.

He turned to Jenny, who looked up as he walked toward her. She didn't smile. It seemed her hand was going up to hold him away. He didn't try to kiss her, or even get too close.

Zoe slapped her hands on the tabletop. "You're right, Dora. We've got to help here," she said, half ignoring Tony.

He took the chair next to Jenny reached over to touch her, only for a second. Her hand was quick to get away.

"Girl's probably home already," Tony said to Zoe. "Wouldn't worry if I was you."

Zoe dropped her head into her hands and looked up, her blue eyes staring hard at him through her fingers. "The kid's gone."

"They come back usually."

Zoe shrugged. "That's what I thought at first. Now . . ." She shook her head.

"Did Ed get the driver who killed Janice Root?" Jenny wanted to know.

He hesitated, wondering how much he could tell.

"What's he heard so far?" Zoe asked, almost absentmindedly, as if there were many tracks of thought competing inside her head.

The look she gave him when he didn't answer was deep and probing. "Murder, huh? Am I right?"

He nodded. "Not a hit-and-run. Been dead two days already. No trauma on her body. And she wasn't lying in the road for two days. Rigor gone. Lividity gone. She'd been moved. Probably brought to the highway from where she died."

Zoe sighed. "I knew it. Knew it before I got out of bed this morning. Didn't want to believe it though. Awful thing."

"Now, Zoe . . ." Dora chided.

"What did she die of?" Zoe went right on.

He shrugged. "ME's calling as soon as she knows."

"Two days?" Zoe sat with her head in her hands. "Then dumped on the highway sometime last night."

Tony nodded.

"A crazy teenage thing? Overdose?" Jenny demanded something logical she could hold on to.

"Then where'd they stash her body for two days? And why?" Zoe asked.

Tony shook his head. "There *is* something else, but you can't tell anybody." He looked toward Zoe. "When they found her, she was wearing . . ."

He shook his head, hesitating to go on.

"What? What was she wearing?" Zoe urged.

"A strange outfit. Not like anything a teenage girl would wear."

"You mean, like she'd been redressed?" Zoe kept at him.

He nodded.

"In what?"

"A dirty white cotton dress. Ed said it was like something you'd see on an old doll, or in some historical movie. Lots of lace and long, puffed sleeves. Pearl buttons down the back."

"A religious outfit? Like that?" Zoe's head was scrunched down into her body, her eyes almost closed. "Maybe something those polygamist groups out west make the women wear?"

Nobody spoke.

"Remember, you can't tell Ed I told you any of this," Tony warned.

"Some kind of religious outfit." Zoe said to herself.

"Not a clue. One thing though, Myrtle ordered me out to her kitchen and told me that Pamela's mother and father belonged to some religious sect. That's a kind of tie-in."

Dora nodded. "Terrible people, Tony. Awful. Abandoned Pamela when she had the baby. The whole town chipped in . . ."

"Myrtle thinks they could be the ones who took Cammy. They've been seen in town lately."

Dora made a face. "Why would they want anything to do with her now?"

Zoe's eyes were only slits. "And where's that leave Janice Root? She sure wasn't killed over some old family feud."

"Probably only one murder," Jenny said.

"Should know soon if Cammy's home," Dora said.

They were on to other things by the time the phone rang and Dora answered.

"She's not here," Dora heard Pamela say. "She hasn't been here. She's still gone . . ." Her voice cracked.

Dora turned to the others and shook her head.

Tony called out, "Tell Pamela we'll be out searching in the morning. We'll find her."

Dora relayed the message but wasn't certain Pamela heard.

"Tell Miz Zola and Jenny to come tomorrow, will you? I want them to know my Cammy. They have to understand her. If anybody can find her, it will be Miss Zola. I felt it, just talking to her. She's a little like Cammy. You know, with that kind of different brain."

Dora promised to tell them and then promised to call in the morning. "And Pamela, if she comes home—any time of the night—let us know. Please."

"So, Cammy's not there yet." Zoe stared at the floor. "Didn't think she would be. We'll go to her house tomorrow, all right?" She checked with Jenny, who nodded. "Just like she said. I want to see the girl's room—maybe something there will tell us who she is. At least we'll know where she liked to go. Maybe find mention of friends her mother forgot about. Or what kinds of things interest her."

"You think we'll find her?" Jenny's voice broke.

Zoe looked at her, and then at Dora. Something inside of her felt as if it was being torn open. Something she couldn't make herself think about right then.

Chapter 9

That evening after dinner, Zoe was back from an afternoon of trying to absorb more of Jane Austen. Jenny cleared the table and Zoe started the dishwasher. Because it was spring and even though it was cold, there was light beyond the windows. All three women had cabin fever and enough fear inside them to need the freedom of being away from the house for at least a little while.

Fida led across the yards, sniffing around Zoe's still empty flower beds, hunting for the fairies that should have been there by now, then looking over her shoulder with an accusing eye at three lazy women who'd done nothing visible all day.

It was agreed that they would each bring a fairy from the winter boxes and set her up in a bed—each choosing their own fairy and own flowerbed.

In the shadowed and icy shed there were a couple of wrangles over the most popular fairies. Dora gave in and took up little Blossom, finding her a tiny house for a front flowerbed. Both Zoe and Jenny wanted Lilianna, but since they were Zoe's fairies and her flowerbeds, she snatched Lilianna away to set her in a tower. That left Jenny with Tara, the fairy queen, which went a little way toward calming her covetousness.

"So." Zoe straightened, signaling an end to fairy placement especially since she looked forward to doing this yearly job alone. "We go to Pamela's about noon? Tomorrow. That okay, Jenny?"

Before Jenny could agree, Dora stood up very straight, eyes wide. She clapped a hand over her mouth.

"How could I have forgotten?"

"Forgotten what, Mom?"

"I promised Keith Robbins we'd all go with him to that new mansion on the lake at one o'clock tomorrow. For crap's sakes, how did I forget all about it?

"Sometimes it's like everything falls on your head all at once." She threw her hands up. "I wish I could forget the whole thing now but . . ."

"What 'whole thing'?" Zoe frowned, only half paying attention. She still had most of the evening to get back to *Pride and Prejudice*. Time to learn more patience as she got deeper into Austen's women, finding them far more ruthless than the men—a thing she held against them until another idea cropped up: that maybe ruthlessness came from desperation.

What lay beneath all that hysteria? She had to face the question, had to push hard for truth, teach herself to accept what was, and not judge the victims too harshly. And what did Jane Austen really think about her world?

She never married.

Oh, mess after mess after mess . . .

And then a different thing was whirling inside her. Something to do with Camille. She was trying to stick a pin in it, to hold it down. It had nothing to do with anything going on right then, but yet she couldn't shake the weird feeling.

Dora was saying. "The three of us. Along with Keith and Bernadette." She thought a minute. "And I think Minnie Moon and Dianna are going, too."

Jenny, impatient, asked, "For what, Mom? If it's like a welcome committee—honest, there are other things . . ."

"You're right about that. What you're doing is more important than a couple of million dollars coming to Bear Falls for a civic improvement, but I was hoping . . ."

"A couple of million?" Zoe tried to whistle but couldn't work up enough spit.

"It's that new man. Fitzwilliam Dillon. His friend came to see Keith."

"You said a couple million." Zoe tried to whistle again then gave up.

"Keith asked for both of you. In fact, he was very firm about you, Zoe."

"Never heard of a Fitzwilliam Dillon. Who's the man Keith saw?"

"Charles Bingman."

"Never heard of either one of them." Zoe scowled.

"Let me tell you first—Mr. Dillon hopes to be well received by all Bear Fallsians."

"Really? Bear Fallsians?" Jenny couldn't help but laugh.

"It's not just the improvement he's offering. He needs help throwing a party for the whole town this spring."

"Hmmm," Zoe was considering. "Did he say what the money had to go to? This civic improvement?"

"He wants Keith to spearhead a meeting where everybody can give their ideas and then vote."

Zoe frowned and thought a long time. "This Dillon man must be a real loser if he has to buy his way into our good graces."

"Two million should do it." Dora grinned over at her. "I can't imagine our 'good graces' costing more than that."

Zoe stood still, considering two million dollars.

Dora nodded. "An hour of your time. I promise. That's all he's asking for. If you go to Pamela's before one o'clock the search won't be over anyway. Nothing will be known."

Zoe was quiet. She blinked her eyes fast. She put a finger to her chin. "An hour? You promise?"

Dora nodded.

"Okay." She turned to Jenny. "I just thought of something we should do tonight."

"Tonight? I want to go call Tony. I was rude to him earlier."

Zoe shook her head. "You can make up any time. Mine is more important. I want to visit Reverend Senise, the one at the Baptist Church."

Jenny made a face. "If you're having a religious crisis leave me out of it."

Zoe stared until Jenny started squirming. "It's Pamela's parents," Zoe said. "I think we should find 'em. I'd like to know what they were doing back in town. Remember, Janice Root was dressed in an odd dress—maybe a religious outfit. Can't get it out of my head."

Dora made a face. "Blamed Camille's . . . well . . . her slight deficiency on Pamela's sins not a slight lack of oxygen at birth. How is that for Christian people?"

"Camille's a teenager now." Zoe frowned, trying to figure out the thing in her head. "Maybe they got to thinking she could be an addition to their goofy sect. Get her away from Pamela. Sometimes people are that twisted."

"Makes me sick to my stomach," Dora said. "Just the thought of poor Camille with those terrible people. She doesn't even know them. She wouldn't understand what was happening."

"Anybody else who might have an interest in Camille?" Jenny asked.

"Maybe her father," Zoe said, looking down at her hands, spreading her fingers so five perfect dots of nail polish flashed in front of her. "There's always that."

"And maybe the searchers will find her in the woods in the morning and we can stop worrying."

Dora was tired and wanted the evening over.

Zoe wanted to move. To do something.

Jenny didn't take long to decide that her evening wasn't going to get any better. *Oh, Tony.*

She hurried back home to get her purse as Zoe gathered up Fida, pushing her into Dora's arms. "You don't mind, do you? We won't be long?"

Dora stood at the curb waving as the women pulled away in Jenny's car. Worried, she hoped they would come back with something, anything that led to Cammy Otis being found.

Then came the new, and very vague, thought of a library in Bear Falls. *Wouldn't that be the best gift ever to the people of town?* She smiled for a minute. She squeezed Fida to her. *Who could argue with a library?*

Behind Dora Weston's closed eyes, a building began taking form—low and long, with a walled garden along one side . . .

She smiled wider. She squeezed Fida again, until the little white dog began to whimper.

Chapter 10

"Two million," Zoe said as Jenny turned down Oak toward Pastor Everett Senise's church, and the manse next door. "We could have a tremendous garden in the park. Maybe an arboretum. Think of that. We could offer master gardener classes right here and the gardens would bring visitors from everywhere."

Jenny made a noise. "Think about the kids. We could have a great gym. A swimming pool . . ."

"They've got Lake Michigan right outside their door."

"You ever try to swim there in December? Town needs a pool."

Jenny parked in front of the house where the Reverend Everett Senise lived with his wife and two children. Made of local river stone, the house was over a hundred years old. It stood next door to the Reverend's imposing stone church.

Zoe rang the bell and cocked her head to one side, listening to a serious gong beyond the door. She'd been to Reverend Senise's church a few times when she first moved to Bear Falls, but she didn't fancy it much. Predictable sermons—the reverend wasn't an imaginative man. And then there were the same people every week, and those same people gaped at her the first two weeks she attended services. Enough was enough, was what she said to Dora who begged her to give them a little more time to get to know her. Zoe was going to give the other Senise brother's Evangelical church, over behind the police station, a try but she told herself one night that her church might as well be her own home. Quiet there. Nobody preaching at her. Nobody staring at her. Nobody telling her she'd committed sins when she knew she hadn't committed any of those particular sins, but would gladly have owned up to her own, much smaller sins: like calling tall people terrible names when they stepped on her; like laughing at a group of relatives she'd never met when they learned their grandma left her—an unknown to all of them—the house in Bear Falls. Nobody mentioned any of those particular sins.

Elizabeth Senise opened the door to Jenny and Zoe, smiling broadly.

"Come in. Come in." She held the oak door wide. The woman, who wore a cardigan draped over her shoulders, a string of pearls around her neck, and looked as though she was held together with an old-fashioned girdle, was genuinely welcoming.

"We're here to see the reverend." Jenny stepped into the stone-floored vestibule and looked around. "Is he in?"

Elizabeth threw back her head, laughing. "That man. He's in his study, writing his sermon for tomorrow. Can you imagine? He always waits until the last minute and then berates himself for laziness. Week after week. But every Sunday morning he surprises me. Always such a wise and well-thought-out message to his congregants."

She tipped her head a little. "But that's a wife for you. I'll go ask if he can take a few minutes." She looked back over her shoulder, stopping. "It will be only a few minutes, won't it? Please have mercy on him or he'll be up all night."

Reverend Senise, his thin, red face drawn up in a smile, came from a room down a side hall. He trailed behind Elizabeth, then took Jenny's hand and then Zoe's into his, greeting them warmly.

"I always welcome talk with Bear Fall's most famous writer," he said, bending over Zoe's head. "Come on back. It's time I took a break. Elizabeth here is a slave driver." He grinned at his wife.

"Hmm. Slave driver. I'd like to see you, just once, stand up there before the people and fumble for words. That would teach you a little humility."

She walked away after being turned down on the coffee or tea question.

"So good of you two to call." In his office, the man rested back in a huge leather chair. On the large desk in front of him were pages of work fresh from the computer, an open Bible, and other volumes which—embossed with gold—looked to be ecclesiastical.

"My books." He slapped first one, and then another, of the books lying open in front of him. "I get so engrossed reading, preparing for my sermon, it takes me hours more time than it should each week."

"Sorry to say we're not here about religious matters." Zoe frowned across the desk at the man.

"No matter. I'd love to sit with you both a while. We'll have a talk. Maybe about the awful death that's happened." His thick eyebrows shot up.

"It's gotten worse." Zoe nodded at the man. "A girl from town has disappeared."

His eyebrows came together over his nose. "You mean a girl other than Janice Root?"

Zoe nodded again.

"Camille Otis." Jenny slid forward on her chair. "Pamela Otis's girl."

"Why, that's awful. But what do you mean by 'disappeared'? Kids are forever running off, you know."

"Pamela doesn't think so. This is the second day she's been gone."

"A sweet kid. Pamela is a member of our church. I'll call her after you leave. So terribly sorry. Good woman."

He raised his eyebrows, taking the news deeper. "This . . . now . . . on top of the hit-and-run. What can I do to help?" He leaned forward, knocking his knuckles on the desktop.

"There is something in Pamela's history . . ." Zoe took a deep breath. "I've heard . . ."

"You mean her parents, I suppose. I know about those people. Everyone in town does. And please don't hold cultists, such as the Otises, against the rest of us. What they got themselves mixed up in has nothing to do with a real faith in God. Most of the time they are personality cults, you know. Strong personalities like that terrible Jonestown man."

"Can you tell us where they might be? Her parents?"

"I suppose you mean the cult itself. I heard, in the last few years, that the group couldn't get along and a number of them left to start a new church. I don't know which sect the Otises went with. I could call my brother, Robert—see if he knows anything. Or I could even call a few friends, other ministers. It won't hurt to ask. As I said, I want to help in any way possible. Knowing Pamela's background, I admire the way she's turned out. A very nice woman. A good mother. And a hard . . ."

"Could you do that? Call around? See if you can find where they are now?" Jenny leaned in closer, breaking into what might have become a long rumination.

"I can certainly try, can't I? And I will. I promise you, I will do my best." He smiled from woman to woman.

Zoe gave him her number, writing with a flourish on the pad he pushed across the desk. "We appreciate your help. We've got to find Camille. And poor Janice . . ." She left the rest unsaid, remembering their promise to Tony not to let out the news that Janice was most likely murdered.

They followed the Reverend Senise back down the hall to the front door. Mrs. Senise was nowhere in sight.

"And, Reverend, one more thing." Zoe turned to him. "Do you know if any of those cults wore a particular kind of dress?"

He thought a minute. "Dress? You mean a uniform?"

"I mean, did any of them wear long, white dresses?" Zoe watched his face as he thought.

He shook his head. "I don't think so. I could be wrong; I know so little about them. But I'll ask. You can be sure I'll ask about that, too, and let you know."

He leaned toward Zoe, smiling. "I've read your books, Miss Zola. You have quite a mind for delving into lives and thoughts buried in our literature. I salute you. And to see that mind of yours trained on evil makes me feel more secure in this world. You may be on the small side, but your footprint is large. You two will find Camille." He nodded to include Jenny. "I have every confidence in you both."

Zoe, looking up at the pleasant man, turned bright red. She scowled to cover her mix of pleasure at his kind words and embarrassment at all the things she'd thought about his sermons. She promised they would do their best as he closed the door on them.

"I've got to get back to church, at least once in a while," Zoe mumbled to Jenny as they walked out to Jenny's car.

"For your soul? Or for a few more compliments?"

"Shame on you. Nothing but a heathen. Never see you out of bed before noon on Sunday morning."

"God knows where to find me."

"What if she's not looking?"

CAMILLE

The girl lay perfectly still on the bed, a cold dirty pillow at her back and a thin pink blanket over her bare feet. She mostly sat with her eyes closed so she didn't have to look at the room, nothing but concrete walls and one dim and flickering light fixture on the far wall. There was a table. There were three chairs—like the three bears. There were metal shelves along the back wall with old boxes of crackers and cans of soup split up the sides and other stuff she couldn't identify and didn't care about because she wasn't hungry. She wasn't anything but scared.

Mostly she sang while she waited for him to come back and let her out of this damp hole in the ground. One song after another, especially "That's the Way It Is" because Mom liked Celine Dion and sang the song all the time, and when she thought about it now she liked best the line that went: "Don't surrender 'cause you can win" so she sang it again and again because it was like having Mom in her head with her, singing a duet.

She hummed to the soft shirring of air coming in up high on the wall, where it was too dark to see, making new songs in her head when she couldn't think of old ones.

She was dressed in a dress that wasn't hers but was all he'd left her. A white dress with lace around the neck and lace in ruffled layers down the front. Lace and lace and lace until she saw nothing but lace when she looked over her body, and dirty lace ruffles tripped her bare feet when she tried to slide off the bed. It was a dress far too big for her. She would have pulled it off, but there was nothing else in the chilly room for her to put on except the pink blanket, which was far too puny for warmth. And he said her clothes were gone.

From time to time she pulled the dress up over her head and off her arms and nested inside where her breath warmed her.

63

She'd thought the man was a new friend, but this wasn't the way friends treated people. She knew what a real friend was like. Her mom told her so many times, "You'll find a friend. Just you wait." Then she found Kent. Kent was a real friend. Maybe he was a boyfriend.

Mom told her to treat people the way she wanted to be treated. That was Mom's golden rule. Kent treated her like that—just the way she wanted to be treated by a boy.

At first, she'd thought the man was nice, too. But he brought her here. He brought her out to the middle of the woods where she was supposed to dig for dinosaur bones with a bunch of college students. He was going to pay her five dollars an hour and that seemed like a lot of money; money she would share with her mom—surprise her with the first check.

She shut her eyes and sat up against the stained pillow to think as hard as she needed to think. One thing was, she found her imagination. Miss Shubert, in the eighth grade, said she had a lot of it and said that it would take her far, but she didn't think Miss Shubert meant this far. Maybe too much imagination.

When she met the man outside her house, the man who said his name was James, he told her he'd found her flyer at the super market: LOOKING FOR A SUMMER JOB. He offered her a job, though she couldn't tell anyone about it because there were no other dinosaur digs in Michigan, and he didn't want people to know what they were doing.

He brought her to the woods and that was all right, but she didn't want to come down here with him. He said this was their laboratory and everything was set up, but right then she knew she'd made a mistake and kicked and screamed but she couldn't do anything about it. He pushed her through the double metal doors and down the metal ladder.

Once she was at the bottom of the ladder, she grabbed on to his leg and pulled until he kicked her in the head, knocking her out. He must have picked her up and carried her to this little bed in the corner of this strange room. When she woke up her clothes were gone. Gone, like magic, *and she wore the dress. And he said her clothes, and her phone, were in the woods so somebody who really needed them could find them.*

Her arms hurt a lot and there was one more thing. It was a good thing. There was an old teddy bear on the bed beside her. His fur was worn off over his stomach and stuffing stuck out of his back, but he had both of his shoe button eyes and they were friendly when he looked up at her.

With no watch and no clock, the girl had no idea what time it was, nor even how many days she'd been here. Maybe one whole day. Maybe two. She tried to count on her fingers but didn't know which finger to start on and which to end on. It all seemed so much to think about. It was better to sit on the bed or sit in one of the chairs at the little table and think of ways to get home.

She stopped humming and reached a hand out to feel for the bear. He was as soft as anything she'd ever felt. She held the old bear to her cheek and, though it smelled funny, she felt at peace with the bear close by, like she wasn't alone in this cold room with concrete walls and crisscrossed curtains over painted-in windows.

There was nothing for her to do but wait until Mom came for her. She was sure that wouldn't take long. Mom was a fighter. Look how she'd fought the grandparents. Mom would fight anybody for her, she knew that much, and the idea kept her happy when there was no way to measure time, so she sang and counted—one and two and three—until she knew how long a song lasted. If she kept singing that song and counting at the same time, she knew how long a half hour was until she got tired and didn't care and stopped singing. She wrapped the pink blanket up around her, over the dress, and thought what she could do to pass the time was write stories in her head. So, she wrote little stories and then bigger stories until she heard the metal door open. She buried her face in the pillow, as he told her to do. She wouldn't look at him nor talk to him, nor to the person he brought with him, who had a soft voice and called her Mandy though she mumbled over and over again that her name was Camille.

She was handed a meatloaf sandwich and a carton of milk and told to eat with her back turned to them.

When they were gone, she lay on the bed telling herself a story about a young girl who was trapped in a house in the woods and animals and people kept coming to the door. The three bears came and she ran out of the house. An old witch came and cackled at her and pointed to a stove where she was going to cook her, but she ran out of the house again and got home safe.

There was a grandmother who lived in a house in the woods and she was there when a wolf walked in and ate the grandmother but didn't eat Camille because she was hiding under the bed. Then a little girl in a red cape came in with a basket filled with strawberries that she'd picked for her grandmother and she kept asking, "Where's my grandmother?"

Pretty soon the little girl went back outside and came in with a wood-cutter who found the wolf hiding in a storeroom and cut him open and let the grandmother out and everybody was happy.

That story was wrong, so she had to start over and make the wolf dress up as the grandmother, and when the little girl came with her basket of strawberries and asked where her grandmother was, she pointed to the wolf and said he ate her grandmother. The little girl ran out to find a woodcutter who came in and killed the wolf and let the grandmother out and everybody celebrated.

That was pretty good because when she fell asleep all she dreamed about was sitting in the middle of a field of forget-me-nots, in a big pool of sunshine. She ate the whole basket of strawberries by herself.

Part 2

"Surprises are foolish things. The pleasure is not enhanced,
and the inconvenience is often considerable."

—Jane Austen, *Emma*

Chapter 11

From the beginning, nothing about this trip to the mansion on the shore felt right to Jenny. If she had ever sensed a rolling wall of doom coming at her, this afternoon felt like that slow-motion wall. Part of it was Janice Root. She couldn't keep her mind off what happened to the girl. It made no sense. Not a crazed rapist. She wasn't raped. Not an accident—she was deliberately left by the highway. Why, when there were miles and miles of woods to hide her body, would someone put her by the road?

Then Camille Otis—gone. Just gone. Still gone. This one with a man involved. Wouldn't any girl have told someone about him? Her mother? Her boyfriend?

The black Chevy behind them honked and Jenny remembered what she was mad at next. Gladys Bonney and her daughter, Tammy, were following them. She'd heard Minnie Moon shooting her mouth off in Myrtle's, about going to a meeting at the mansion. "Figured if we were all being good neighbors, why, me and Tammy should be among the first," Gladys said when they came to the door, earlier, came in and stood, waiting to go, as if butting in was the most natural thing to do.

"You all know my Tammy, don't you?" She had smiled and pushed Tammy forward. "Probably already heard she won first prize in the tile-painting contest in Traverse."

Tammy gave a slight bow, a sweet smile, and a nod of her head. Jenny watched the girl and felt so deeply for her. Town gossips called her "Poor Tammy." Jenny, who knew her from high school, had heard it many times. And sometimes the gossips shook their head and whispered that "Poor Tammy" was a born spinster. *The kind of girl who doesn't look you straight in the eye. Too shy to look at a man her age.*

69

Jenny remembered hearing one teacher suggest Tammy Bonney wasn't too smart. Another teacher countered, "No, personally I think she's way *too* smart. You know, one of those women who can't be bothered with regular things."

Zoe came in the front door behind them, ready for the meeting in a long, striped-green dress with a green bow in her hair and clunky green shoes.

Gladys took a step back, looking her up and down. "You must be that Little Person people talk about."

Zoe slowly turned to Dora. "Is this woman going with us?" She tipped her head up in Gladys' direction.

"Well, I . . ."

Gladys didn't have sense enough to leave it alone. "Got a blueberry cobbler in the car, Dora. You know it's the first to sell out every bake sale. Want to give it to the new people."

Gladys leaned in close to her daughter, covered her mouth with her hand, and said, "That's Zoe Zola, you know, the dwarf you've been hearing about. She's helping the police chief look for that missing girl."

Zoe flew out the front door. She sailed down the steps, stomping on the hem of her long dress. The green bow tilted to one side.

She was in the back seat when Jenny and Dora came out.

"Off to Rosings," Zoe crowed. "What fun! A pompous ass for an owner and now a retinue of slithering mothers with daughters to auction off. What fun! What fun!"

"You and Jane Austen better behave yourselves, Zoe Zola." Dora turned around to warn her, then turned to eye Jennie. "Minnie and Gladys aren't the only desperate mothers who might be hoping to marry off a girl or two, you know. Of course I'll play up your assets as best I can."

"I've got assets?" Zoe almost growled.

"There's your good temper, Zoe. How's that for an asset? And your wonderful manners. That's two right there."

Zoe thought a while. "Not bad for a dwarf," she said.

*   *   *

Zoe was the first to spot the long stonewall, and then the wrought-iron arch above the open gate with ROSINGS etched among wrought-iron flowers.

She chortled, "'Rosings.' Look at that. Lady Catherine de Bourgh's home: Rosings Park in *Pride and Prejudice*. Talk about putting on airs. Can't wait to meet this Fitzwilliam Dillon."

She watched as the long drive curved one way and then another. She snickered at the pathetic gardens, nothing but piles of sand with sand sculptures on top: funny animals and castles, half washed away. *A big, pathetic sand box*, Zoe told herself then muttered "Fool. Not bright enough to know about Lake Michigan winds and wild storms. Blow those things away first thing."

There was a final curve ending in a circular drive, where Jenny stopped, pulling to one side, making room for Gladys to park beside her.

Up and up, Zoe looked. The house was big, but not as big as the fictional Rosings Park must have been. About what she expected though, a house of stone and brick, chimney after chimney, two stories, rows of casement windows stretching from one end of the house to the other. More space than any single man needed. But like Jane Austen's friends—this manor house wasn't about need, nor even about comfort. It was about thumbing your nose at your friends.

She tipped her head sideways to see the steep roof of red shingle. A house to impress. A house to declare the man who owned it wealthy enough to wall himself in; to keep the masses out.

More and more she was determined to dislike this Fitzgerald Dillon.

They got out and stood beside the car until Gladys and Tammy joined them, Gladys pointing and exclaiming over the biggest house she'd ever seen.

* * *

Minnie Moon and Dianna parked behind Jenny. Minnie turned off the motor, and blew out a deep breath, then recognized the black Chevy parked ahead and swore under her breath. Of all the . . .

She sputtered. Not the day she'd hoped for. Not at all. Here she was, still mad at Dianna—all floozied-up in a playsuit kind of thing that Minnie couldn't name, but short enough to show her underpants if she bent over—which Minnie told her emphatically not to do. And that makeup. If the girl started to sweat, her face would be down around her neck.

Now Gladys Bonney. *Could the day get any worse?*

Dianna got out and whistled. "One hell of a house if you ask me. Who do you imagine cleans it?"

"You could have a place like this if you played your cards right."

Dianna reared back to give her mother the look she always used when Minnie was delusional, a roll of her eyes and then a bat of her long, stiff lashes. She glanced at the place again. "You think I'm nuts?"

The other women were almost to the large, carved, front door. Minnie put on speed, catching up with Dora. "What's *she* doing here?" Minnie demanded in a voice meant to carry to Gladys' ears.

"She heard you talking in Myrtle's. What did you expect?" Dora shrugged, turning away from her. "She wants to be part of the welcoming committee, just like you and Diana."

"See that girl of hers?" Minnie hissed near Dora's ear. "Thinks she's going to marry Tammy off rich. Talk about high hopes!"

Dora pushed the bell. She turned to smile nervously at the others. Gladys straightened the shoulder of Tammy's pink sweater and poked her in the ribs—to stand up straight. She looked around at

Minnie and that girl of hers, dressed in some little playsuit fit for a three-year-old.

Out of nowhere, Gladys sighed, "Least my girl's a virgin," she said to no one in particular, but loud enough for everyone to hear. "That's a quality nobody here can claim."

Chapter *12*

Charles Bingman threw the door open and greeted their guests with his arms thrown wide. "Welcome to Rosings," he called out, smiling from woman to woman, then beckoning them inside. "Come in. Come in."

Dora was drawn in close to the tall man, into a hearty hug. His blond hair was newly shaved at the sides, the rest swept up and draped across the top of his head. He wore a blue turtleneck over dark blue slacks.

"Welcome! Welcome! I'm Charles Bingman, a friend of Fitzwilliam's. Please come in. Come in. We've been waiting for you." He drew them, one by one, into the long front hall.

Behind Charles, her red smile wide, her hands held out to take Dora's, was a woman who looked to Dora like an old movie star she couldn't name. The woman was dressed in what Dora took to be "casual afternoon chic"—a pale cream pantsuit with a soft, green scarf at her throat. Her makeup was pale and understated. At her throat, over the scarf, she wore a green broach, and green stones in her ears.

Probably emeralds Dora guessed, not with envy, more amazement—that the woman was here in Bear Falls, and that Dora was about to shake her hand.

"Lady Cynthia Barnabus." Charles stepped back to introduce the woman. "Lady Barnabus arrived from London this very day. She's been dying to see Fitz's new home." He turned to smile at the pretty woman.

Lady Barnabus clapped her hands, her pointed red nails flashing in front of her. "I'm so terribly happy to meet all of you Americans. What a treat! This gorgeous house, and now Fitz's new friends."

Both Lady Barnabus and Charles Bingman put an arm out to shepherd the group down the hall—talking to one after the other as they moved, making their guests comfortable, leading them to a huge, tiled room where a wall of sparkling windows looked out on nothing but water.

Oohs and aahs met the view; all of Lake Michigan spread out in front of them. Light blues and dark blues and deep greens shimmering in layers as the lake moved. Sun rode white-capped waves, then small waves spreading over the horizon. Slivers of watered sunshine danced across the ceiling of the room.

Zoe thought she was going to be seasick and turned away as fast as she could.

"For Christ's sakes!" Dianna barked at the view. "That's a lotta damned water. Kind of makes me feel wet all over."

Jenny gave an involuntary gasp at the room; not enough to embarrass herself, though embarrassment wasn't really a worry as Minnie and Gladys gave big rushes of breath and then—with Gladys a step ahead of Minnie—fell over themselves to clap their hands. Gush at the "beautiful vista." "Never saw such a view." "Wouldn't know it was the same lake . . ."

Zoe, stomach churning, preferred to get a good look at the room around her.

Shiny dark tiles. Dark paneled walls. Paintings—large and small—everywhere. Some she recognized. Those had to be prints. Some she didn't recognize and went closer to get a better sense of this Fitzwilliam guy. If there were only portraits of generals, she would run. If softly viewed countryside's—she might stay but think less of him.

There was a Willem de Kooning on the back wall, one she didn't know. Not bad. But beside the de Kooning—the unexpected: a Georgia O'Keefe—early work: *jack-in-the-pulpit*, the flower not as sexualized as her later works.

The next two paintings took her breath away. *Hairy Locomotion* and *Star Catcher* by Varo Remedios, one of her favorite painters—a woman. She almost didn't dare look any farther, fearful she would be disappointed.

And she was—the opposite wall was hung with Manets and Van Goghs. Old gold-stamped men staring across the room at wild women.

Fitzwilliam was a crazy man, Zoe told herself, smugness creeping into her opinion of the owner. What kind of collection was this—a wall of female artists facing a wall of male artists—a sexist face-off? She wasn't sure about the man, maybe a rabble-rouser, a man who liked to watch artistic battles.

"Isn't this something?" Bernadette Robbins, Keith's wife, a small woman, her brown hair cut bluntly around her face, joined Zoe in front of the last of the paintings.

"Imagine, a place like this is in Bear Falls."

Zoe thought a minute. "Makes you wonder, doesn't it?"

"About what, Zoe?"

"About why the rich get money without the good taste to go with it."

"Really?" Bernadette frowned at the paintings. "This is bad taste? Could have fooled me. Looks like an art museum."

"True." Zoe nodded, agreeing because there was nothing more to say and she was too wrong to defend herself.

"And I'll bet you anything he's got a huge library. I hope Dora gets to see it. I mean, first editions, signed copies. He wouldn't have those out where just anybody could touch them. I'll bet you anything he'll give Dora a tour."

A long table stood in front of the big windows. The table was covered with a startlingly white tablecloth, an array of silver, and a stack of white plates. Silver, domed platters were lined down the center of the table. A maid brought a bowl of iced shrimp, busied herself rearranging salt and pepper shakers, then plumped up white linen napkins.

Uncovered, the platters held meats and cheeses done up in little rolls. And plates of relishes. There were platters of charred asparagus and plates of thin sliced, raw-looking meat.

Charles Bingman and Cynthia Barnabus called to everyone to come help themselves as maids filled plates.

Minnie was especially effusive over the "black stuff" in a silver bowl. "Have one of those crackers with it," she whispered toward Jenny. "It'll go down better that way."

Charles Bingman seemed satisfied with the compliments as the guests helped themselves then stood around, juggling plates and glasses while smiling and carrying on conversations going in all directions.

Charles offered champagne at the far end of the table, though most took mimosa tea. It was, after all, early afternoon.

When everyone had a dish and a glass in their hands, Bingman raised his own glass.

"To Fitzwilliam Dillon—the owner of Rosings, and my very good friend."

Glasses were raised, with difficulty. The toast was seconded with a "Here, here."

"Fitz fell in love with this side of Michigan," Charles went on. "Another friend of ours, Nathan Wickley—whom you will meet shortly—brought him over from Chicago to see Northern Michigan and the places he knew as a child. Fitz couldn't get this lovely state out of his mind after that. And now he plans to stay here a long time, maybe one day retiring to Bear Falls. And that's why . . ." He spread one arm out to include everyone, confirming Dora's first impression that he was a well brought up and a very mannerly young man. "Fitz hopes you will welcome him to your town. And not just because he wants to do something special as an introduction, but because he hopes you'll happily share your beautiful lake and woods and air."

"The man's got a real castle here," Gladys gushed out loud while elbowing Minnie aside.

Tammy, prodded by Gladys, stepped forward and curtsied, holding her skirt out, then lowering her head so Charles couldn't see her face.

Jenny watched as Charles took Tammy's hand then bent to say something to her, making Tammy blush, then smile a little, and even look up at him. The smile on Tammy Bonney's face made Jenny feel better about the day. Maybe that smile signaled a change.

"Fitz and I have so looked forward to this." Charles beamed from face to face then turned to Jenny, saying he was especially happy she and her mother wanted to be a part of Fitz's gift to the town and the party to follow. From Jenny, he moved on, stopping to talk to everyone, making each person laugh a little and nod along with him. Soon Jenny was sure it wasn't only the food making her friend's faces a little red, the voices a little happier. Charles Bingman was the perfect host.

When Charles came to Zoe, he bent forward so he could look directly into her eyes. "And you are Zoe Zola, the famous author. Fitz is eager to meet you. He has ideas, himself, about how novelists and poets mirror our society. I believe that *is* the kind of thing you write, isn't it?"

Zoe didn't exactly nod. She wasn't sure what it was she wrote—things that moved her.

"I'm sure you'll enjoy your discussions with him," Charles said as Lady Barnabus came over, with Gladys frowning behind her.

Lady Barnabus took Charles' arm and held it, bending down to hear what Zoe was about to say.

Zoe, her annoyance leaving at Charles' interest in her work, was highly pleased at their attention. She accepted the praise with no modesty at all and was about to say something learned and wise but they moved on to Dora.

"And, of course, Dora Weston," Lady Barnabus greeted her. "Librarian of the town. You have those darling Little Library boxes so many are putting up, I hear. Keith tells me you will be our main mover and shaker."

They moved on when Dora, struck dumb at hearing the description of herself, couldn't come out with a single word.

Charles bowed over Minnie's hand and held Dianna's a little

longer than necessary, making Dianna wind up her motor and give her behind a shake.

"Please, all of you, make yourselves comfortable." Charles, having completed his circle of greetings, raised his hands for quiet. "Fitz will be down soon. Some unexpected business. He's a very busy man. So . . ." He clapped his hands together. "In the meantime, please help yourself to more shrimp or caviar. Or mimosa tea—hot or iced."

He turned to point to a door where three maids entered with more plates.

"Strawberry tarts, and cookies ordered from our favorite Chicago bakery. Fresh fruit, of course. Please help yourselves."

Minnie moved sideways toward the tarts. Gladys followed, pulling Tammy along behind her, then pushing her toward where Charles Bingman stood with Lady Barnabus, beaming as their guests gingerly lifted tarts and cookies to their plates and declined more mimosa tea.

Zoe, full and ready to get out of there, heard Gladys ask Lady Barnabus if she and Charles were engaged; then smile ear to ear when the lady demurred. "Heavens no. Only friends."

Dora leaned toward Gladys and whispered in her ear that she'd forgotten her cobbler. "Don't you want to present it to them?"

Gladys glared at her. "You see those little cookies and those tarts? Some damned pastry chef made all that stuff. Makes my tart look like a toadstool."

*　*　*

As Dora looked for a place to pour out her mimosa tea, someone poked her in the back. She looked around, then down, into Zoe's squeezed up face.

"How long are we expected to wait for this Fitz man?" Zoe's irritation was growing. "I say we give him ten more minutes then get out of here. I don't like this place. Rosings—huh. Do you get the feeling we're trapped in somebody's old movie?"

Jenny was about to answer when a rather short man in a pale-blue unstructured blazer, pale-blue shirt, perfectly pressed blue pants, and a many-colored ascot around his neck, walked in from the hall. The man, who had to be in his sixties, wore his too dark, obviously dyed, brown hair slicked back. His face approached ugly—too much forehead, too little chin. Still, he gave the impression of being well pleased with himself as he raised his hand in greeting to everyone.

Jenny nudged Zoe. "This must be him."

Behind the older man, entering from the hall, was an even older woman, a very pale, and very lined, version of a former beauty. Her light—almost white—blonde hair was piled on top of her head in a complicated waterfall of curls. Her blue eyes, circled by wrinkles, were wide open, even startled, as she looked from one face to the next, pulling a little closer to the man, taking his arm, and holding on tight.

"Ladies and gentlemen, let me introduce two of Fitz's oldest friends. Nathan Wickley and Delia Thurgood. They go so far back they were friends of Fitz's father. Business, wasn't it, Nathan?"

Charles turned to the couple, who bowed graciously and beamed back at Charles.

"Yes. At first." Nathan, a short man, threw his head back and smiled to the left and then to the right, inviting them all to take part in his superiority. "But then we became such good, close friends. A pleasure to be here today."

He raised his arm over his head in a wave while the woman held on to him.

Then came a new line of introductions as Jenny watched the short man and the statuesque woman beside him move in unison from one to the other of their groups, nodding regally after being given the name of each person, then stepping on, nodding at the name, going to the next without a word.

Jenny, when introduced by Charles, gave a little bow of her head and passed the odd couple on to Zoe. Zoe's eyes went wide with a mischievous idea trotting through her brain. No prim dismissal here. She looked up at them, straining her neck to see directly into Delia Thurgood's face. She fixed both with a curious stare. "From Chicago?"

Zoe's question was for Delia Thurgood, but Nathan answered. "Yes, Chicago. Delia comes from—where was it now? Oh yes, New York City. I'm teasing because she loves to lord it over me, that I'm a country boy, originally from right here in Michigan, while she's a New Yorker through and through. Fitz will be only too happy to tell you I was the one who brought him to Michigan in the first place. The man fell in love with your conifers."

He smiled and bowed low taking credit for the trees and all of Michigan.

Zoe clapped her hands and leaned back, smiling from ear to ear. "Ah yes. Our conifers. But don't forget our maples and oaks and cherry trees. Our ash and basswood—oh, don't forget our birch and . . ."

"Well, yes. Michigan does have a lot of trees."

Delia had left Nathan behind, moving on to Minnie, who gave a deep bow and called her "ma'am."

Jenny, behind Zoe, pinched her arm. "I saw what you did. You stop it right now," she whispered. "You're going to ruin everything for Keith and the whole town if you make fools of these people."

"Phooey. This is all nothing but phooey. I give that man ten more minutes to appear or I'm gone. Ten minutes and I'm off to call Tony. Then Pamela. I can't stand here wasting time like this . . ."

Zoe didn't finish. Charles Bingman was back at the doorway calling out, "And here is the man of the hour, ladies and gentlemen. Let me introduce you to our host: Fitzwilliam Dillon."

Zoe murmured, "About time," as she turned to the doorway, saw Fitzwilliam Dillon and thought, *Now, what fresh hell is this?*

Chapter 13

Fitz Dillon was a little man, only a bit taller than Zoe. He wobbled through the doorway and stood with one foot hanging in space. He put his foot to the floor as if to do a dance step—toe down, then turning slowly from left to right, examining the people gathered in his house. Fitz had large, misshapen brown eyes that moved from person to person, going quickly to Zoe, who was closest to the door. He hesitated, then frowned at her. He didn't nod or smile or address Zoe in any way, just looked her up and down, gave a superior sniff, and turned back to the others.

At the table, where some were still mingling and eating, Minnie hesitated with a shrimp on her fork as she pinched Dianna, leaning close to tell her to keep her mouth shut.

From the confused looks around her, Zoe, her face red at being passed over, could see the man wasn't what any of them expected. That single fact pleased her, that it hadn't been bandied about he was a Little Person. Money obviously bought a man more than just a few paintings. Maybe a lot of respect. Maybe a little fear. As least a little privacy.

Zoe grinned behind the little man's back as Gladys's eyes bugged out and her mouth fell open. What joy—watching Gladys's dream of a grand marriage for Tammy sizzle and burst while Tammy, sweet Tammy, gave a quick smile and a very polite bow of her head.

Fitzwilliam maneuvered around the table toward Charles, clapping his hands as he went. Zoe enjoyed the immediate dislike she felt for this Little Person—maybe one of her people but not like her at all. His head was long and narrow—his face ugly, ugly, ugly. His jaw jutted out oddly. His dark eyes were close together though, above his eyes, his very nice hair hung in a brown sweep over his forehead—his best feature: that head of thick, neatly trimmed brown hair. What Zoe didn't allow herself to do, as she watched narrow-eyed while Charles introduced him with glowing words and obvious friendship, was admire the self-assured way the man walked—with a bounce, not only as if he owned the room, but with a certainty that everyone there must be happy to see him.

Zoe pulled in one deep breath after another. He'd paid no attention to her. What happened to how much he wanted to meet the famous author?

She waited impatiently as Fitz, arms out wide, invited his guests to help themselves to more food, to enjoy themselves, while he ignored the popping eyes of Gladys and Minnie, and the laughter half hidden by Dianna's hand over her mouth.

Two million dollars wasn't enough to buy *her*, Zoe huffed to herself. Two could play his obvious game.

"But you've missed our writer." Charles turned Fitz back around to Zoe.

They faced each other, neither saying a word.

With slow, mincing steps, Fitzwilliam Dillon walked toward Zoe, stopping in front of her, then looking her over from her little green shoes to the crooked green bow atop her head.

"You're about half the size I expected," he said.

Zoe narrowed her eyes, looking him up and down in return.

"And what the hell are you, I'd like to know? Making us wait all this time. Seems you think a lot more of yourself than your size deserves."

"I wouldn't talk about size, Miss Zoe Zola." He wasn't smiling now. His dark eyes simmered with battle. "The biggest thing about you seems to be your mouth."

The very little man reached out and patted Zoe on top of her piled-up blonde curls. He knocked her green bow so it hung over her ear. She ducked away from his hand, then grabbed it and twisted.

"Ow." Fitzwilliam pulled back, complaining. "That wasn't necessary, you know."

"Oh, yes it was. Nobody touches my hair but me."

"But it's your best feature. I wanted to touch it."

"It is pretty. And it's mine. If you are this Fitzwilliam Dillon they've been talking about, I think you'd better act your age and get down to business."

"My age has nothing to do with it." His voice was aggrieved. "I was told you were coming and was looking forward to meeting you."

"Then say hello and stop patting me on the head." By now Zoe's face was red and swollen into a fine snit. "You should be ashamed of yourself. All these people here and you keep us waiting then come in like a clown. You are not what I expected, Mr. Dillon."

"And you are not what *I* expected, Zoe Zola. Miss Famous Writer, whom I have never heard of."

"Why are you acting such a fool, Mr. Dillon?" she demanded, almost nose to nose with him.

"And why are you so mad, Miz Zola?" He stepped back. "I was very happy when I heard that the famous writer of Bear Falls, Michigan, was a Little Person like me. I thought we could have long heart-to-hearts about smallness and talk about the big world around us; that I would finally have somebody to commiserate with about high curbs and fast cars turning corners and people who pat me on the head."

"Like you just did to me?" Zoe's mouth opened and stayed that way. "You need lessons in politeness."

"Oh, well. I've been disappointed before." Fitzwilliam Dillon shrugged, straightened the white shirt collar sticking out around his neck, straightened his child-sized gray sports jacket, pulled at his gray and white striped tie, and moved to the head of the table, where he knocked briskly, demanding attention even as he grinned at each new face. "Well! Now that we are all happily acquainted, let's get to work."

Chapter 14

Fitzwilliam led everyone into what Charles called the study, a room of deep chairs and soft lamplight. They were ushered to a round, polished table circled with upholstered seats. Charles took a chair at one end of the table and Fitz sat, scowling, at the other. Zoe found herself exactly at the middle of one side, Jenny at the other side, next to Dora. The others filled in.

"May I ask why we're here?" Zoe raised her hand then brought it down and stood up, waving at Fitz, who ignored her.

She turned to Charles and repeated her question.

"I would say we've gathered to set up a town meeting where all of our neighbors might make a suggestion as to what the village most needs. Two million dollars. That's a lot to consider." He motioned for Keith to stand and begin the meeting.

Keith, his face a bright, nervous red, cleared his throat over and over, then looked to Bernadette, who smiled encouragement toward him.

He began by talking to Fitz, which irritated Zoe. "I just want to say thank you, Mr. Dillon, for your generous gift to Bear Falls, where we hope you will live a long and very happy life . . ."

Minnie Moon waved her hand and got to her feet, bursting to talk. "Me and Dianna would be happy to plan that party you want to have here."

Gladys Bonney was on her feet. "I think you'll find me and my highly cultured daughter, Tammy, would do the best job of party planning." She motioned for Tammy to stand and show herself. She didn't.

"Why don't we talk about that when we've finished planning the meeting, shall we?" Charles acknowledged both of them but didn't smile.

Keith volunteered to chair the town meeting. A date of May

eighteenth, at seven PM—the following Friday, was chosen. The place to be the town offices on Oak Street.

Minnie Moon was asked to put up flyers all around town announcing the meeting. She frowned but agreed. Dianna was to help her, though Dianna made a face that seemed to put in doubt her enthusiastic cooperation.

Gladys offered to do refreshments for the meeting, adding that she would make her famous blueberry cobbler because of the auspiciousness of the occasion.

Keith said he thought it might be a good idea to put up a box in front of the town hall, where people could write their ideas for something the town needed and drop them in. He went on to suggest the Elks Club could help with traffic control that night and maybe they'd put up the chairs and take them down afterward.

"And—to make the evening go easier," Keith said, nodding seriously. "Bernadette and I will sort suggestions from the box ahead of time. Kind of get out duplicates—things like that." He cleared his throat. "The night of the meeting people can speak out, supporting their favorites, until we've got it down to two or three, and then we'll have a show of hands in favor. Be easy enough."

Next on the agenda, as Fitz yawned, Charles brought up the open house to be held there at Rosings in June. Gladys and Minnie's arms shot into the air again. They shouted over each other.

"Barbeque," Gladys offered.

"We'll do it," Minnie shouted. "Me and Dianna."

Dianna, inspired now, called down toward Fitz, "I'll do the whole thing myself, Mr. Fitz. How hard can it be? A couple of kegs. Bunch of pizzas."

Fitz frowned and covered his mouth with his hand. His eyes were huge. His body shook.

Keith turned to Dora, almost begging. "I thought maybe you would take over, Dora, since you're the first to have offered help."

He repeated what he said to Dora over another shouting match between the Moons and Gladys Bonney.

"I'll be happy to plan the party," Dora said, forcing Gladys and Minnie back into their chairs, mumbling at each other under their breath. "As long as I get plenty of help."

"Be happy to help out," Minnie called first.

"Us, too," was all that was left to Gladys. "We'll do invitations. Tammy's a wonderful artist—as you all know."

Delia Thurgood, seated not at the table but in a Queen Anne chair in front of the smoking fireplace, spoke for the first time since the meeting began. "I'll do the flower arrangements," she offered, then stopped, searching around for Nathan.

"Maybe you shouldn't take on something that strenuous, Delia." Nathan leaned around Fitz. "You know how you get in the spring. Your allergies."

She took time to consider before saying out loud, "And I am so sensitive to bee stings. And you are insisting on having the party outside, I understand, Fitz." Her voice held accusation.

Fitz shrugged and looked away, out the nearest window.

"No, no, Fitz. I do understand. So many people. Where would you put them all in this house?" She thought a while longer, as everyone waited impatiently for her to make up her mind.

"And who knows how long I'll be staying, after all," she said. "I do have business in New York to attend to. Everyone here knows I am from New York City, don't you?"

Nathan hurried to her side, leaning forward, telling her not to think of doing anything for the party. "These people are used to things like this, I'm sure. They'll take care of flowers and the other necessities. You're much too delicate for stressful things like throwing parties, dear." He took her hand in his and held it until she smiled and nodded graciously.

Nathan then said he, himself, would see to the liquor but was stopped by Fitz, who insisted he'd already hired people to take care of staging the house and ordering wines and liquor.

"All is in order," Fitz insisted. "Food, too. All we need is a date and maybe soon a round number; how many people might come."

"Oh, everyone, Mr. Dillon . . ." Gladys gushed toward Fitz. She winked at him. "There isn't another place anywhere near as grand as this. Not within miles and miles. They'll all be dying to meet you. And your wife, of course."

She raised her thinly drawn eyebrows and waited and waited, but Fitz turned to Bernadette, beside him, ignoring Gladys.

When things were settled and Charles had thanked them all for coming, Fitz leaned on the table, his chin resting on both of his crossed arms. He looked toward Zoe. "I see you plan to do nothing, Miss Zola." He raised his voice to make sure everyone heard him.

"Zoe," she growled at him. "And I will certainly be of help, but with a book deadline . . ."

"Ah, yes. You obviously want us all to know that you are an important writer. But could we stipulate that fact and get on to more important things?"

"Like a municipal garden," Zoe pushed her chair back, facing Fitzwilliam Dillon. She sniffed. "And an arboretum. That's what's most important here. To add beauty to Bear Falls. Bring tourists. Make a lasting impact on our town and its people."

He mulled over the idea, then slowly shook his head. "Weak. Very weak. All that money to have people walk through flowerbeds? And that only a few months out of the year? Surely," he looked at the others, now standing, ready to escape, "We can come up with something better than flowerbeds."

Zoe was gone. Just gone. She didn't know how she moved so fast, or how she found the front door. She was in the car, waiting for Dora and Jenny, huddled in the back seat, swearing mightily under her breath, when they came out ten minutes later to drive her home.

"I didn't get to bring up a new library," was the only complaint out of Dora. "And I didn't get to see Fitz's library. All in all, I'd say the meeting was a letdown."

Jenny started the car and drove away before Gladys, or Minnie Moon, could catch up with them.

Chapter 15

Almost lost in the pines between their houses, Zoe called back to Jenny. "Got to get moving, you know. Can't keep wasting time like we've been doing. Poor kid's out there."

Zoe let her voice fade as she climbed the back steps to her house and heard Fida throw her body at the door then scramble in place when the door was opened.

She grabbed up her dog and hugged her, happiest when holding Fida who asked for so little. She buried her nose in the somewhat dirty fur and murmured things to Fida she never dared say to another being: "Snuggy-Wuggy! I love you best in all the world."

With Fida in her arms, she pulled out her cell and called Pamela, who answered on the first ring sounding scared and tired and all the things a mother frightened to death about her daughter would sound like.

"Jenny and I will be there as soon as we can. Did you hear from the police chief?"

"Tony Ralenti and the searchers found something." There was a long pause. "Cammy's phone. In the woods. I guess it was damaged. Ed needs the password and I don't know it. Oh God, Zoe. I don't know my own child's password."

Zoe said nothing. She listened to Pamela's breathless silence.

"And they found her jacket. It's got a blue bear on the back. They found her jeans."

Her voice broke. "I should get over to the station . . ."

"That won't change anything right now. We'll take you," Zoe promised. "Let's look at Cammy's room first."

"Whatever you need. I want my girl back. I've been awake all night waiting. And thinking—as you asked me to do." There was a long intake of breath. "She should be running up the steps right now, but . . . nothing."

Her voice cracked.

"I've left the room the way it . . ." She was saying as Zoe's back door opened and Fida went into a barking and growling frenzy. Tony stuck his head in, putting up a hand to say he didn't mean to disturb her.

Over Fida's noise, Zoe told Pamela again that they'd be there soon, hung up, and motioned Tony to a chair while she shushed her dog.

"Heard you found some of Cammy's belongings," she said.

He looked tired. His hands were clasped together between his knees. He nodded. "Clothes. Her phone."

"Could she have used the phone?" she asked.

He shook his head. "Damaged. Couldn't get into it but Pamela gave us the color—blue. We know it's hers."

"And the clothes?"

He nodded. "Found everything . . ." He pulled out a map with a series of Xs written in black marker. "Right here," he pointed down a dotted logging road, east of Shore Drive. "The jean jacket's got a blue bear on the back. Hers all right. I'm still trying to think of a way to make this a good thing. Maybe she got confused. Got so scared she didn't know what she was doing."

He looked up, almost hopeful.

"What was Janice supposed to be wearing, instead of that thing they found her in?"

"Black tights. Black skirt. Pink-and-white striped top. And—I think—some kind of hoodie. I'll check with Ed. I think it was black."

"But you didn't find Janice's things."

He shook his head. "Nothing to do with Janice."

He examined his rough hands. "Jenny said you're going over to see Cammy's room. Could you pick up the girl's computer? Ed's got a forensics guy coming in an hour or two. He'll get in it; see what's there. Could be a connection to somebody or something. He went through Janice's. Not a thing out of the ordinary. Kid stuff."

She nodded. "We'll bring Pamela, and the computer, to the station when we're done at the house. I want Ed kept on top of everything we find. Hope he feels the same about us."

"Ed does. He's concentrating on Janice Root's murder, but keeping his deputy going on Cammy's disappearance. He called Principal Stoves. No plays going on at the high school. Hadn't heard of anything requiring a costume like Janice was wearing. Anyway, Sally or Jay would have known—but they're both still a mess. Ed's got a state cop talking to any kids who knew her. He plans to ask the Roots if Cammy and Janice were friends but Sally won't come out of her room or talk to anybody—and Jay's—well, not much help either. Janice is their only child, you know. You'd think a mother . . . well, any mother, would want to help."

"Maybe she can't."

She should have offered coffee or something, the way everybody did up here—reflexively, as if people couldn't begin to talk when they sat at a table unless they had a cup in their hands. She didn't have time.

"I've got to get going," she said.

Tony kept his head down. He didn't move to leave. "The chief had ten guys out looking last night—just here in town. I had fifteen high school kids out searching this morning, along with a bunch of other people. The ones who knew Cammy said they liked her. Some thought she was a little . . . well . . . one kid called her a little nutty. Not because she's different, he said. Just—this is what he said: "You never know for sure where she's coming from. Smarter than she seemed.""

"Any suspects? Ed say anything?"

"Got a couple of calls. But he doesn't want it getting out. People could be hurt."

"Hurt? How? You mean they could be suspects? Who?"

"Roach."

"The man who found her?"

Tony nodded.

"Why?"

Tony nodded. "Something Ed was told, and then remembered, about Harold Roach."

Zoe winced. "A lot of dirt comes out when a thing like this happens. People have secrets."

"Yeah. Secrets. And in a small town it isn't easy to hide them."

"What about Roach?"

"A rape charge. Years ago."

"Did he go to jail?"

"No. Dismissed. Girl was the same age. First offense and the girl's father didn't want to press charges after all."

"What's Ed think?"

He shook his head. "He was asking why would Harold call in the body if he had anything to do with what happened? And the girl wasn't raped. That's not what this is about. When you think about it, even if Harold didn't have a thing to do with the girl, he could have been too scared to call, because of his past. He did the right thing. Ed thinks Harold's just a wrong track to take."

Zoe took a deep breath. "It's going to get ugly, isn't it?"

"Already is. The chief got a call about Jay Root, too. Anonymous. Something from a long time ago that Ed's looking into. Has to do with Janice, but Ed wouldn't say what it was. Didn't want to be a part of spreading rumors." Tony looked up at Zoe. "I'll tell you one thing, though. The chief is wondering why Jay's not more help. His daughter—but he doesn't seem that interested. Clams up when he's asked questions."

She made a face. "That's what it's going to be like here in town, everybody suspecting somebody."

Tony nodded. "Myrtle's must be boiling like a volcano. Rumors and meatloaf. Kind of what she's known for around town."

"When evil leaks out, everybody gets a little slimy."

"Yeah, well, thing about that is, everybody's trying to help, too."

Tony cleared his throat, leaned back, ran his hands through his thick hair, and cleared his throat again.

"What is it?" Zoe asked. "You want to tell me something or ask me something?"

"Maybe both. I was wondering if you and Jenny might go back out in the woods where we were today. Maybe you two could go over our search area. Look for places we didn't think of. My group's heading in a different direction, but I've got this feeling we shouldn't give up on those woods yet."

"Course. In the morning."

He leaned forward, pulled his map to him, and smoothed it flat with his broad hands. He pointed to places he'd outlined, showing Zoe where they'd been, where they were going next, and where she and Jenny might look, covering the area at least one more time.

"Does Ed know what killed Janice yet?" She took the map and folded it back the way it was.

"She died of asphyxia."

She thought about the word. *Asphyxia.* "Carbon monoxide? Choked to death? Strangled?"

"That's all the ME said: 'asphyxia.'"

"No wonder Ed's calling it murder. She sure wasn't asphyxiated out there on the road."

"Even if it was an accident, somebody was with her when it happened, and that somebody moved her body."

"Could she have been left in a running car, or in some kind of closed space?"

He shrugged. "Could have been a huffing party or she choked to death—something like that. But," he went on. "No drugs in her system."

"Got stomach contents?"

"ME couldn't tell for sure but she thought the girl had some kind of burger, some vegetable with it. Maybe green peppers. Found a partially dissolved hard candy, like she choked on it, but that didn't kill her. Too small, what she found. Said it looked like she'd eaten only a few hours before she died."

Zoe quietly filed away the information. She massaged her forehead until she could think again. "Any ideas about that outfit she had on?"

"Nothing. Ed checked with Jay. He just kept shaking his head. Made Ed mad. Then Jay said she didn't own clothes like that as far as he knew, but that's all he'd say about it."

"How about a Halloween custom?"

Tony shrugged. "Wrong time of year. She always wore normal teenage garb, Jay said. Nothing unusual going on in her life, he told Ed. Good kid."

"I was hoping that old dress might be a link between the girls."

"Like how?"

"Through Pamela's parents. Can't get those people out of my head. They made Pamela's life hell after she got pregnant. The old man—well, some things just make you sick. Those people have never seen Camille. But they were back in town recently. Stranger things have been done by groups like that—scorn the kid they couldn't be bothered with until it dawns on them: *Hey, we've got a grandkid who we could save. And maybe enslave while we're at it.*"

"Could be," Tony answered. "You think that dress was something from a virgin sacrifice? Or a wedding dress? But that's mixing up the two girls again. Camille—okay. Could find her in something like that. But Pamela's parents don't have a thing to do with Janice. And Janice didn't have anything to do with Cammy, far as we know."

Zoe stared at Tony without seeing him. "I know I'm clutching at straws here . . . but maybe Janice Root was a mistake. They didn't know what Cammy looked like. Same age. About the same height. Stranger things have happened."

"So these two old people kill Janice when they find out she isn't Camille? Doesn't make any sense."

"What were they going to do with her? Turn her loose?"

"I guess it's worth looking into. If for no other reason than Camille Otis might still be alive, if they've got her."

Tony got up to leave.

"Anybody tell you what happened at that Dillon house today?" she asked.

He nodded. There was laughter in his eyes. "Ran into Keith on my way over here. I heard you don't like our new neighbor."

"*Like* him!" She exploded. "The man's a . . . tapeworm; sucks the life out of everything around him. Not my fault he's a first class turd."

"Keith's worried about losing that money. With everybody knowing two million dollars might be coming to the town, it could be pretty hard, letting everybody down if this Fitzwilliam guy takes it all back."

"Why would he take it back? Makes him a big hero."

"Keith got a call from a friend of Dillon's. Said Dillon didn't feel exactly welcomed."

"Because of me?"

Tony shrugged.

"Not my fault." She felt a tiny prick of guilt. "He's the idiot."

She stopped talking and watched Tony's face, trying to figure which side he was going to take in the war ahead of them.

"You've got a lot on your plate, Zoe. I'd say the Otis girl's more important that any of that stuff with Dillon. Why don't you let the others take him on and stay away? For myself, Bear Falls is great just the way it is. Don't want to see our town messed up by fights over money."

"You're so right." She slid off her chair. "I've got no time to think about a sleazy millionaire."

CAMILLE

What she decided to do was peek around the rag the man tied over her eyes when he came with that other person. She couldn't tell for sure if that one was a woman or a man because the voice was high, a pretend sound, but now there was the strong stink of perfume in the room.

The thing about the other person was that when she or he came there were hard candies left behind in a basket on the table. Which was a good thing because then there was something to eat if nobody came back when she got hungry.

There were games like checkers left on one of the chairs, but when she was coaxed to play she shook her head, put her hands over her ears, and wouldn't move from the bed.

That other person—when the voice got low—said things like, "Mandy. You know this is your favorite game. We'll play for a little while, until you get too sleepy."

It sounded as if the person was crying, but that was no reason for her—whose name wasn't even Mandy—to say more than, "I need to go home now, please."

And then the person would sing a little song, in a funny way, about a cradle falling, probably killing the baby, and ask her to sing along, but all she did was fold her arms and sit there at the end of the bed saying it was time for her to go home.

Cammy had a bigger story floating in her head so she didn't think about how cold she was or how hungry she sometimes got when he didn't show up with a sandwich for what she thought was hours, or how he'd tricked her with his dinosaur bones, or that he stole her clothes and only gave her this old white thing to wear and didn't let her go home when she asked.

Today's story went back to when she read all the Nancy Drew books. Every single one of them.

When the other person—she thought it was really a lady—tried to talk to her she took herself out to an inn with her best friend Kent. There they found that an old woman had gone missing. So they looked around the inn, going out into the woods until they found a metal door in the ground that Kent knew to pull open. When they called down into the hole below, a voice answered and an old lady came over to look up at them. Then, Kent went down the metal ladder to get the lady and brought her out. They took her back to the inn where policemen were waiting to arrest the old woman's son and his wife, who had talked him into getting rid of his mother so they could have all her money and own the inn.

Another time she was thinking that Kent was named after Superman, like Clark Kent, and maybe he was looking for her right that minute. She lay back on the pillow and thought about him breaking through the ceiling until she was sure she heard him above her, but it was just the small man opening the door and bringing her more meatloaf.

Part 3

"Facts are such horrid things!"

—Jane Austen, *Lady Susan*

Chapter 16

Jenny parked in front of Pamela's small house: white aluminum siding, green shutters at the two front windows.

There was a long porch already set with wicker armchairs and enclosed, at either end, with trellises where newly greening honey-suckle vines climbed.

The winter-burned lawn was divided into two rectangles by a straight, cement walk. In front of the porch, tulips, in various stages of growth, filled half-moon flowerbeds. It was a neatly kept house, the kind of small place most Americans chose for their first home; or the kind of place old people scaled back to, or the proud home of a single-mother who has put her child before her own life.

Jenny knocked at the front door, leaning back toward Zoe. "And one more thing you should know," she said, as if there had been a conversation going on the way over instead of silence.

Zoe sighed. "What now?"

"About this Fitz thing. Mom said to tell you that Minnie came up to her and whispered she thought Fitzwilliam was a jerk. Didn't like him at all. Dianna said she'd like to kick him all the way around that trumped-up house. And . . ." She put a finger in the air when Zoe tried to break in. "And even Gladys said she sure was happy she knew the man better, before she let Tammy marry him. She called him a 'pint-sized creep.'"

"Well, well, well." Zoe swung her head up to Jenny. "Feels good to have friends. But I betcha anything if he looked at either one of those girls cross-eyed they'd turn on me in a flash."

"Tammy, too?"

"Nah. You're right. There's a girl with a whole lot of sense. She keeps her mouth shut." Zoe smiled as Jenny knocked again.

"You don't have to worry," Jenny said over her shoulder. "Gladys and Minnie have moved their traps into Charles Bingman's territory anyway."

"Hmmm. Let's see. Charles's got three feet on Fitz; is a lot better looking, much nicer. Maybe just as rich. Good choice."

A very different Pamela Otis answered the door. Her hair hung in uneven strings. Her eyes were dead. When she looked out at them, she didn't seem to remember who they were. She was about to say "Yes?" as if to strangers, when she shook herself, and pushed the door open, inviting them inside.

"Of course, Zoe Zola. And Jenny Weston." She muttered the words then looked hard at the two standing in her living room. "I was expecting you but time seems to stand still . . ."

She motioned toward a white sofa.

"They found Cammy's clothes, and her phone. What am I supposed to hope for?" she asked once they were all seated, as if there were nothing tragic to the question.

"Hope that next we'll find *her*," Zoe answered, not buying into depression.

"They think she's dead." She put a fist to her mouth.

"I don't," Zoe said.

"Then where is she, with no clothes? She must be so cold . . ."

"We don't know what happened yet." Jenny reached to touch one of Pamela's icy hands. "Zoe and I are going back out there in the morning. Tony Ralenti's group will be north of where they found her clothes. She's out there, Pamela. We're going to find her."

Pamela eyes raked Jenny's face. "I've been thinking about my parents. If they took her, they would make her change her clothes. She'd be dressed in something awful, like they used to make me wear. They would do that to punish me, make me pay for my sins." Pamela choked on the words. "Next they'll be dropping her, like Janice, beside the highway. Maybe that's what they do now, after they've saved a girl."

"Cut it out," Zoe said. "We'll find them. Every minister and cop up north is looking. And then we'll see. For now, it's the woods. She might be out there. There are places she could be hidden . . ."

Pamela wiped her nose with a tissue she pulled from the sleeve of her sweater. She sat staring at her visitors. "I can't even tell you what my father did to me when I was a little girl . . ." The words were whispered "*And my mother protected him . . .*"

Nobody spoke.

"If he's got Cammy, I will kill him."

Pain, like smog, hung in the air around them—*The thing that can't be told.*

Zoe pushed herself forward on the sofa, head down, for once unable to talk.

Jenny closed her eyes. She shook her head. "I don't know . . . I can't imagine . . ."

Pamela sat with her feet together, hands clasped in her lap. A little girl shamed. A little girl who was supposed to keep quiet.

It took a few minutes until Zoe could talk. She cleared her throat. "Remember what I asked you to think about?" The words were nothing. The thing that had been let out between them didn't drift easily away. Zoe's voice was different.

Pamela nodded. "Where she liked to go. There's a broken down cabin or maybe a house, she told me about. Has to be from a hundred years ago or more. Cammy liked to talk about the birds nesting in that one. And there was something about the wind playing around the chimney. But I told her not to go there."

"Do you know where it is?"

She shook her head. "If only I'd gotten smart earlier. I want to think she's in the woods. But I wish they hadn't found her clothes. I just wish *that* hadn't happened."

"We came to look at Cammy's room." Zoe got up, Jenny beside her. "Then we've all got to go to the police station . . ."

Pamela led them down a hall to a small, not too neat, room with a single bed covered by a mussed, white chenille spread. The walls were a soft green. There was a round green rug on the wood floor—wrinkled up in the middle, as if someone had slid on it. A pile of clothes was thrown across a small, slipper chair upholstered with sunflowers.

"I haven't touched it. I won't until she's back home."

The bed was loaded with stuffed animals—mostly bears of all sizes. There was a three-drawer bureau against one wall and a dressing table with a single drawer and a plain straight-backed chair drawn up to it. Zoe looked around slowly, very carefully, taking in the room where the girl had spent most of her time. Nothing on the walls. No photos. No drawings. But the dressing table was piled with what looked like school papers, a stack of books, and a crude, handmade cup holding pens and pencils.

"No computer?" Zoe turned to Pamela, standing in the doorway, not entering the room. "Tony asked for it."

"I took it away the morning she left. She was spending too much time on it. I bought it for her to do her homework. I told her I'd give it back if she promised to cut down the time she spent writing to people I didn't know. To tell the truth, I was getting a little afraid. You hear about those awful predators waiting to get ahold of kids. So trusting and so caring. All it would have taken was a sad story and Cammy would try to fix things. With one girl she met online last year it was a new dress for her graduation. Camille drove me crazy until I got one on sale at Vernie's Dress Shop and sent it to the kid. Cammy never got so much as a thank you in return. It didn't bother her. As long as the girl had a dress for graduation—that was all Cammy wanted."

"Do you have the computer?" Zoe asked.

"Yes."

"We'll take it to Ed. Could be important."

Jenny and Zoe exchanged a look when Pamela left the room.

"Think that could be it? A predator?" Jenny asked in a whisper.

"Happened to other girls."

Jenny shivered. "Not Camille. Oh good lord! Not Camille."

"Remember the clothes. This has something to do with the woods. Has to."

"Still, let's just pray there's nothing on it."

Zoe opened the top drawer in the bureau. Underwear. Two dried corsages. A bunch of pens and what looked like prizes from a fair.

Next drawer: sweaters, a couple of shirts with emblems on them.

Bottom drawer: A jumble of toys and games and dolls.

Zoe looked around the room, wishing something would jump out and say: *"Here's where I am. Please come get me."*

Jenny, at the dressing table, touched the homemade pencil cup. Camille must have made it in grade school. She shuffled through the top school papers, down to papers beneath. She pulled out one, read it, and flapped it at Zoe.

"Look at this."

LOOKING FOR A SUMMER JOB
  BABYSITTING
  ARCHEOLOGY
  YARD WORK
  HARD WORKER
  WORK FOR LESS MONEY THAN MOST PEOPLE
  CALL ME: CAMILLE OTIS

At the bottom were her cell phone number, address, and a smiley face.

"Think she got any calls?" Jenny asked, holding out the paper for Zoe to read, then frowning at it.

"Pamela didn't mention this. Think she would have. I wonder if she even knew. Maybe that boyfriend of hers would know. What girl her age doesn't share secrets with her boyfriend?"

Zoe carefully and slowly folded the paper in half to stick in her purse.

"We'll see in the morning," Zoe said. "He'll be back by then. I'm getting the feeling that kid's like a plug in a dike. Bet he knows Camille better than her own mother."

"You've got a feeling, or just hoping, the way I am?"

Jenny went through the other things on the dressing table. All she found was a colorful calendar with teddy bears on it. No dates circled for any of the months. No plans noted.

She opened a drawer and found a collection of lipsticks and eye makeup—most of it new. She didn't imagine Camille was the kind of girl who wore much makeup, but maybe she tried it on when she was alone, looking at her face, trying to decide who she looked like—with her painted face.

There was a small quilted box holding jewelry in the drawer. Inside was a locket with Pamela's picture in it; a handmade bead necklace, and a small gold pendant set with a blue stone.

Without knowing why, Jenny picked up the gold pendant and stuck it down into the pocket of her jeans, her hand warm around it until she let go.

Zoe was going through the closet: the usual hoodies and jeans and tee shirts, when Pamela came back, standing in the doorway, laptop in her hands.

Zoe checked under the bed—only an old pair of slippers. She got to her feet, brushed at the knees of her slacks, and ran her hands under Camille's thin mattress, her fingers going over what felt like the edges of a book.

Zoe drew the book out to take a look. A book on dinosaurs. A thing any kid could get fascinated by. She pushed it back between the mattress and box spring and turned to ask Pamela directly, "What were Cammy's dreams?"

"Dreams? Of what? You mean movie stars and being on Broadway?" The woman made a face and clutched the computer closer. "Cammy's not like that."

Zoe shook her head again. "What does she want to be when she finishes high school?"

"A college student. At least, that's what I'm hoping."

Zoe shook her head. "But what does *she* want to be? Was Camille a planner?"

Pamela took a deep breath at the question. "She talked about digging for dinosaurs but every kid does at one time or another. She asked about joining the forestry service and being a fire-lookout person. You know, living on one of those fire towers. She does love being alone in the woods though. The way she loves bears . . . well, I sometimes wondered if she would do something dangerous. You know, like try to save a bear in trouble. Or get too close to one . . . I warned her enough times and she said she wasn't dumb. She said she knew that bears in the woods aren't teddy bears."

Pamela was distracted for a minute. "I just thought of something. Probably has nothing to do with anything, but Kent asked her to go to a farm near Grayling with him this summer. His mother's taking them. She got all excited and told me she could hardly wait."

"Would she head over there by herself?" Jenny asked. "To that farm?"

Pamela shook her head. "We talked about it. The fun was to be going with the others. There's nothing stupid about Camille. I don't want anyone to get that idea. She's different. That's all. Sees things differently."

"Got the name of the farm?" Zoe asked. "Wouldn't hurt to call. See if, just by chance, she showed up there."

"She's been gone since Friday!" Pamela shook her head. "She wouldn't just keep walking. She would have called me by now." She stopped and put a hand to her mouth. "But she can't, can she? Ed's got her cell. And no clothes."

"Anyway, what's the name of the farm, Pamela?" Zoe's voice was low and insistent, not wanting to lose Pamela to despair.

"Blakely's. It's like an old time place. Kids churn milk and feed the goats. Things like that. But that's not even . . . possible."

Zoe turned to Jenny. "Could you call there? See if a girl of Cammy's description showed up. She might have hitchhiked. We don't know . . . anything."

Jenny pulled her phone from her pocket, and went out to the porch to call Blakely's.

"Any other plans for summer?" Zoe turned back to Pamela, who had moved into the room.

Pamela thought a long while. "The kids at school were talking about summer jobs and how they were going to make money. You know how kids are. She said she wanted a job, too. I told her I'd give her an allowance if she kept her room clean but she wasn't thrilled about the idea."

Zoe pulled the paper from her purse and put it in Pamela's hands. "Found this in Cammy's dressing table."

Pamela shook her head. "She didn't show it to me but I don't think she ever did anything with it. Actually, she stopped talking about a job when Kent asked her to go with them to Grayling. That was the last I heard of a summer job. Maybe Kent would know if she put the flyer out. You can ask him, but I never heard anything about it. That's not like Cammy."

Jenny was back, shaking her head. "The farm was closed but a woman answered. She said she hasn't seen a young girl who seemed lost or who hung around. She's asking the others. I gave her my number."

Jenny glanced quickly at Zoe. "And the chief called. He knew we were here and wondered if we'd be coming over before long. Pamela, too."

"Something new?" Zoe hated asking, not knowing what the answer might be.

"He's got a forensics guy coming pretty soon to pick up the computer."

With a quick intake of breath, Pamela, computer in hand, hurried out of the room. "I'll meet you on the porch," she called over her shoulder. "Don't be long. Please. There could be something on here . . ."

Chapter 17

Deputy Fortes looked up when the women walked in, his young face almost scared, as if dreading more bad news.

After he made what he thought was small talk, the deputy led them back to Ed's office. They came in on the chief bending over items spread across the surface of his scarred desk.

As the women filed in, Ed quickly pulled sheets of newspaper over the things on the desk and got up, almost embarrassed as he nodded at Zoe and Jenny. He took Pamela's arm to lead her to his chair, took the computer from her hands, and thanked her, explaining the man would be there soon to pick it up, then they'd see if Cammy had anything going on that maybe Pamela didn't know about.

Pamela nodded but didn't take her eyes from the paper-shrouded desk.

She whispered toward Ed. "Are these her things?"

He pulled the newspaper away. Pamela put a hand on his arm, stopping him.

"Before I look, can you tell me if you found anything else . . . ?"

"Like what, Miz Otis?" He bent down to answer her.

"Like blood on the clothes."

"No." He drew out the word. "Nothing like that. Just the clothes and the cell phone. A lot of dirt on everything."

"The jacket has a bear on the back. Did you see it? She loves bears."

Ed pulled off the rustling paper, while keeping his eyes away from hers. He folded the paper, again and again, until he laid it on the floor.

Pamela leaned over the desk, her body stiff. She looked at the clothes and the smashed phone, lying there. She touched the phone.

She reached out to put a finger on one after the other of the folded clothes. She looked up at Ed. "Should I? I mean, may I touch them?"

Ed nodded. "Phone's been fingerprinted. We just don't have Camille's prints yet."

"Her fingerprints are everywhere in the house. All you have to do . . ." She stopped talking.

"I'm sure that's her phone," she said.

She looked away from Ed's face and back to the articles on the desk, reaching out to pick up one after the other.

"Her favorite shirt." She held up the plain blue T-shirt with WTOM across the front, her fingers locking tightly to the fabric.

She folded the shirt, laid it down, patted it, then picked up the jeans.

She barely touched the white bra and panties, but took up one of the dirty white sneakers and ran her finger over the toe.

"These all belong to Cammy. And the jacket . . ."

She picked up the jacket, turning it in her hands to show the blue bear on the back.

Pamela tipped her head up, looking hard into the faces gathered around her. "Why would she leave her clothes? As far as I know, she didn't have any other things with her."

No one could look at her.

"Where did you find her things, exactly?" she asked Ed. "Was it near an old house? Or maybe a cabin? There is an old cabin, I think it's a cabin, or a ruined house, she liked to go to. I was just telling Zoe . . ."

She took a deep breath. "Not much left of it, that's what she said. I warned her. But if she went there maybe she found other clothes to wear. You know it's still only in the thirties at night." She looked up at Ed. "Is that where you found these things, by an abandoned cabin?"

Ed shook his head. "No, ma'am. They were at the side of one of the logging trails coming off of Shore Drive."

Pamela nodded and slowly stood. "I'd like to go home now," she said. "Cammy's probably there. She doesn't like to be cold. She wouldn't stay away for long . . . not without her clothes." Her voice broke. She stumbled, grabbing for the back of the chair, then stood with her head down.

Jenny and Zoe popped out of their chairs.

Jenny held Pamela—an arm around her slumping shoulders. "Maybe you shouldn't be alone."

Pamela straightened and shook her head. "I'd rather. I can't seem to concentrate when people talk at me."

Pamela looked slowly from face to face. "She's not dead. I'd know. If Camille wasn't in the world, I'd know right away. That's what being a mother is."

She walked out, Jenny hurrying behind, turning in the doorway to tell Zoe she'd be back for her.

Zoe and Ed waited for the sound of footsteps down the hall to disappear.

"Think we'll ever find Janice's clothes?" she asked, keeping her voice low.

Ed shook his head. "You never know."

"Anything else out there? Where they found those?" She nodded toward the girl's clothes that looked like nothing more than a pile of rags.

Zoe wasn't a mother, but looking at a pile of cloth that stood for a living daughter—it made her sick all over again at what Pamela Otis was going through.

"What do you mean?"

"Summer homes? Year-round places?"

"Some, but not many. Too many swamps. Roads not good in winter."

"Are there other logging roads?"

Ed nodded. "Three or four two tracks. A couple of dirt roads. Some bisect each other. There are old ruins back there, I understand. Places abandoned years ago. Shacks, mostly. That's what Tony told me."

"Did they search the entire area after they found Cammy's clothes?" Zoe asked.

Ed frowned. "Did the best they could."

"I heard about an abandoned house . . ."

He nodded, turned a county map around, and drew a crooked blue line from town out to a big X. He handed the map to her. "That's what Tony wants zeroed in on right now."

She nodded. "How far is this from the Root's orchard?" She looked hard at him.

Ed hesitated, thinking over what she was asking. "I'd say about fifteen miles. Why?"

"Just thinking. That's not close."

"Not real close."

"We're after a murderer, aren't we?" Zoe looked up at Ed. "And a kidnapper?"

He nodded.

"You think there's a chance she's still alive?" Zoe didn't like the taste in her mouth.

"Hope so." Ed's head dipped to one side. "Can't bear to think otherwise."

"How about Kent Miller? Maybe he knows where she went, or who she went with. Maybe he knows if Camille and Janice were friends."

"Already asked kids from the school. The girls weren't friends. At least not close friends. They knew each other but nobody ever saw them together away from school. I'll talk to this Kent in the morning. His mom's bringing him in. You want to be here?"

"We'll go to his house after you're through with him. Jenny and I will be back in the woods after that."

He nodded. "Let me know what's going on."

"You've got missing flyers up around town?"

Ed nodded.

"We need them in every town near here."

"Already done that."

"Traverse City, too?"

He nodded. "Everywhere. And we'll get the rest of this to the state police for testing in the morning—the phone and clothes. Probably get at what's on her computer yet tonight."

Zoe rubbed her eyes.

"What do you think happened?" She asked after a while.

"Don't like to think about it."

Zoe took a breath. "And what's Cammy wearing if all her clothes are here?"

He shook his head again.

"You think it could it be an old white dress with pearl buttons down the back?" she asked.

Chapter 18

Only a few hours until dawn and her mind wouldn't let her sleep. Zoe turned from one side to the other in the bed, rolling over Fida, who complained and jumped to the floor, snorting and circling until she fell down in a heap.

Zoe squeezed her eyes shut and tried to become Camille—picturing herself wearing a white dress and being surprised at what she was wearing. She tried to push further into Camille's mind, but ran into a dark wall: up and down and left and right. Like a frightened mime, she couldn't find her way around it.

The thing was, she didn't have enough information about the girl. She needed to know Cammy Otis. There was that bear on her jacket . . .

Did she collect bugs?

Was she allergic to anything that could make her sick?

What would she be thinking if someone was keeping her where she didn't want to be? Would she try to escape?

Or—was that dark, endless wall in Zoe's head there because Camille couldn't think anymore and it didn't matter who she'd been or what she'd dreamed?

Maybe she'd given up hope and would soon be dumped on a highway, in an old white dress, asphyxiated in some way that wouldn't leave trauma on her young body, by someone who'd done the same to Janice Root.

Zoe got out of bed, stepping on Fida, who gave a resigned growl and would have nipped at her foot if Zoe hadn't hopped beyond her.

She grabbed up her robe from a chair, and headed to the kitchen.

She wanted to make a list of everyone to talk to—at least in her head. Then she wanted to sort out how Janice and Cammy were alike and how they were different. There was no accepting that the two weren't connected. And that fatal connection meant there was no time to lose. Somebody knew the area. Somebody knew both girls had limitations. Were friendly. Were vulnerable.

The race to find Cammy was running through Zoe's blood and brain. Jenny and Ed moved at a small-town pace. Even Tony, it seemed, had shed his big city hurry.

She had to think, and work, and walk in the woods until she found her.

Another part of her brain was thinking about Jenny. And Tony. And why there seemed to be so much distance between them. Not the kind of thing a friend should stick her nose into, but maybe there was another way.

And Dora. She was going to let her down—putting off the whole business of Fitzwilliam's gift and a party and all that nonsense. Her line of importance was straight—and it didn't go anywhere near that terrible Fitzwilliam. She owed nobody anything. Certainly not more of her time.

Well—maybe Dora.

*　*　*

The answering machine flashed one call. The message was from Dora. Some of the mansion people were coming to her house at one o'clock to discuss plans for the open house.

"They probably don't trust me to get it right," the message said. She asked, almost begged, "Please come over, Zoe. One o'clock. I really need you with me. Jenny says she can't be here."

Zoe groaned when she heard the message and then put it out of her mind. She was tired. And, the last thing she wanted to think about was facing any of those awful people again in the whole of her lifetime. And there was Kent Miller to see, and then they were going into the woods. No. No time at all for those obnoxious people.

But as if on cue, Zoe's cell rang at eight.

"Will you be here, Zoe?" Dora's voice sounded frantic. "I left you a message . . ."

"Not on your life. Got to talk to Kent Miller. He'll be back. Supposed to go into the woods after that. And, by the way, Jenny's going with me. At least she said she would. I hope she hasn't changed her mind."

"I guess I'll have to take care of things . . ."

Dora's disappointment colored her voice.

Zoe still wasn't sorry. The less she had to do with that awful man and his group, the better. A young girl's death and another girl kidnapped or dead in the woods—that trumped a snob's money and his need to impress a bunch of small-town yokels.

Then she was ashamed of turning on Dora, but told herself there were some things a person had no control over. Meetings with Fitz's people didn't come under that heading. She had control. She would have nothing to do with any of them. Dora was a big girl and could handle her own commitments. As for Zoe Zola . . . free as a bird!

It was still early. She went to her office to think of things that needed thought. She created new files—a list of people to talk to and questions to ask and places to check. She saved the files and thought about Tony and Jenny and how she could maybe help them sort out whatever was going on between them. Usually she knew better than to get involved, but this was her friend. Maybe a little screwed up—all of this 'finding herself' stuff going on. But there were times in every woman's life when "screwed up" was the nicest thing that could be said of her.

Zoe filed that away in her brain—a thing to think about when there was not much else to think about.

She went to the living room, being barked at by Fida who was bored and ready to take on a more interesting activity. Zoe ignored her dog and sat down to read the notes on *Pride and Prejudice* again, scouring them for quotes and scenes to use. Even with her book deadline marching toward her, she found very little help from Jane Austen. Maybe in her letters. Zoe made up an appropriate comment in her head:

And then the pathetic women set about securing husbands without thought to how their daughters might be treated, or might be betrayed—all for money.

Nothing that honest in the texts so far. Nothing, though it had to be hidden somewhere in Austen's sentences. A snicker here. A single word jab there. Zoe could almost put a finger on Austen's real thoughts—but then they slipped away, well hidden by a cynical snicker, an unladylike sneer. The woman was a master of deceit.

She opened a history she was using. Going back into the eighteenth century in England was like a trail into darkness—unfamiliar landscape: silly dresses that must have dragged in the dirt of the streets, certainly dragged through tons of horse manure. And body odor—no deodorant. They didn't bathe often. She imagined the bedding that got washed every six months, and poisonous food sitting in overheated kitchens. And bugs . . .

An olfactory swamp, she told herself and snapped the book shut, thinking: *Fitzwilliam Dillon. Now there's a villain who would fit nicely back into that time. Both he, and his silly friends.*

Chapter 19

Nine thirty and they were at Kent Miller's house.

"We're working with Chief of Police Ed Warner," Zoe said to the skinny boy with sloping shoulders who stepped down carefully to the porch from inside the house. "He asked us to come talk to you . . ."

"I was there already this morning. Told the chief I'll do anything to help Cammy." The kid frowned from Jenny to Zoe, then back. "The chief asked me questions. I . . . I didn't even know there was anything wrong with Cammy. Now I've got to find her."

Kent stared openmouthed at Zoe, and then at Jenny—back and forth between the two of them again and again. His red-striped tee shirt stretched in wrinkles across his narrow chest. His jeans were too big, the legs loose and dipping down over his sneakers. He was very tall, even for a seventeen-year-old high school senior, and gently nice looking: soft brown hair, light brown eyes, a face without deception. He blinked a few more times at the women, then called out, "Mom, come see who's here! They want to know about Cammy, too."

He waited, then gave a pitiful wail. "Mom! I need you."

A woman hurried from the house, stepping out to the porch, wiping her hands on a dishtowel. She touched Kent's arm.

"Yes?" Mrs. Miller's asked, looking from Zoe to Jenny. And then, when told why they were there, she said, "He's already talked to the police chief. He doesn't know anything about where Camille could have gotten to. He's awfully upset about this whole thing. If you're from a newspaper . . ."

Mrs. Miller's face was worn like so many women who lived in the country. In her forties, she looked like a woman who had lived hard—every one of those years. There were lines around her mouth and eyes;

her gray-streaked hair was drawn back into a short ponytail. Her body had melted into a square—a thing that happened when people were on their feet a lot, and wore bad shoes. Mrs. Miller looked to Zoe like a women used to fighting her way through unwelcomed territory. But not tough. Nothing harsh or coarse about her. Only tired.

"They want to ask me questions, Mom." Kent's voice quivered. "They say they're helping Police Chief Warner."

Pearl Miller looked from Zoe to Jenny, her tired eyes leery. She stared at Zoe. "You're that writer, aren't you? That Zoe Zola. I've seen you in town."

Zoe nodded.

"You work with the police sometimes, that's what I heard." She turned to Jenny. "And you're one of Dora Weston's girls."

She pushed the screen wide, inviting them in. "The chief says to help you in any way we can."

Inside, she pointed to two large, very worn, chairs, offering what she had.

"Life's taught me to be careful." She gave a weak smile.

The room was small, but very clean, filled with homemade afghans and frilly lampshades.

"Is your husband home? Maybe we should speak to him . . ."

"We're divorced."

Kent sat in a rocking chair, where his mother pointed. He began to rock, at first slow and then faster and faster. He tipped his head to one side—waiting for questions as he rocked.

"Do you want me to tell you the same things I told the police chief?" he finally asked, slowing.

Zoe nodded.

"Okay. Good, because I want to help find Camille. I want to do anything to bring her back. I don't know where she went." He looked directly at Zoe, tucking his chin in to see her better before he turned to Jenny.

"I just want her home," he said, a plaintive note behind the words. "We've got all kinds of plans to do things this summer. I don't want her to miss any of those things."

He nodded hard and then shifted his eyes to Zoe, friendlier now. "We were going to a farm where they churn milk. We talked about that a lot, how we were looking forward to churning milk."

"You have any other plans?" Jenny asked as she pulled a small notebook and pen from her shoulder bag.

He looked at his mother before answering. "We were talking about a lot of things. I told her about going up to the Mackinaw Bridge. Camille said she never went there, you know, because her mother has to work a lot and Camille is alone. You know she doesn't have a dad? You heard that didn't you? I do. I have a dad. He just doesn't live here anymore."

Jenny nodded.

Zoe asked. "I heard Camille wanted to get a summer job."

"Yes, she did. She was looking hard but then she got afraid that maybe she wouldn't have time to go to the farm with us but then she said she wanted to make some money to help her mom."

"I saw a flyer she put together."

He nodded. "I did most of that. She liked it a lot and we went around together and put it in some people's mailboxes, or we handed it to people on the street. I had the idea to put one up at Draper's store. They've got a whole bulletin board for flyers like Camille's. Lots of places. A lot of them she took around herself when I was busy with Robotics after school." He smiled an almost shy smile. "I'm pretty good at working on engines and that's what I had to do because we're going to be in a big match next month, and everybody has to do their best so we can win and maybe go to Missouri for a worldwide match."

"Do you know where she put up her flyers, when you weren't with her? Which mailboxes she put them it?"

"She told me she stuck 'em in mailboxes where she thought she might get a gardening job. That's all. Oh, and she said they were places with a lot of weeds."

"Here in town?"

He shook his head. "I don't know. I'd guess so 'cause she doesn't drive."

"Did she get any responses that you know of? To the flyers?"

"Said she had somebody talking to her the afternoon I left with my dad. I called her when we were driving. I was thinking about her a lot and hoping she got a really good job."

"Did she tell you who she talked to?"

"All she said was she was still waiting to hear."

Zoe watched Kent's face as she questioned him. If she ever saw a human being struggling, this kid was that human being. It was almost a letdown, having him so believable, as if they'd lost another trail toward Camille.

"Kent, do you happen to know the places Camille liked to go to be alone?"

"Mostly the woods. I asked her once if I could go and she said no. She had these places that were just hers and she wasn't going to share them with anybody. Not even me.'

"Special places?"

He thought a while, biting his bottom lip. "Well, one house. The last time I talked to her she started telling me about it. It was a place she liked to go but that's all I know."

Zoe sat up. "She didn't tell you where it was?"

He shook his head again, trying to remember then giving up.

"Any other places the two of you talked about?"

On a suspicion Zoe asked, "You sure you never went to the woods with her, Kent?"

Beside him, Mrs. Miller frowned. "I don't let Kent go in the woods alone. He goes hunting with his dad, that's enough. They don't get a lot of time together. But I have strict rules about going into the woods. Too many kids get lost."

Kent put his head down and worked his hands, one within the other, until Jenny asked a question.

"Did she have any other friends that you know about?"

He knotted up his face and thought very hard. "The kids at school like her a lot. Everybody likes Cammy."

"Anybody in particular?"

He thought hard again, looking off, then back. He shook his head. "Nobody in particular. Except me."

"What about Janice Root?" Jenny asked, pretending it was a question she just threw out. "Was she Cammy's friend?"

"I know Janice Root. My mom told me what happened to her. That's very bad. I wonder why things are happening to girls here in Bear Falls. Hit-and-run. Getting lost."

"But Janice and Cammy weren't close friends?"

"No. She was really nice and Cammy liked her, but Cammy said that Janice had to work in her family's orchard and didn't have a lot of time for friends."

"Did Janice have time for boyfriends?"

"I don't know." He shook his head.

"You wouldn't know if Janice liked any certain boy in school, would you?"

"Nope. I didn't get into a lot of things like that. I'd say girls talk about that stuff."

"Was Cammy one of those girls who talked about that stuff?"

"Nope. That's why she was my friend. She wasn't like other girls."

"Did people know that you and Cammy were . . . eh . . . friends?"

Kent looked at his mother and blushed.

"Are you tired, Kent?" His mother leaned toward him.

He shook his head. "I've got to help find Cammy."

Zoe took a deep breath. She asked: "Would she run away from home?"

"Cammy? Run away from home? What for? She loves her mother an awful lot. Always said if it wasn't for her mother, nobody would have taken care of her."

"Cammy ever say what she wanted to be after high school?"

Kent nodded. "A archeologist. Or a zookeeper. She likes bears a lot."

"Did she ever say which college she wanted to go to?"

He looked perplexed and shook his head. "She didn't think she could make it in college. She wasn't going to go."

Zoe and Jenny turned to each other, silently wondering if there were more questions.

"Did you know about Cammy's grandparents?" Zoe remembered to ask.

He rolled his eyes and made a face. "Terrible people. Cammy said she'd never have anything to do with them, not even if they came back to town and apologized to her mother."

"So you don't think she would go see them if they got in touch?"

"Hmmm." He bent forward, as if he hadn't heard right.

"Would Cammy ever go see them?"

"Without telling her mom?" He shook his head. "Nope. That's one thing I can say for sure. Cammy would never want to see those people. From what she said, they hurt her mom pretty bad."

"Could we come back another time, if we have more questions?" Jenny finally asked.

"Sure. And bring Cammy with you, okay? I'm really missing her now and want her to come back to her mom. I'll bet her mom misses her, too."

"She does. She really does."

He stood to politely shake hands, first bending to take Zoe's hand, and then Jenny's.

"You get a turkey?" Zoe thought to ask when they were back out on the porch.

"I don't kill things," he said. "I just go along to be with my dad. I don't see him much. But I don't watch when he shoots." He made a face. "I don't like it when something dies."

Mrs. Miller was closing the door behind them when she stopped to ask, "How are Jay and Sally? I don't know when to go see them. This is a terrible thing. Is it true that Janice was . . . ?"

She looked behind her. Kent, standing at her shoulder, listened, concerned about everything.

Zoe nodded, not saying the word "murdered" aloud.

Chapter 20

"No signs of sexual attack. Abrasions around her wrists and ankles," the chief read from the ME's report. Jenny and Zoe sat across from him, listening hard. Tony was behind them, looking down at his hands.

Ed Warner cleared his throat and sniffed.

"Both wrists and ankles had been taped but the ankles show deeper scratches and deeper cuts. Probably from being dragged." Ed studied the faces in front of him, looking up to add more that he knew. "We didn't recover the tape at the crime scene so the tape was removed before dropping her at the road."

Ed shook his head. "You know? When I took this job the one thing I was happy about was that I'd probably never have to deal with a crazed serial killer. I don't know if that's what we've got here or not, but with two girls—one already dead and the other one in more danger every day we don't find her, well . . ."

He leaned back. "I was half-hoping it was some teenage thing gone wrong. But this was deliberate. No overdose shown. We know the stomach contents—nothing there that would have killed her: some kind of burger and greens. Half a hard candy."

"No chance of poison." Zoe said. "How about something that could have knocked her out?"

He shook his head, going over the papers—page by page—as he searched for anything that would suggest a different outcome.

"So we don't know what, exactly, killed her." Tony shook his head at Ed. "Nobody hit her on the head with a rock. Nobody stabbed or shot her. She wasn't strangled. Didn't choke on her own vomit. Wasn't drowned."

"Yeah. Well. She says 'asphyxia,'" Ed said looking up again.

"But what does that mean?" Zoe demanded. "The medical examiner can't do better than that?"

"What she did say was that carbon monoxide leaves the body pretty fast. Two days and it would be gone from her blood. Except maybe a tiny residue. That doesn't mean it wasn't what killed her, only that she can't say for certain. Here's what she called it: *environmental asphyxia. Lack of oxygen.* Comes down to something cut off her oxygen and she died. Suicide's not even in the equation. No strangulation marks on her throat. One thing's for sure—one way or the other, the kid couldn't breathe. ME says "homicide.""

Zoe looked at the thin man whose head kept steadily drifting to one side until he jerked it back. "Do you think Cammy's dead?" she asked.

The question dropped like a spent bullet between them.

"No. No," Tony, from behind Zoe, hurried to assure her when Ed couldn't find an answer.

Ed rubbed his hands together. "I'm not giving up. We've just started looking. We've got her clothes and her cell phone . . ."

Ed stopped talking.

Tony said, "Just because Janice's dead doesn't mean Camille Otis is, too. Different kind of thing, the way Camille disappeared. Unless we find a body, I'm going to keep thinking she's alive and put someplace. Probably out in the woods. Lots of places to search yet."

Jenny looked from Zoe to Ed. "Maybe we're kidding ourselves. It's the 'clothes and cell' that worries me. How'd the phone get broken? It's still down in the thirties overnight, what's she wearing? It's been four days." She shook her head. "You talked to Kent this morning, right Ed? He tell you Camille was looking for a summer job?"

Ed leaned back and closed his eyes. "That boy's got no part in any of this."

"I don't think so either," Zoe said. "But he knew just about everything Cammy was doing. Likes her a lot and is broken up about her being missing. No way he took her somewhere, killed her, and then went hunting with his dad."

"Kid said he and his dad left at eight a.m. Friday morning. I could check . . ."

"Not necessary," Zoe said. "Pamela was still home at eight o'clock. Boy is telling the truth."

"We don't have a real timeline—Friday afternoon, is all," the chief said.

Zoe drew in a long breath. "Still . . . I think Kent's holding something back. I can feel it. Couldn't look me in the eye. A kid like that—they don't like to lie, they're so straight forward—more black and white that most kids. Maybe he promised he wouldn't tell anybody about that summer job. Or something else he promised not to tell. We've got to talk to him again. Could take two or three times to gain his trust."

"Anything else you can think of?" Ed pushed papers around on the desk, obviously having other things to do.

Zoe started to rise but stopped to ask, "Has the tech gotten into the phone yet?"

"Working on it. It's the computer I'm pinning my hopes on. I thought it would be easier. Should get something today."

Tony lifted his head, his dark-circled eyes taking Jenny in for a long minute, and then turning to Zoe. "How's the thing going with the rich guy?"

"You mean Fitzwilliam Dillon? Ask Jenny."

Jenny shrugged and said nothing.

"Dora's got friends of Fitz Dillon coming over around noon." All she could do was make a face, then turn to Zoe. "Good thing we'll be out of here."

"Yes. Well." Zoe looked down at her hands with bright purple polish on her nails. "I hate to do that . . ."

Ed broke in. "So, you two going out to where Tony found the clothes?" he asked Jenny. "Got Google maps of the area. Looks like there are a few houses outlined every so often. Maybe abandoned places. If you can get to it, you could take a look at them while you're out there."

"Pamela said there was one place Cammy liked to go especially. A ruined building or house or cabin."

Tony nodded. "She told me, too. That's why we were in that area."

Zoe took a deep breath and jumped in. "You know, I've been thinking. Maybe I could cover more ground if I looked at some other . . . things."

"What other things?" Jenny asked. "You said as early as we could go . . ."

Zoe was playing games she usually didn't play and wasn't good at. She turned to Tony. "I was thinking, if you went with Jenny you'd know right where to start. I could go see the Reverend Senise. See if he learned something about that religious group."

Tony shook his head. "Already lined up a search group. We're going north."

"My deputy will do that," Ed jumped in, avoiding Zoe's eyes.

"And then I can go out and talk to the Roots," she said. "There is something going on with those two."

Ed nodded. "I'll be in Traverse City. Me and Chief Simpson are working up a predators list—seeing if there are similar MOs to cases seen already. Anybody who took a teenage girl and hid her, or even approached a young girl."

Ed slouched in his chair and looked really hard at Zoe. "But I don't know about you going out to the Roots. Sally won't get out of bed and Jay's no help at all. Every time I'm there he looks at me as if I've got no right asking. Makes me wonder. And I got a phone call . . . but I don't want to go into any of that. Not yet."

"It won't hurt for me to try." Zoe pressed her fingers to her forehead.

Jenny's eyes were closed. Zoe was bailing on her and she knew why. Playing cupid. She knew her friend well enough—this was all planned, damn her. Some fouled up idea of getting her and Tony together.

Just what she didn't need right now. Resumes out to four more Chicago law firms. A host of resumes out to firms in Traverse City. She had to do follow-up calls. She could hear any day, and be gone within the week. What she needed, more than anything, was to know where she was going and what she was doing before she talked to Tony, explained why she had to get her life moving.

Guilt was shaming her, as if she'd already betrayed him.

Damn Zoe Zola. Likes to mess in everybody's life.

Zoe was saying, "After I see the Roots I think I'll go to Draper's Superette. Kent said she put her flyer up on Draper's community board. Cammy could've met that guy right there. And I think I'll go to your house. You know, those mansion people. Be there for your mom. She's always there for me."

Jenny pulled herself back to what was important right then, ignoring what Zoe was doing. "About that flyer, does anyone remember Cammy put her address on it? She didn't have to get phone calls. All the man had to do was watch her house and go there when Pamela was at work."

Jenny hurried on. "I'm thinking it's more important for me to go with you to see Sally Root. I know her . . ."

Zoe shook her head. "Waste of time. No, you and Tony search around where her clothes were found. Then look for that place Pamela mentioned. An old house in the woods. Birds in the chimney. What if she fell and got stuck in the foundation? What if she broke a leg? Who's going to hear her back in those woods? What if there's an old well and she fell in?"

"Naked?" Jenny scoffed. "Accident isn't the answer."

Exasperated, Tony threw his hands up. "Don't need you two

arguing over me. I say, Zoe, you get going to the Roots and wherever else you need to go. Come on, Jenny. You two can fight out whatever's going on between you another time, okay?"

Zoe smirked behind Tony's back as he headed toward the door.

Jenny made a face at her, hesitated, then got up and walked out behind him.

Ed raised his eyebrows at Zoe when they were gone.

"What?" she said. "I'm going over to Dora's. I felt bad, letting her down."

"Then where?"

"Roots."

He shook his head ever so slowly, got up, and put his jacket on.

He headed for the door. "We'll share what we know later. Got to keep our heads going in the right direction. All of us. You know, Zoe, we're not in the romance business."

"Really?" She lifted her eyebrows at his back. "Seems to me . . ."

But he was gone.

Chapter 21

Jenny said nothing once they were on their way. She looked at her phone, checked emails and hoped, as she did every day now, there would be an answer from one of the places she'd applied to. This whole thing was too drawn out. Once she'd made up her mind to move on with her life, she wanted it over with, not this deceit—a long lie to Tony. This wasn't who she was. And if she did hear, was offered a well-paying job, maybe in Chicago, what then? *Been nice knowing you . . .* She looked over at him—his profile. He stared out the front window, thinking, frowning, his dark brows drawn together, his lips set. She saw the scar running down his cheek and knew what that had cost him. But pity couldn't be allowed to sway her. She had a life to plan.

She said nothing. Neither did he.

Out her window she watched as Bear Falls moved past—the stores, the movie theatre, the town offices, Myrtle's. It was all home to her again. Be hard to leave.

She leaned back against the seat and took a deep breath. Something in her wanted to reach over and put her hand on his but she couldn't. That would be another lie—that there was something lasting between them. She couldn't promise anything.

"Think we'll start with Orrin Road." He stared hard out the front window, searching for a road sign. "Me and Ed went over the map." He pointed beside him on the seat. "That's where they found Camille's things—that star." He pointed again. "About a mile in from Shore Road."

"Here?" She saw smaller stars. "Are those houses?"

He nodded.

"Where's that other team searching?"

"Toward the lake. Then north. Into the woods around there, and the swamps."

"There are only two of us, Tony. How much can we cover?"

"Do what we can." He looked at her but turned away immediately. "If we need more people, we've got just about everybody in town ready to help. Ed says he'll get 'em together and send 'em out if we find anything."

She searched the Google map, trying to make out the shapes of roofs hidden under canopies of trees. One or two were possibilities.

One new driveway stood out, but not old driveways—those were only guesses. She searched for spaces between the thick trees.

Tony parked the truck off Shore Drive, on Orrin, a narrow dirt road where loggers once pulled felled logs out in winter, by horse. He pointed directly into the woods, motioning for Jenny to follow, then marched off without waiting for her.

"Do you at least have a compass?" She called when they were a few hundred yards into the trees, fighting snapping limbs, and uneven ground.

"Won't need one." He climbed over a fallen tree, coming back to take Jenny's hand, helping her through the dead branches.

"People get lost out here, you know."

"Got my cell," he said over his shoulder.

"No service. This isn't Detroit."

He pulled the map from his pocket. "We're headed straight for Elder Road. The depression where they found her stuff is between here and there. Beyond that is something called H Road."

Jenny followed with only a few grumbles about him moving too fast. "And if we get lost, all I brought is a candy bar," she called toward his taut back. "A small one. Too small to share."

"That's okay." He yelled over his shoulder. "I'm bigger than you. I'll just take it."

She slowed after a while, moving under a very old Basswood tree, tripping on a root and falling to the ground. He was back beside her, his rough and blunted hands out to help her.

She tried to pull her hand from his.

"What's going on, Jenny?" His voice wasn't friendly. His eyes were angry. The scar on his cheek turned an ugly red.

She said nothing.

"Look, I'm too old to play games. Whatever it is, at least be honest with me."

She still said nothing. She couldn't look at him.

"I thought everything was back to being fine with us. Now I get the feeling you want out."

"No." She shook her head. "That's not it, Tony. I'd tell you . . ."

"Then what? You do your best to keep away from me. Barely talk to me." He took a step back, letting go of her hand. "I don't play games, Jenny. I didn't think you did either."

She shook her head again and again. No tears—that was too easy. "I've got to get a job, Tony. I'm almost to the point of living off my mother. That makes me feel really great about myself."

"Look." He moved closer. "I can try to pay you more."

"You're not making anything as it is. Maybe someday."

"I've got my pension. I could help you out."

She looked away. "You don't get it. It's not just money. It's me. I have to function the way I used to—before Ronald. I need to make my own decisions. I guess, I'm saying . . . Oh Tony . . . I can't . . . I can't be a wife until I know I can be somebody to myself."

"I never asked you to be my wife." He said, but softly. "I never pushed you, Jen. I . . . can't . . ."

He turned and walked away.

Rain began to tap down through the new and tiny leaves. Rain ran over her face as she watched his bent back. He headed toward another copse of aspen without waiting to see if she followed.

Chapter 22

On her way to Dora's, Zoe walked slower than she might have between the pines, thinking of things she should be thinking about—like hoping Jenny and Tony would be smart enough to put whatever was going on between them aside and concentrate on Cammy Otis while they were out in the woods. And hoping the Roots would talk to her. And how Dora so easily made her feel guilty. What she hated most about life was guilt. Always came so easily to her.

How dare you leave your mother alone? "Why, shame on you little girl," said the minister, who came to spread the word of God to Zoe's mother, Darla, as she lay in bed, sick and aggrieved at the world.

"You know she needs you with her," said the social worker, who couldn't figure where to put Darla and decided her daughter could very well attend to her. After all, what was college going to do for her?

Later, from a neighbor: *Shame, shame, Zoe. You don't need to be out working. You could get welfare, you know. What with your deficiency and all.*

Zoe shook her head and thought of other things. *Of cabbages and kings.* Chapters of the Austen book she should have sent to her editor, the ever-patient Christopher Morley.

She bent to straighten a tulip head, draping it over a neighboring tulip, then stood looking at the two flowers—dependent on each other.

* * *

They were there already, three of them sitting at Dora's kitchen table, making noises about Dora's "sweet little house."

Nathan Wickley pulled himself to full, unimpressive height as she walked in. Delia Thurgood straightened her cashmere shawl across her shoulders, and smiled—slightly. Lady Cynthia Barnabus tipped her head to one side, leaned toward Zoe, and made kissing gestures in the air.

Dora fluttered nervously back and forth offering iced tea or coffee as Zoe took her chair atop phone books and nodded to each of the guests.

Delia, wrapping the shawl around her shoulders, made mewling sounds, then leaned over to take Zoe's arm in her hand and squeeze.

"I can't tell you how sorry Fitz is that the two of you got off to such a bad start," Delia gushed at her. "Now he feels that he won't be welcomed into his new home, and that it might be best if he sold Rosings and went back to Chicago. This is a true catastrophe."

Zoe scratched her nose. "That's his choice. Might be best for all of us."

"Oh no, don't say that!" Delia threw her hands in the air and looked straight at Nathan for help. "Fitz knows how hospitable the North Country can be. Nathan has such fond memories of his boyhood. It would be a shame to deprive Fitz of such an experience. You know, Zoe, he's not always had an easy life."

Nathan nodded but looked to Lady Cynthia for help.

"Surely, Miss Zola, you don't want to see what were wonderful plans for this amazing town destroyed because of a little misunderstanding," she said.

Nathan spread his small hands wide. "I can't help but agree with Lady Cynthia, Zoe . . . er . . . Miss Zola. You can't be allowed to ruin things for everybody. Why, Delia and I were just talking about maybe settling near here ourselves. Maybe find adjacent properties. Another loss. Just imagine what people will think of you? My friend, Fitz, is a fine man, a kind man, a generous man, just like his father before him. It does seem to me that you could show a little compassion."

Zoe held up one of her hands, blocking Nathan's face. "What has any of this to do with me? When did you all decide I was responsible for your Fitzwilliam's whims?"

She bit her tongue by mistake and then tried to think of nothing but the pain in her mouth, hoping there was blood she could spit into a napkin in front of them to make them feel sorry for picking on her.

It was after a very deep breath—with no blood appearing to help her—that she smiled at Nathan. "I have no control what-so-ever over your Fitzwilliam."

"But you stormed out . . ."

"Really? You call that a storm?"

Delia looked to Dora for help but Dora, watching and listening to what was going on in her kitchen, clamped her lips shut and stared down at the floor.

Delia made a sad face at Zoe. "Word has gotten back to Fitz of your . . . shall we say 'antipathy' to him. Such a shame. And with your notoriety . . ."

"Notoriety? What on earth makes me notorious?"

Dora made a noise while Delia demurred, putting a finger to her lips. "I chose the wrong word." She laughed slightly, rolling her eyes Lady Cynthia's way.

"What Delia means to say, I think, is that you are probably the best known person in the entire town. Who better to direct people to the perfect choice for everyone?"

Zoe zeroed in on what the woman had said, probably not meaning to be unkind. "Best known for what?" She crossed her arms and sat back.

"Why, for your scholarly work, of course."

"Ah, yes. My scholarly work. I'm sure that's what your Fitz admires most about me."

"Oh, but he does. And if there is any misunderstanding about it you have only to ask him. I heard him myself, last night, saying how badly he felt that the two of you had gotten off to a terrible start."

Lady Cynthia smiled, laughed, and shook her finger at Zoe. Across from her Delia shook her head, too, agreeing as hard as she could.

Lady Cynthia leaned across the table. "He can be impossible," she said. "But he is the most generous man. Though . . . at times . . . well . . . testy. He works very hard, you know. Not an easy life at all—being that wealthy."

Zoe watched the nervous woman flutter her eyelids. It was a moment to savor—for every perverse reason she could come up with. For some reason, she rattled these people and that felt good.

"We all do so much want to stay. If you would only call him." Delia's hand was on hers again, but not for long. Zoe dropped her hands to her lap while wishing she'd brought Fida with her. Fida knew people. She would certainly have been nipping at Delia's very narrow ankles by now, sinking her tiny, but deadly teeth into those many-strapped pink shoes.

"I have to agree with Cynthia and Delia. One simple phone call." Nathan nodded.

"Maybe he should come to my house." Zoe looked around the kitchen, leaning back and poking one very straight finger into her hair. "I think he should ring the bell, then ask prettily if he may come inside."

"Fitz is an important man. You don't understand who you're dealing with," Nathan blustered.

"Oh," Dora, upset at what she was hearing, interrupted, frowning at everyone around the table. "I'll bet you understand well enough, don't you, Zoe?"

Zoe nodded. "And when I open the door to Fitz, the first thing I'll do is introduce him to Fida, my dog. She'll know if he's important enough to be let in."

"What a good idea," Dora said, clapping her hands. "Leave it to Fida. I've never known her to be wrong."

Zoe moved around on her chair, as if ready to get down. "But I'm very busy right now—something more important than Fitzwilliam's moods."

Delia looked to Nathan.

"I've heard," he said. "How terrible . . . I mean about the dead girl."

He spoke louder. "And another girl missing. I understand that both you and Dora's daughter are helping the police. Have you found the girl yet?"

"We will."

"I'll have to admit," Delia broke in to add, "It does give one pause. Moving to a place with so much crime. Really, for such a small town . . ."

"Frightening, I'd say." Lady Cynthia put a finger to her lips. Her light eyes were wide. "I wonder what happened . . . strangers, I'll bet. Always a terrible stranger lurking somewhere. Needless to say, even in England we've had our share . . ."

Dora watched as each added an opinion.

Nathan interrupted his friend. "But really, with one girl already dead—don't you think you shouldn't be interfering? I mean . . ." Nathan blinked hard at Zoe. ". . . with the police trying to do their work?"

Zoe, her round-eyes huge, looked straight at Dora. "What do you think, Dora? Should Jenny and I stop looking for Camille?"

Dora bit at her lip. She thumped her hands on the table and stood. "I think," she said, "we should all have a piece of pie."

She got up to get the pie, still steaming, sitting on top of the stove. She pulled five plates from the cupboard and five forks from the silverware drawer. With everything—including the pie and a very sharp knife in hand—she came to the table, fussing, setting things down until she stopped, knife in midair. She slowly set the knife down and bowed her head.

It took Dora a minute to take a deep breath, to look from Nathan's bland face to Delia's icy eyes, to Lady Cynthia, who was out of her depth and looked bewildered.

Dora turned slowly to Zoe, letting her anger bubble up.

She shook her head. "I have to tell the truth, Zoe. I don't think you should call Fitzwilliam Dillon at all. Not for any amount of money. I think the man's a nasty piece of work. If he wants your forgiveness then I agree, let him come himself and ask for it."

She nodded again and again as she very slowly picked up the pie and took it back to the oven. She came back to the table for the knife and took it to the sink. She picked up the forks and returned them to the silverware drawer. Then it was the five plates—back to the cupboard, one by one, until she shut the cupboard door with a satisfying slam.

When she turned to the people at the table, it was with a grievous sigh. "What I really think is that the three of you should leave."

She nodded to Nathan and then to Delia Thurgood, and finally to Lady Cynthia, who sat very stiff, her mouth hanging slightly open.

"Oh, please don't get us wrong, dear Dora. We understand everyone's anxiety but . . ." Nathan Wickley tried to smooth the waters.

"That's enough for today."

"Oh, of course. Maybe you'll be able to talk some sense into your friend with us not around."

"Please leave my house." Dora's face was red from her hairline to her neck.

Nathan and Delia muttered under their breath as they got out of their chairs at the same time and headed for the kitchen door, with Lady Cynthia close behind.

In the archway, Nathan stopped. He looked back, giving the women a sad smile. "This is unfortunate, you know. So sorry that we couldn't make you see . . ."

Zoe slid from her chair, feet hitting the ground with a thump. She headed around the table to stand next to Dora.

"Oh, but there was something else." Nathan turned again, putting a hand into the air, smiling broadly as if nothing had happened between them. "That woman with the charming daughter . . . could I have her telephone number?"

Dora and Zoe exchanged puzzled looks.

"Nathan means the woman with the demure daughter. Dear, dear soul," Delia leaned around him. "I'd like to know her better. She seems so . . . well . . . dear."

Zoe kept her face straight when looking up at Dora. "They must mean Minnie Moon. Sounds like Dianna, doesn't it? I mean, demure."

Dora's smile was wary. "Yes, of course." She turned to Nathan. "Do you want to invite them to something?"

"We thought a nice little dinner . . ." Delia said. "We'd like to know the townspeople better. Maybe get help to change your mind, Zoe, about Fitz."

Dora quickly found Minnie's number and copied it for Nathan.

"Thank you so much. And, Miss Zola, if you would only reconsider and reach out to him. It would be so much appreciated by everyone. I, for one, would love to stay in this quaint little town."

Zoe smiled as wide as she could get her lips to go. "Oh, I'll think about it all right. And, in the meantime, you have a wonderful dinner with the Moons."

Chapter 23

Jenny didn't hurry to catch up with Tony. The old leaves were wet. Rain dripped from her long hair down her back, making her sweater damp and cold.

From time to time she slipped, eventually walking slower, losing sight of Tony.

Still she followed, though she might have taken a wrong turn for all she knew.

In half an hour the rain stopped. Sun came out, making skinny shadows of branches, a crisscrossed camouflage pattern that hid the places on the ground that might trip her.

He was there. Ahead of her. Standing very still. He put a finger to his mouth, and whispered, "Look," then pointed to a place beyond where the quaking aspens thinned.

She saw nothing but wet leaves and bowing branches.

He beckoned. "Through there."

He pointed again, "See that?" he whispered.

There was a ruin. She held her breath. A house. The roof was gone. Two floors were open, like a monstrous dollhouse.

Waving strips of wallpaper and shreds of curtains fluttered from upstairs windows along the intact back wall. Siding hung everywhere, peeled away from broken laths. From the remnants of an old stone fireplace, birds flew up into the trees and sat there, watching them silently.

Jenny shivered. An unnatural place. Houses shouldn't be cut in half and opened for everyone to see. Walls should be where walls are supposed to be.

"Cammy!" she called, then stood still, finger to her lips, listening hard.

She called again.

Nothing. Not even the birds stirred.

Tony called—his deep voice echoing back at them.

Across the middle of the house one wall was still half intact. It formed a dividing wall between the front rooms and maybe a kitchen.

"Could this be the ruin Cammy told Pamela about?" Jenny whispered. "Plenty of birds around that fireplace."

He shrugged, holding his shoulders tight while he thought. "The kid could've got herself killed here."

"Or hidden," she said.

Jenny took a deep breath, put her hands beside her mouth, and called out one more time, "Camille! Camille! Camille!"

A noisy crow squawked back at her from the top of the broken chimney.

Tony collected a pile of boards—one by one. He set them in front of the house and, with his hands on the decayed floor, leaped up to stand in what must once have been the living room.

Without a look back at her, he worked his way around mounds of fallen plaster to the back wall where he disappeared through a skewed doorway.

She held her breath because she couldn't hear him.

"There's a Michigan basement back here." He stood in the doorway. "Looks like stone walls, dirt floor."

"Can you get down there?"

"Got the door open but there's nothing left of the stairs."

"Did you call her?"

"Did that. No answer. Wish I'd brought a flashlight."

"Use your phone."

"Tried that. Can't see much."

"How far are we from the place where they found her things?" she asked. "This may not be the right house. Maybe it's too far from there."

He shrugged. "We went right by the place on the way here."

"Why didn't you say something?"

He looked off across the yard, then shook his head. "She's wasn't there. And she's not here."

"You don't know for sure." She'd lowered her voice, anger making her throat tighten. "She could be in that basement. Maybe hurt." She walked away as he crossed the floor then jumped to the ground, tripping as he jumped, falling to his knees when he hit the ground.

With the first moan he rocked back and forth, his left ankle in his hand. He rocked until he got himself together enough to sit up straight, sticking his left leg in front of him and swearing.

"I broke something." His voice was strained, and mad. "Or twisted my ankle. Help me up." He pushed with one hand at the ground and held on to Jenny's bent arm with his other hand. It wasn't easy to get him to a standing position, and then not easy to move him as he leaned heavily against her.

"Which way do we go?" Jenny asked as she tried to take on his full weight but stumbled.

Tony blew out a painful breath before motioning with his head, not the way they'd come, but in the opposite direction.

"Gotta find a road. Too far back to the truck. I don't think I can make it."

She tried her cell phone but had no bars. Jenny put her arm around his waist and clutched his belt as tightly as she could.

At first he hopped, then put a small amount of weight on that foot, and soon was walking—painfully—but without his whole weight on Jenny. They could move, ever so slowly.

"There has to be a driveway leading in from a road otherwise how would these people have gotten back here?" He grimaced but didn't stop moving.

He pulled the map from his back pocket.

"H Road ahead. Looks close."

She pointed to an opening between large trees. "There? That way?"

He nodded, took a deep breath, and pushed on.

Before they left the clearing, Tony had her star the place they were on his map. She circled the star, then drew a box around the circle. "We'll find it again," she promised.

"Let's keep moving," Jenny said, helping Tony from the clearing as the birds, settling back around the fireplace, set up a nasty chorus behind them.

Chapter 24

The ground was slippery, and uneven. With every step a fallen branch threatened to trip them. And still no road. They moved, hunting for other houses, for signs of human habitation—any place where they could get a phone signal, or where people lived and they could call for help.

"H Road must be just ahead," Tony kept saying, pointing to different places on his map when they stopped. It wasn't long before they stumbled into another clearing, large enough to hold a house, maybe a barn—but empty, nothing but tall grass and piles of blackened boards laying over the ground, some sticking into the air, rusted nails threatening.

"Fire," he said, looking around. "House burned down. Happens a lot to ruins. Lightning. Kids."

Jenny pointed to a pile of dead brush at the far end of the open space. There was nothing else around. Not an outhouse. Not a chicken coop. Nothing left of the farm or homestead that once stood there.

They made slow passage among the charred boards and through the broken remains of what must once have been furniture or more broken and burned bits of the house.

Jenny called, "Cammy!" Then stood still to listen to nothing but leaves.

Tony called, too, his deep voice echoing across the clearing and into the woods. "Not here," he said. "And nowhere to hide."

"Or be hidden." Jenny said.

* * *

They went on, through what looked like a straight opening in the trees. An old road. A driveway. Tony hopped on one leg, giving Jenny a break as he checked the map, then shook his head.

"Should have planned this better." He turned to Jenny, apologetic.

"Accidents happen."

"Think we should take that way?" He pointed off between a stand of maples.

"Where's it go?"

He shrugged as he folded the map. "Let's just find a road. Okay? I'll figure it out." His voice was hard. Jenny understood it was the pain talking but gave him a pinch anyway. He got it, turned to look straight at her, and smile.

The way they chose led through thick beds of wet leaves, and through thickets of brambles tearing at their clothes. Tony kept moving, though he grunted from time to time.

They stumbled into the dirt road. Almost fell down into it. Not knowing they were on H Road until they looked both ways and saw it was a curved dirt road.

Tony took out his cell. No service. They checked the map again and chose right—north. Quite a ways, but it looked as if they'd get back to Orrin Road.

Jenny walked steadily even though her shoes were caked with mud, her feet felt like solid lumps of ice, and both arms ached—one from reaching around Tony's waist, supporting him, the warmth of him coming through her jacket. She held his am with her other hand, feeling his strength push against her, and then a pulling away when he must have felt he was hurting her.

"Ed'll be all over that house soon as we get ahold of him," Tony said between grimaces.

"He's in Traverse, meeting with the police chief."

"Flores will get people out here."

"If Cammy was in one of those places she would have answered," Jenny said.

"Could have been sleeping. Or knocked out." He thought a minute. "I imagine she's found something to wrap up in."

"Like a white dress with ruffles?" she couldn't stop what she was thinking. "Like Janice Root? A white dress with lace on it?"

"Maybe not. More and more I think Zoe's right about Pamela's parents."

"You have to think that. We all do. And even that's horrible."

She closed her eyes but kept walking.

"No solace there for Pamela." Jenny couldn't help herself. "If her parents have Cammy, it will kill her."

"If Pamela's parents hurt Cammy *they'll* be the ones we find dead." Tony grunted.

Chapter 25

It was at a crossroads where a bent-over road sign said Orrin and H that Tony leaned against the metal post and pulled his pant leg up. His ankle was red and swollen, puffing over his shoe. He slid to the ground and looked as if he meant to stay there.

Jenny figured she was on her own. He needed to get to a doctor. She had to call the chief and get people out there. They'd lost so much time already. Maybe very precious time when Cammy could have been saved.

How far back on Orrin to get to the truck?

"Not going to make it any farther," he said from where he sat on the ground. "Maybe you should get the truck . . ."

"If I can find it."

She turned first in one direction and then in the other—up and down the road that looked like the road they'd just walked out on. In one direction there were trees and bushes. Trees and bushes everywhere. She knew she had to go west, but which way was west, toward the lake? She'd never been good at directions, nor even good at reading time on a clock that didn't say: one, two, three . . .

Tony sat with his head down, his hands shoved into the pockets of his jacket; his back slightly bent, dark hair blown by the wind. He pointed to a place in the woods.

"Looks like a driveway over there—kind of overgrown—but maybe there's a house."

She checked where he pointed. Old weeds grew down the middle of the old pathway, but the ruts were clear and deep. Worth a try.

She crossed the road.

"Don't be long." He called to her. "Call Ed first, if you find somebody. Get people out to the house."

"And you to a doctor."

"Yeah," he nodded. "But not until we show the searchers where that house is."

At a bend in the two-track driveway, Jenny saw a small house set in a clearing; a cedar-sided cottage with mullioned windows, with dug-over flowerbeds around the house and down the sides and along a walk that went out of sight.

A white arbor stood at the head of a stone walk leading to the low, front door. On either side of the arbor were tall lilac bushes, flower heads just appearing on leafing branches. If it hadn't been for the coil of white smoke coming from the chimney Jenny would have thought the place was empty. No car stood in the side yard; no dog barked.

She walked through the arbor, up to a small covered porch, and a front door where a sign hung: UNLESS YE BE OF PURE HEART, DON'T BOTHER KNOCKING.

Refusing to examine her conscience, she lifted the brass knocker, and dropped it heavily against the worn wooden door.

A tall woman, maybe in her late thirties, wearing a gray tunic and trousers answered at once. She wore her gray streaked hair pulled up into a sweeping chignon at the back of her neck. *Not your ordinary woods woman*, Jenny couldn't help but think, taking in the lady, her thin nose turned up, chin out, looking Jenny up and down before narrowing her cool, gray eyes and saying, "Yes?"

"I'm sorry to bother you but . . ."

"I've been watching you," she said. "Are you Jehovah's Witnesses? Found me at last? I've been expecting you for years." She smiled a sly smile.

"I need help," Jenny said.

"With what?"

"My friend and I have been out all morning looking for a missing girl and got lost. He's hurt."

"Who is the girl?" The woman's strong face showed immediate concern. "From time to time kids come by here. I often worry. And by the way, my name is Selma Grange."

Jenny gave her name and followed it with Cammy's. "Cammy Otis. She's sixteen and been missing four days now."

"Come in. Come in. How can I help?" Selma blinked fast, and frowned. "These woods can be treacherous." She motioned Jenny to take a seat on a sofa that looked as if it hadn't been sat on—maybe ever. There wasn't a pillow in the room that wasn't squarely set in its chair. Not a speck of dust on the end tables. Photos on the walls were straight. The wood floor gleamed as if it had been freshly waxed.

The room was in perfect order, somewhat like the woman who stood across from her.

"What happened to your friend?"

"He's waiting at the crossroad. He hurt his ankle. May I use your phone? I have to call the police in Bear Falls, get them out here."

"Of course. Anything I can do. And I have a car."

Selma Grange pointed to a phone on a side table and told Jenny to help herself.

Ed's wife answered telling Jenny Ed was still in Traverse City. She put Deputy Flores on. Just back from the afternoon search.

Words spilled out of her as she tried to get across to him that they needed help.

"Bring as many people as you can gather. We think Cammy Otis might be in this ruin of a house out here."

"Where?" was all the man wanted to know after taking down what Jenny told him—that they would be waiting at the corner of H and Orrin.

"Tony's hurt his ankle. He should get to a doctor. But I can take you to the house. There's a Michigan basement. She could be down there—maybe hurt bad. She didn't answer when we called."

Deputy Flores said he would get ahold of Ed and tell him where he was going and why. "I'll be there in half an hour," he figured. "Wait out on Orrin. I'll find you.

She put the phone down with a deep sense of relief. At least it was out of her hands. The deputy would come and bring others with him; the woods would be populated.

Maybe they would find Cammy Otis, or at least they would rule out another place she might have gone, but didn't.

"You live out here by yourself?" Jenny couldn't help but ask the woman when she turned around.

"Yes," the woman nodded. "I'm an ornithologist. I study birds. I find them more pleasant to live around than most people."

"And you're a gardener." Jenny smiled as she headed back to the door thinking how this could be a woman Zoe might like to meet. Or not, depending on Zoe's mood.

Selma shrugged and raised her chin a little higher, looking down her nose again. "That was my mother. She was the gardener. I keep it up in her memory. And the birds love flowers. Especially the hummingbirds—red flowers for them. If you were to pass by in another month you'd find red roses climbing the arbor, and the lilacs in full bloom."

"Must be beautiful." Jenny felt as she sometimes did with Zoe, in a little over her head, but awed.

Selma nodded. "And necessary. But now that you know who I am and I've satisfied your curiosity, please tell me about this search you're on. You said for a missing girl?"

"She loved coming to the woods. Her mother told us about a house out here, where birds lived in the chimney. We think we found it but she didn't answer when we called."

She stopped talking as Selma Grange nodded quickly. "The old

Tollis place. Down H Road. Maybe two miles from here?" She nodded when Jenny agreed.

"It's been derelict a long time. Really nothing but a ruin. My
mother knew the family, but not well. I visit from time to time because
the birds love nesting in those old rafters and in the chimney stones.
I look forward to seeing which of them come back each year. You
would be surprised that they recognize me, sometimes flying near my
head to greet me."

She hesitated, narrowing her eyes. "I do have to say, though, I don't
really like that place. If it weren't for the birds I don't think I would go
there. There can be a terrible sadness around a house in ruins."

"Any other old houses that you know of? We're checking everywhere we can."

"Many—in all states of repair. These woods are my textbooks."
Selma shook her head. Her smile was apologetic. "But I don't have
perfect knowledge. My mother was the one who knew the area for
miles around."

She grew thoughtful. "This missing girl. Her name is what?"

"Cammy Otis. Sixteen. Loved the woods. Blond hair."

The woman thought a while. "There is a girl. Every once in a while
she comes into the yard because, she tells me, she heard about what I
do—that I love birds. One time she told me about a bird she'd seen
the year before. But what she described was a bird that only lives in
Hawaii. I thought she'd been reading up on birds to impress me, or
else had a truly astounding birding experience." She smiled.

"I really hope it isn't her. I never asked her name. Marvelous child
with big blue eyes and a sense of wonder too large for such a young
girl. I really hope she's not missing. Tell me, did she wear a blue
pendant?"

Jenny's hand dropped to her jeans pocket where she'd transferred
the pendant, wanting something of Camille's close to remind her how
desperate their search was going to be.

She pulled the chain and pendant out slowly, handing it to Selma Grange, who draped it through her fingers.

Selma looked close, bending to make sure. She nodded. "That's the necklace. I once commented, I think, how pretty it was. I remember she said a friend gave it to her and that it was her all-time favorite piece of jewelry." She thought hard and gave Jenny an odd, suspicious, look. "I suppose some would call her challenged. But they don't understand that some are greater beings. I was drawn to the magic in this girl. We all meet them—the magic people, but most don't recognize who they are and simply call them a name and let them go."

Her long face was sad. "I don't want her to be missing. How can I help?"

"If you come on anything, or hear anything, please get in touch with the police chief in Bear Falls, or call my friend, Zoe Zola. She lives in town and has been looking for Cammy since the beginning of all of this."

The woman nodded. "The writer. I know of her."

Jenny was out on the porch. "One girl is already dead, you know." She turned back to Selma.

"I heard." The woman's thin eyebrows rose, her shoulders hunched protectively up to her ears. "Is her death connected to Cammy's disappearance, do you think?"

"We don't know. But that death was a murder."

A look of horror moved from the woman's eyes to her mouth. She bit her lip and rubbed one hand up and down her arm. After a while, she caught her breath again. "I can't bear to think of that child . . . that beautiful, otherworldly child . . ."

She didn't add the word "dead."

CAMILLE

The man yelled at her when she was slow putting the blindfold on. He said she should get off the bed and sing a song with them, but she stayed curled in a ball. She stuck a finger into each of her ears and kept writing her newest story, which was about a girl who hunted dinosaur bones in Michigan. People didn't think there had ever been dinosaurs there so they didn't believe her at first, until she took a big bone into the Dennos Museum in Traverse City and the person there in charge of accepting displays was so overwhelmed he got tears in his eyes. The next day her name was in the newspaper and the phone was ringing with calls from bigger newspapers saying they wanted to print her story . . .

He pulled her hair until she fell off the end of the bed and hit the floor so hard it knocked the breath out of her. The other person, who smelled of awful perfume, screamed like a woman, saying that he was too stupid to do anything right and he'd done it again . . . or something like that, but she didn't pay a lot of attention because her back hurt. She crawled up on the bed. The other person was still yelling at him and Cammy heard some-body get up and go back up the ladder. The man followed behind saying he was sorry this one wasn't right either and the other person said, "What would you know? She was *my* sister!"

And then they were gone with the metal door clanking shut behind them.

She undid the blindfold and lay down, making her breath get back to normal. She thought about climbing the ladder and trying to push that door open, but knew it wasn't any use. The man—who said his name was James, but she knew that wasn't right because the other one called him a different name when she got mad—always pushed something heavy on top of the door. It wouldn't budge. It never budged when she tried it.

But at least she had half the dish of hard candy left. They forgot to bring meatloaf.

"That's the way it is . . ." she sang as she sucked slowly on a candy.

Part 4

"Our scars make us know that our past was for real."

—Jane Austen, *Pride and Prejudice*

Chapter 26

Zoe turned in beside a closed roadside stand with a crooked ROOT ORCHARD sign nailed to the front. That her phone rang at that somber moment seemed like the height of intrusion but she had to answer, stopping her car beside the stand to hear a woman's voice.

"Hi, is this Zoe Zola? This is Cassandra Hatch. I work at Draper's. You'd know me if you saw me. I know you. Anyway, I just talked to Pamela Otis. I've been dreading running into her but she said maybe I could help . . ."

"How?"

"Well, you see. Last Friday I saw a car I didn't recognize parked across the street from Pamela's house. I didn't think much about it, but it wasn't one of the neighbors. This was a black car. Just thought . . ." Her voice ran down. "Well, anyway, Pamela said it was okay to call you."

She sounded as if she was about to hang up.

"Cassandra. Wait! Of course it helps. What kind of car was it?"

"Don't know one from the other."

"Did you get a license plate?"

"Never thought of it. Didn't hear about anything until Saturday."

"Still, it helps to know that a strange car's been in the neighborhood."

"Might not be so strange. Just a black car."

"But not a car from the neighborhood. Oh, Cassandra. While I've got you . . . Cammy put up a flyer, looking for a summer job. Did you see it on the bulletin board?"

She thought a while. "There're so many flyers all the time. I never look at them."

"Have you seen Cammy in the store lately?"

"Sure, a couple of times last week. Don't remember when exactly."

"Was there anybody with her?"

"Don't think so. But then I see so many people . . ."

That was it. Cassandra, who'd been nervous, was gone.

Zoe put down her phone.

A black car. How many million of them were everywhere? How many damned black cars? Why couldn't it have been orange? Or purple . . .

She sat where she was and squeezed her brain hard, trying to recall everybody in town who drove a black car. Reverend Senise drove a shiny black car. Keith Robbins. The new principal at the high school drove a black car. Delaware Hopkins, Myrtle's day waitress.

She gave up counting.

She drove in to the little house set under tall oak trees beyond the fruit stand. Everything so strangely quiet. No one sat on the porch that wrapped around the front of the one-story house. No dog ran out to greet her. The black pickup by the barn looked as though it hadn't been moved in days; dead leaves were blown around the tires. She couldn't see anyone in the orchard behind the house.

She walked to the door.

Jay, on the short side, older, more stooped now, answered the door in a wrinkled plaid shirt and wrinkled jeans. When he saw it was Zoe, he held on to the door handle and looked at her, saying nothing.

"Jay," she finally said. "Do you know me?"

He nodded, but still held tight to the door.

"I'm helping Police Chief Ed Warner. We want to get whoever hurt your daughter. Should I have called first?"

He looked beyond her, way over her head. "You mean killed my daughter, don't you? Not just hurt her. Somebody killed my daughter."

She nodded. "May I come in and talk to you and your wife?"

Jay took his hand off the inner handle but didn't push the door open.

"Sally can't talk to people. She's just not able . . ."

Zoe nodded. "I heard." She waited for him to make a move, not leaving the porch.

It took him a while until he finally pushed the door open, inviting her to come in without saying another word.

Inside the house, he still said nothing. He turned his back and led her across the small living room where at least ten photos of Janice were set about on dusty tables.

There wasn't a sound in the house but their footsteps. No music coming from any of the rooms. No TV.

Sally Root was nowhere in sight.

In the kitchen, Jay pointed to a chair at the empty oak table covered with coffee rings.

The sink overflowed with dirty dishes.

The room smelled of garbage.

Jay didn't sit with her; he leaned against the sink, arms folded, his head down. "I know you're looking for help but I have to tell you, Miss Zola, me and Sally aren't up to much of anything. Sally never comes out of the bedroom anymore. She doesn't get dressed. Won't hardly eat."

"I'm so sorry." Zoe put her hand out. He ignored it. "I'm here about Camille Otis, too. She's still missing."

"Don't know anything about that."

"Maybe you could help . . ."

"Doubt it."

After a while, Jay took a deep breath. "What do you need from me?" he asked.

The air in the room lightened just a bit.

"I wondered if Janice knew Camille? If they were friends."

He shook his head. "Never heard Janice talk about her. Same school. Must have known each other. But nothing I can tell you."

"Cammy was looking for a summer job. Somebody contacted her and offered her work. I need to know who that somebody was. I thought maybe you could help. She wanted work gardening—things like that."

He thought a while.

"Janice was talking about doing that but she worked here in the orchard all summer."

"Did you pay her?"

"What I could."

"Was she happy with that?"

"Seemed to be."

"Did she ever say she wanted to babysit or help people in their gardens? Do anything at all to make money of her own?"

Jay looked around the room as if something there would give him an answer. "We needed her here. First in the orchard—spraying and trimming the trees; keeping the weeds down. Then all summer at the stand. Needed her every day right through the fall. No time to do much of anything else."

"You sure she wasn't looking for something she could do in between helping at the stand?"

The man shook his head. Terrible eyes looked beyond her out the back window toward the orchard and the rows of trees. When Zoe turned to look, the orchard was as empty as the house. Everything out there, and in this house, seemed to have come to a dead stop.

"I'm not sure of anything anymore," he said, his voice catching at every word.

Zoe couldn't speak for a while. The pain she was seeing was too terrible. The man was living in his own circle of hell.

"What about her room? Cammy had a flyer she'd put up around town. Maybe Janice . . ."

She stopped at a sound behind her. Jay Root's face fell even deeper into sadness.

Sally leaned against the doorframe, staring hard at them. Her gray streaked hair was uncombed. She caught a colorless robe at her waist, holding it with one hand. Her feet were bare.

"Did they get him?" was all she asked.

Zoe stood.

"Not yet, Sally," she said.

"It's because my girl limped. Somebody said that to me. Because she limped and somebody didn't like that she limped or they thought she was weak. Jay dropped her when she was a baby. I called the police, did you know that? Broke her leg in so many places. That's why she limped. Always said it didn't matter. But it did. Somebody didn't like that limp. That's why it happened to Janice. Because she limped."

"Now, Sally . . ." Tears stood in Jay's eyes.

Sally was gone. Zoe heard her bare feet treading softly across the living room floor, and then there came the sound of a door closing.

"You see?" Jay spread his hands wide. "I can't help her. She's blaming *me*. After all these years, she's blaming *me*."

All she could decently do, Zoe knew, was leave.

On the porch, Zoe offered the only thing she could think to offer. She turned to Jay, in the doorway. "I know Dora Weston would come. She'd talk to Sally."

Jay nodded. "Anybody besides me. I'm being punished. Tell Dora I'd welcome her though it probably won't do any good. Sally hates everybody."

Zoe left. She wasn't like Dora. She didn't have words kind enough to help him.

Chapter 27

Dora was alone, sitting on the sofa in front of her TV with Fida in her lap. Zoe peeked in the front window and felt something like a hand squeezing her insides. Just Dora, with Fida lying beside her, on her back, four feet in the air as Dora's hand absentmindedly tickled Fida's stomach.

Simple, homemade bliss without hatred and guilt weighing the air; a sweet-faced woman trying to make life pleasant for her peevish neighbor's dog. And she was peevish. Zoe didn't mind admitting it. Especially when she was out in world, away from her literary work, and made aware of the things people really did to each other.

Zoe stood an extra minute. After the misery of the Root house, she was ready for this simple scene.

But Dora must have felt a pair of eyes on her, she look up, saw Zoe, and started off the couch, dumping Fida to the floor, who then began to bark—mostly because her world of stomach scratching had come to so abrupt an end.

Dora must have taken notice of Zoe's sad face and the hint of tears in her eyes.

"You scared me. You look like ten miles of bad road." She held the door, then pointed to a chair. "It's been wild back here. Jenny and Tony got lost in the woods. They found the house Cammy used to go to but she wasn't there. People went out and searched. Tony hurt his ankle. Sprained. Now he's limping. It's been quite a day. Sit. Sit. Tell me how you made out with the Roots." She bent to look closer at Zoe's face. "I can see you didn't do any better than anybody else."

"Where's Jenny now?"

"She's with Tony. Said she was going to stay with him a while."

Zoe rolled her eyes.

"Now, Zoe. The man is injured. He probably can't get around too well."

"You want to bet?"

Dora ignored her. "What about Jay and Sally? Wouldn't they talk to you? How are they doing?"

Zoe told her about that awful, hate-filled house. "I don't think they'll stay together. Can't. Something inside that house is so awful."

"Anything I can do?"

Zoe nodded. "I told Jay you would come out and stay with Sally for a while. I didn't mean days, just sit with her, talk to her."

"Did he agree?"

She nodded.

"When?"

"Soon as you can."

"Poor Sally. Imagine losing your child the way she's lost Janice. Terrible."

"Imagine losing your child and your wife. That's what he's facing."

Neither said a word for a while.

"Keith called. It looks as though everything's set for this Friday."

"Why the rush? We've got more important things to think about than a meeting."

Dora nodded. "Keith's heard about the feud . . ."

"Feud? You mean between that terrible man and me? No feud." She insisted, shaking her head until her curls bounced.

"Keith's afraid we'll lose the money."

"We wouldn't be losing something we already had. And if it's going to be this bad from now on, I say tell him where he can stick his money."

"Now Zoe. You know about expectations. The town's fired up about this wonderful asset we're going to gain."

Zoe made a face as she sat thinking. "You hear anything more from those people?"

Dora shook her head.

"What nerve. Trying to get me to call that awful man and make nice."

"I wonder if Fitz sent them."

"A possibility."

"He should call you."

Zoe got up and put her arms around Dora's shoulders. "If he rescinds the offer it will be on him. I say let's go on as if we expect everything to continue as planned."

Dora had to think a while. "As long as that awful little man leaves you alone."

Zoe nodded. "As long as he leaves me alone. A deal. And as long as we get a wonderful arboretum out of him."

"Hmmm." Dora didn't hesitate. "A library. Every town should have a marvelous library. Flowers replenish themselves. Books don't."

Chapter 28

Morning. Five thirty. Too early to call anybody. And Cammy was still lost. That was the saddest thing Zoe could think of at the moment.

Jenny was with Tony. That was a good thing, she supposed. Maybe Jenny was finally getting her head together. Or maybe she had a job, was going back to Chicago—only one big lake—Michigan—between her and Tony Ralenti. A predicament, certainly. But not the end.

She threw an arm over her eyes to think, and to keep Fida from licking her face. One overwhelming concern—and they couldn't be allowed to forget it: Cammy Otis wasn't home.

The next thought was who killed Janice Root? Could it have been her own father? She had to talk to Ed Warner. See if he found out anything about Jay. Seventeen years ago. First thing to attack today: was there a record of his past somewhere? She gave in to Fida's little nips and barks, got up to let her out, and then made herself a whole pot of coffee.

At six fifteen, Zoe looked out her window, checking to see if Jenny's car was in the drive. It wasn't.

Dora's lights weren't on either. She went to her office, intending to spend at least the next four or five hours working on the book. She climbed into her high office chair, snapped on the computer, and sat staring at the array of icons, without the will to open a file.

It was too early to do anything, she decided. Comedy and tragedy—the stuff of the best fiction—was everywhere around her but she couldn't write. Not a word. Jane Austen eluded her. Mrs. Bennett, Elizabeth Bennett's deplorable mother, sat at the edge of Zoe's desk and smirked, whispering behind her hand that the women in Bear

Falls, Michigan, (wherever that could possibly be in England) knew nothing at all about arranging advantageous marriages for their girls.

And then there was Caroline Bingley.

How could she write a word about the awful Caroline, who fawned over Mr. Darcy until Zoe wanted to throw up or throw the computer at the wall, or, at the very least, jump up and down on top of the manuscript?

How was she supposed to deal with a woman who told Darcy what a great writer he was, meaning how beautifully he gripped his pen?

If she could shrink the years between the centuries she would have Caroline Bingley driven into Lake Michigan for the crimes against intelligence she committed. Better to call the book *Pride and Stupidity*.

Austen divided a single woman's characteristics between them all, as if by lottery. If she, like Austen, took the traits of women she knew: one part Jenny's confusion, one part Dora's worry, one part Minnie Moon's pushiness, one part Gladys Bonney's rapaciousness, and then threw in one part the audacity of Dianna Moon and one part the shyness of Tammy Bonney . . . and one part that awful snob, Delia Thurgood. What kind of woman would that be?

She shivered at the thought of such a being set loose in the twenty-first century.

Money. Money. Money. Here the centuries were alike—that was easy enough to write about. Everyone made into a figure of currency, judged by the clothes they wore, by their bank account, turned to fawning bootlickers at the sight of a fancy car.

Maybe a black car.

She thought about what Cassandra told her. A black car. Out of the ordinary in their neighborhood? What could that mean? In which neighborhood was a 'black car' out of the ordinary?

Zoe rolled back her chair, climbed down, and went to the kitchen to pour another cup from her enormous pot of coffee.

Silly, she told herself, bending to scratch Fida's stomach.

Phooey, she told herself and rubbed one hand up and down her arm as if cold instead of frustrated.

Hmmm. Nine o'clock—whether she'd accomplished anything or not. Small children were playing in the street. Children from any century: chasing a ball, chasing each other, a dog joining in the fun. A street in Hertfordshire, in the eighteen hundreds. What would Jane Austen be doing? What a conundrum! Jane Austen could be writing about people like Zoe, but she would be sending her off to an institution, sensibilities be damned. Prejudice to the forefront—no dwarves allowed. She would condemn Zoe to servitude—scrubbing the stone floors of back halls as anyone who was different was treated back then.

Or no—she would make her a star in a freak show. One of Princess Lena's Living Dolls, on stage along with the likes of Alice Bounds, the Bear Lady; or Hairy Mary from Borneo.

Compared to those poor souls, Zoe knew herself to be a fortunate woman—born in the United States. Born in the twentieth century. She knew herself to be amiable and friendly. She was . . . hmmm . . . not against having money but not obsessed with it. She wasn't after a man, having learned to live alone and like it. She was a human being with the full rights of any other human being and from that moment she decided to hold on to her prejudice against Jane Austen and not write another word that day.

Until she heard from Jenny, or could go over to ask the chief about old records—she would garden. It would be a much better place to spend the next few hours, until Jenny got home and they could talk over what to do next.

She left Austen's women to fend for themselves and went to change into work clothes: old shoes, old socks, pants with holes at the knees, a yellow flannel shirt washed out to a sort of beige, and a big hat. When she got outside, Fida shivering at her feet, there was no sun to bother her, only gray clouds and the spring wind back to blowing seeds everywhere and flapping her hat around her head.

How good to be on her knees in the dirt, completely engrossed with cleaning last year's clutter from around Liliana's new house, then straightening the tower where Rapunzel lived. How good to see the world through a swirl of last-year's leaves.

How good . . .

A black car was parked at the curb just down the street. She sat back on her heels and stared that way. Not an ordinary black car but a large black car. A shiny car. New. Tinted windows. She couldn't see if there was anyone inside.

The phone in her pocket rang, distracting her. It was the chief, calling to tell her that the Reverends Senise was in his office. They had news to share with everyone and could she get right over.

"I called Tony," Ed said. "He says he's limping but on his way."

"And Jenny? Did you call her?"

Ed cleared his throat. "Didn't have to. She was with Tony."

She said nothing, letting him deal with his embarrassment himself.

On the way back to the house she reminded herself not to grumble at the twin reverends just because she was in a foul mood. When she grumbled, her head hung down, her back went up, and she walked like a very small robot, which wasn't a look she favored. She would be endlessly sweet . . . The word grated, like a piece of loose sandpaper, in her head. 'Sweet' wasn't a word she could tolerate—like "cloying" or "syrupy." So she would be herself.

Somewhere between her grubbies and a poppy print dress and bright red lipstick she began to feel better. All in all, she didn't have a bad job. As she dug a red shoulder bag from her closet she reminded herself she was a lucky woman. If she wanted to, she could turn her thoughts from the dark and bloody recesses of the human mind to women busily clawing each other to land a rich husband.

She checked her face and fluffed her curls. She could be anybody she wanted to be, at any time, she reassured her reflection. That was the benefit of a lively imagination, as she'd always told herself.

And then, coming down from the lofty place she'd let herself soar, she confronted the terrible proposition of Jenny leaving town.

If she was a decent human being—as she often told herself she was—she would be happy for her good friend. If she was a miserable, selfish person she would be truly, truly happy at the thought that Jenny had given in and chosen Tony; that she'd spent the night in Tony's bed—making promises to him that would cost her everything.

If she wasn't a decent human being she would be truly, selfishly, happy at the thought that Jenny couldn't leave town.

Outside, pulling down the drive, she saw the black car was still parked where it had been earlier. On a whim, Zoe hit the brake and pulled in behind it. She opened the door and slid from the front seat to the street.

Hands on her hips, she stood looking at the car then walked up in back of it, peeked inside, trying to make out a person through the dark windows.

He sat behind the wheel, she was sure of it. Elevated, he stared out the front, maybe not knowing she was looking in with her hands cupped at the glass, or just ignoring her.

At first she swore to herself, and then she laughed. Next she pounded on the window beside where he sat, and waited for something to happen.

Very slowly, the window slid down.

Fitz turned to her and smiled, as if she were a great surprise to him.

"Well, well, well. If it isn't Miss Zola. What on earth are you doing out here, on this odd street, this early?"

"I've been sent to clear the area of riff-raff," she said, angry at being challenged but half-wanting to laugh at the pompous ass behind the wheel.

"Ah. Me, too." He fully turned to her and smiled his crooked smile. "I've been parked here for a while now . . ."

"I've been watching you."

"You have not. You've been gardening and taking care of fairies all set in the very worst places."

"You don't know a thing about fairies."

"Really?" His thick brows shot up. "I don't know a thing about Oberon, Titania, Robin Goodfellow, Peaseblossom, Cobweb, Moth, or Mustardseed?"

"That's only Shakespeare, not real fairies. You are a fake, Fitzwilliam Dillon."

She thumped the door panel as hard as she could, and went back to her car, smiling broadly as she walked, or skipped, away.

Chapter 29

Everett Senise rose to his feet as Zoe walked into the station. He put out his large hand to take Zoe's, then turned to the man beside him, to introduce his brother Robert, the pastor at Bear Falls Evangelical Church, as if he were a visiting dignitary.

The men were dressed in gray tweed sport coats with black turtle neck sweaters beneath. Mirror images of each other: tall, thin, balding, with serious, lined faces.

"Well, aren't you two a pair," she said. "Don't think I've ever seen anything like it."

The men smiled and looked each other up and down, as if noticing for the first time that they'd dressed alike.

"If you came to church more, Miss Zoe, you wouldn't be surprised," Everett teased.

"Ah, but which church, Reverend? How do I choose between you?"

They all laughed, even the chief, who tilted his head to one side, not quite getting what the banter was about but enjoying that short moment of lightness.

With the entrance of Tony, one crutch shoved under his right arm, and Jenny beside him, everyone grew serious.

Jenny smiled at Zoe, who frowned back at her, making Jenny blush, then stick her chin in the air, ignoring Zoe.

There was an electric feeling around the reverends, as they spread a Michigan map out on the table in front of them.

Robert stuck his finger at a place on the map.

"Right here, about fifteen miles north of Alpena."

They gathered around. "No town name, but not too far out of

Posen. Way back in the woods. You see . . ." He pointed to a dark circle drawn inland from Lake Huron.

Everett stood beside Robert, peering over his shoulder.

"We've been told this is what's left of the group the Otises are in." Everett turned to them. "Like most of these sects, they're dying out."

"Not many of them left," Robert echoed, not sure whether to be pleased or sad.

Zoe looked way up, at Ed Warner. "We'd better get out there."

"I've called Harry Fields. He's the chief of police in Alpena. He says he can go and check out the group. See if there's a girl that looks like Camille with them."

Zoe frowned. "He wouldn't have a clue what to ask. He doesn't know Pamela, or those awful Otises. They'll lie and then take the girl where we can't find her."

The chief spread his hands. "What are you thinking?

"I'm thinking I should go. I know Cammy. I know the history of those people. I won't leave there without the truth."

"Not alone," Jenny protested. "I'll go with you."

"Right." Ed said. "But you're not going, Tony."

"Wouldn't be much good. Can you get someone from Alpena to meet them?"

"Come on," Zoe protested. "Just a few old zealots. I think we can handle them."

Everett picked up the map and folded it, handing it to Zoe.

"I'll have a deputy meet you in Posen," The chief said. "What would you say—two hours?"

Zoe looked at Jenny. "Should be about right."

"What's the group call themselves now?" Jenny asked Everett Senise.

Robert answered. "The Children of the New World. Though I hear there's not a child among them and nothing childlike about the group. I spoke to Reverend Adams at Alpena First Baptist. He said that as far as he's heard they are nothing but a small band of angry old people."

"Perfect for the Otises," Zoe said.

"I asked about the Otises, but he wasn't any help there. Some kind of settlement, he said. Thought they might have a cow or two, and some chickens. Oh, and a little chapel, but not much else. The man who led this particular sect died last year. Reverend Adams didn't know for certain how many members were left, but he thought not many."

Zoe felt good about the trip across the state. She'd have a long time to think up nasty things to say to Pamela's parents. And, if Cammy were there, she'd see that the deputy took those two old creatures to the nearest jail and booked them for kidnapping.

Before leaving, Zoe asked Ed about Cammy's phone. "They get into it yet?"

He nodded. "Three numbers Pamela didn't recognize. The rest were to Kent and one to the movie theatre, like she was planning on going Friday night."

"Let me know about those three numbers, will you? What about the computer?"

"Soon," he said.

"Got something from that white dress," he added.

The women waited at the door.

"A fingerprint on one of the pearl buttons."

"Get a match?" Zoe asked.

"Nothing. Checked with the F.B.I. No match."

"When is somebody going to say yes to something I ask?" Zoe groused as she let the door swing shut behind them.

*　*　*

Before they got out to the highway, with Jenny driving, Zoe's phone rang. When she answered a worried woman's voice spoke immediately.

"Zoe Zola, this is Pearl Miller, Kent Miller's mother. Can you come over tonight, Miss Zola? Kent's got something he wants to tell you. I think you need to hear what he's got to say. He's ashamed, really ashamed. He says he didn't tell you the whole truth about Cammy. He won't tell me either . . ."

"Maybe I should send Ed Warner, I'm on my way out of town right now."

"That wouldn't be a good idea. He's upset, Miss Zola. He's very upset. You know, things aren't easy for Kent. Not ever. He likes you." She drew a deep breath. "Will you be back by this evening?"

"I intend to be."

"If you can make it after seven. Is that okay? He's got his chess club and . . . Kent doesn't take well to upsets in his schedule. And, Miss Zola, I have to tell you he's not doing well with Cammy gone. Not well at all."

Zoe thought to tell her Cammy might be home by seven that evening. She didn't. If they brought her back with them—it would be wonderful news for Kent. If she didn't—he wouldn't have known to hope.

One more phone call—to Pamela, who, when she answered, said she was just about to call her.

"I got ahold of Gerald Hoskins," she said, her voice unsteady.

"Who's he?" Zoe asked, trying to recall if she'd heard that name before.

"He used to manage The Falls movie theatre."

"Oh, the movie house."

"Camille's father."

A long, painful silence.

"He's not a bad man." Pamela hesitated. "It was just . . . he was very sad to hear about our daughter." A long breath was dragged in. "But he hasn't seen her. Actually, he's never seen her. I wish Cammy knew his other children. She has a half sister and two half brothers. I always wished that for her. It could have been important, knowing she had family." She hesitated. "I just got to thinking—maybe she went looking for him. She didn't."

"Pamela. We can't get around those clothes . . ."

"Well, there's that. I thought maybe she took other clothes to change into and . . ."

"Out in the woods? If she was heading away from town she wouldn't have gone deep into the woods first."

"Just—I was thinking maybe. Cammy thinks differently than other people."

"Pamela," Zoe stopped her again. "The Reverends Senise found that group your parents belong to. Out near Posen. Me and Jenny are on our way there now."

Silence. And then a deep, anguished sound.

"Pamela. Are you okay?"

The phone was dead.

It was good to be leaving town. Plenty of sunshine as the morning warmed, and very little traffic, except through Gaylord, where there was always traffic.

They settled into the ride, not saying much, pointing out a mother deer and her twins at the side of the road, and then farther along—a field of windmills. Farms and woods and rolling hills and long curves in the road.

During the second hour of the trip, Jenny, driving, said in a near whisper, "Do you think we'll find her alive?"

"Only thing that makes sense—that they'd rear their ugly heads now, just as Cammy's becoming a woman. They must have her."

"And Janice?"

Jenny looked over at her.

Zoe grumbled. "Yeah, there's that."

They drove another thirty miles before Zoe said something she'd been wanting to say. "How are you and Tony doing?"

Jenny shrugged off the question.

"You two okay?"

"Really, my business, Zoe."

"Yeah. Guess there's nothing like a bunch of hormones on fire to quash a life-changing resolution."

"As I said. My business."

Zoe said nothing for another ten miles.

"Just be sure you know what you're doing. I don't want you leaving town any more than he does but I don't want you unhappy either."

"Zoe. I've got enough going on in my head right now. I don't need anybody adding to it."

Jenny looked straight ahead, the road taking a long curve to the left. Another small village. A car repair shop that looked as though it had been there since the days of Henry Ford. A gas station. Back to deep woods.

Zoe'd been quiet for as long as she could stand it. "Did you get a job?"

Jenny shook her head. "Maybe I'm not employable anymore. Maybe I waited too long."

"Baloney. You'll hear."

"I sent out more resumes."

"You'll hear."

"But now Tony and I are . . . okay again."

"Does he know? That you might be leaving?"

She shook her head.

"Maybe you should have said something."

"I told him I've been really mixed up. He understands that much. We're going to talk—as soon as he's not out with a search party and I'm not running to confront some awful people, and a sixteen-year-old girl isn't missing . . ."

Her voice broke.

Zoe looked out the window and kept her mouth shut for the next fifty miles.

Chapter 30

Jenny'd been to the village of Posen once, when she was a little girl. Her dad was alive then. They'd gone to the September Potato Festival. Gone as a family: Jenny, her older sister Lisa, her mom, and her dad. That was when things were normal in their house. When their father's voice was a part of their lives and he hadn't yet been struck by a car, killed by a drunk.

She thought she recognized the town but told herself it looked like every other little town she'd ever been through—a park on one side of the road, a row of stores. To be five meant a lot of her memories were really the memories of others, people who'd told her about their trip to Posen. Or they were made-up memories, the kind a child wants to think happened.

She recalled a campsite. Maybe a sunken lake. And a place where they walked between walls of rock. Or maybe not. The Posen sign looked familiar. The police car, parked along the road at the center of town, was welcomed.

When she stopped in front of the patrol car, a tall uniformed, stiff looking man—from his very straight cap, to his large sunglasses, to his polished boots—got out and walked toward them. No smile.

"Officer Purdy," he said, leaning in Jenny's window, his cap under his arm now, sunglasses stuck in his breast pocket.

"Ma'am." He bent slightly at the waist and took Jenny's outstretched hand, then bent farther down to look in the window. He nodded to Zoe. He sighed, coming to terms with his assignment, as they got out of the car.

"We're going out to The Children of the New World settlement." He turned almost black eyes on them. "I understand there is no reason to believe the two of you are going to make trouble. Is that a fact?"

Zoe, chilled by the rigid man, nodded as Jenny said, "No, no trouble. We're looking for a girl who's been missing, is all."

He nodded his head again and again. "And if you find her? What then?"

Zoe made her hands into fists at her sides.

"We're going to take her out with us," Jenny said.

"In that case, I'll need direction, whether to make an arrest or not. I understand you think these people might be holding this girl against her will."

Jenny nodded.

He cleared his throat. "If she's there, we will be staying until I call for backup."

Zoe, patience gone, got out of the car and walked around to where the man stood, towering over her. She got really close, looking up over a row of silver buttons, straight into the man's flushed face. "A sixteen-year-old girl has been missing for five days now. If she's in there, it will be with her grandparents, who have taken her illegally. What you do about them is up to you. We have one job: find Camille Otis and get her out of there."

He ran a hand over his shining bald head before settling his hat back in place. "Yes, ma'am. Just getting things straight before we go in. I don't have warrants. I was told I was just to escort you in to talk to people who belong to that religious group."

Zoe puffed out her cheeks. "These people don't have custody. We represent her mother—who does have custody, by the way. What you decide to do with the old people is up to you but I can promise you, the girl's mother will press charges."

He nodded. "In that case, you find the girl, I'll get back-up immediately."

"I'm happy that's all straight."

"Follow me," he said, hurrying back to his car."

Down one side road and then a turn at another. All dirt roads cutting through thick stands of oak and maple. They followed for six miles, eating Officer Purdy's dust all the way. At a place where the road ended and a barbed wire fence began, they parked the cars behind each other and walked with Officer Purdy, who kept one hand on the butt of his pistol as he held back tree limbs for the women to pass beneath.

A sign standing above an opening in the wire fence read: THE CHILDREN OF THE NEW WORLD. Around the sign were others—nailed to fence posts every few feet: KEEP OUT.

Ahead of them stood an unpainted, long building—the kind Zoe imagined on ranches out west. Maybe a bunkhouse. There were no chairs on the porch. But then it was only May, not warm enough, yet, for sitting in the sun and rocking.

Zoe saw no evidence of people until they walked toward the house. From a dilapidated barn with no doors, an old man hurried out of the darkness.

"Hey!" He yelled. "Hey there. Whatcha want? Nobody's welcome here. Go on! Get going . . ." He flapped his arms until he noticed Deputy Purdy. His old eyes widened. He turned and ran back into the barn, leaving the three people standing, surprised, in the road.

"Well," Zoe said, looking at the other two. "Guess they don't exactly want converts."

Deputy Purdy took the lead, marching down the center of the dusty street toward the longest of the houses.

Purdy's boots made heavy thumping sounds as he climbed the steps to the house. He knocked hard at the door, making the walls shiver. He kept knocking then shook the doorknob.

The door opened. The elderly woman, standing there, could have come straight from an old Western. She was dressed in a long, wrinkled gray skirt and a dirty white blouse. Her face was tight and angry. Her gray hair was a tangle of fuzzy braids pinned at the top of her head. Her skin was weathered into a sheet of wrinkles hiding sunken and colorless eyes.

"What do you want?" she demanded.

Purdy pulled his hat from his head and leaned toward her. "Ma'am. I'm Officer Purdy with the Alpena Police Department. Is there anyone in charge here I could talk to?"

She sniffed. "What do you mean 'in charge'? We're all free, white Americans in here. Nobody 'in charge' as you say." She held on to the doorknob.

"We're looking for a Mr. and Mrs. Otis. Are they with your group?"

"What do you want to see them for? We don't get visitors out here. Doubt anybody wants to see you, especially."

Zoe, tired of the parrying between the deputy and the woman, pushed around him to stand with her hands on her hips and her eyes about to shoot flames. She looked the woman up and down before opening her mouth.

"Might I suggest," she began. "That you produce the Otises before this whole place is crawling with cops."

"What the devil are you?" the woman stepped back to look down at Zoe, giving her a smirking half smile. "You get going, ya little shrimp, or I'm getting my broom and sweeping you right off this porch."

"Really!" Zoe stood as tall as she could and took a step into the woman, backing her through the doorway. "You don't produce the Otises and we're going to take every bit of this place apart until we find them."

Jenny widened her eyes then pushed right up behind Zoe.

The woman, tiny eyes bugging from her head, turned and called into the room behind her. "Jeddah. There's a little creature here screaming to talk to you. You better come before I step on'er."

Jenny didn't expect Zoe's head butt into the woman's stomach, nor the amount of stale air that came whooshing out as the woman fell back from the door, then came at Zoe, causing Officer Purdy to get between the two of them as noises erupted from inside the building.

There was talking and scrambling, then arguing at the tops of voices. There was yelling back at the woman in the doorway, and then at each other, inside the building. There was scuffling, the sound of chairs being moved, and then a kind of scraping sound.

"For goodness sakes, Jeddah," somebody yelled. "You damned near ran over my foot."

Someone else yelled; another voice called for everybody to quiet down.

The door jerked open all the way and a disheveled old man in a wheelchair pushed the old woman aside and rolled out on to the porch, almost directly into Zoe.

"What in hell the three of you want with me?" the scruffy man in no-colored pants, a yellowed undershirt, and black suspenders, demanded. "I've got nothing to do with you." He looked up at the officer, around at Jenny, and down at Zoe.

Now that she was face to face with the devil, himself, Jenny took a step back.

"Are you Mr. Otis?" Officer Purdy demanded.

"That's my name. What you want with me?"

"Is your wife here?" Zoe asked.

"Wife's dead. None of your business. Not one damned piece of your business." He started to roll back into the house, pushing at the door behind him. "Buried her all legal. Nothing to do with you."

"Sir." Officer Purdy put a hand on a back handle of the wheelchair, gripping hard. "We're here about your granddaughter, Camille Otis."

"Who? I ain't got no granddaughter." His rheumy eyes turned up to stare at them, one after another.

Zoe was immediately hit by the reek of body odor coming from the man, a stink so strong she coughed, then put a hand over her mouth and nose, talking through them. "Your daughter Pamela's child."

The man's chin sank to his chest. His bottom lip slackened. His eyes focused on something beyond them.

"Your daughter, Pamela," Zoe repeated.

"Bitch," the man whispered. "Devil's bitch. Whore. That's the only Pamela I know. Sinner like no other. Killed my wife, that's who done it. Killed her. Couldn't stand to know she brought a sinner into the world. Poor woman. Last year. Dead. One day alive, the next day dead, leaving me behind to fend for myself—the way women do, you know. Most of 'em. Can't trust 'em for nothing. I could . . .'"

"We're here about your granddaughter."

"Got no granddaughter," he repeated.

"Sixteen years ago your daughter, Pamela, had a baby, sir." Zoe stressed the "sir" as if the word was dirty in her mouth. "Sixteen years ago you left your only child alone in a hospital with a newborn baby."

"Sinner. Screwed everything in pants. Deserved to be alone. Me and Dee gave our lives to God because of that girl. We had to make up to Him for the piece of shit we raised. Least we could do. That's what Don Lucas told us. He was our leader. Gone now, too. "*Least we could do*" is what he told us and said to follow him to Paradise—our only way. Now my wife's up there in Paradise without me. And you're here asking about the sinner that sent us on this long hard road we been following. What in hell would I want with that devil's spawn she brought into pollute this world? You tell me, what would I be doing with a thing like that?

"Tell you what." He eyed them one by one, wiping saliva from the corner of his mouth. "Ask God for forgiveness, you coming here disturbing a righteous man. You get down on your knees and you could still have a chance . . ."

"You were there. In Bear Falls. People saw you."

"Yeah, a year ago. Took Dee to see her old doctor. Too late. Cancer. Nothing was going to save her."

Zoe withstood the stink of the old man. She even withstood his spittle landing on her bare arm. What she couldn't stand were the words coming from the ugly mouth. She reached out and dug her nails into the man's bare wrist until the old man yelped. Officer Purdy pulled her away, tucking her behind him.

Jeddah Otis, terrified, rolled his chair back into the house yelling to the others that he'd been attacked. He slammed the door behind him.

"We're going now." Deputy Purdy, ignoring Jenny and Zoe, turned his back and walked from the porch.

"She could still be in there," Zoe yelled after him.

"She's not here, Zoe," Jenny pulled her arm. "You saw that old man. His wife isn't alive. He's in a wheelchair. Nobody from this place took Cammy."

Zoe's mouth fell open, then slowly closed.

She followed Jenny from the porch.

Chapter 31

No girl in the car with them. Nothing to talk about. Every mile stretched twice as long as it should stretch.

Jenny drove toward home.

Zoe felt something much like misery creeping around in her head. She watched the side of the road, thinking how they were getting nowhere. The girl was dead. It was over time for her to be dumped beside a road. Maybe there was another girl picked out already, doomed to the same death.

Why?

Dark ages, she was thinking as she bit at a broken fingernail. That's the time they lived in. Still the dark ages as far as a killer's brain went.

"Someday," she burst out, startling Jenny.

"Someday what?" Jenny asked.

"Nothing. I was just thinking about Janice's killer. They're connected, all right. Janice and Cammy. I just don't know how. I'll get him. Someday I'll get him."

A few miles down the road they were still silent until Jenny's stomach rumbled. "I'm hungry. You want to stop and get something to eat?"

"Let's wait until we get back. We've got to talk to Pamela. And, oh my God, I forgot Kent Miller. I'm supposed to be there by seven."

"It's only three thirty. You've got plenty of time. And time to stop and eat lunch. Call Ed. Call Pamela, too. Why keep her waiting? That's cruel. And my mother. I'll call her."

Zoe shook her head. "Not Pamela. That's not the kind of thing you drop in a phone call. Tell her her mother is dead."

Jenny was quiet for a minute. "The news should be a relief not a tragedy."

"A mother's a mother. There's always sadness."

Zoe hesitated then dialed Ed's number. No signal.

Zoe held her cell in her hands, looking hard at it, waiting for the bars to go up. She scrolled through old texts and checked missed phone calls.

"There's a call from your mom on here. Why'd she call me and not you?"

"Haven't checked my phone. She's probably worried. Call her when you can. She'll tell Tony what happened."

"You're not going to call him?"

"Two birds, Zoe. Two birds with one stone. Mom will do it."

Zoe gave her a funny look, shook her head, then kept her eye on the phone until she had enough bandwidth to make the call to Chief Warner. He answered on the first ring as if he'd been waiting to hear.

Zoe told him the news and got a couple of grunts in return.

"Miz Otis is here now," Ed said. "You want to tell her yourself?"

"No. Just tell her Cammy isn't there. And Tony. Would you tell him?"

"Anything else?"

"Is there even a chance of a fingerprint match on that button?"

"Get the Root girl's murderer and we'll have a match."

Zoe hung up and dialed Dora. She told her Cammy wasn't there. She told her Pamela's mother was dead. She told her she didn't know when they would be back and asked her to let Fida out which Dora said she'd be happy to do with more enthusiasm than the small request deserved.

Phone calls out of the way, they drove without talking, Jenny eventually mentioning she was still hungry only to get a frown from Zoe.

In Indian River they stopped at McDonalds and got diet Cokes.

They used the ladies room and were on their way in ten minutes, going toward Petoskey, then through Charlevoix, and down to Bear Falls.

The ride seemed eternal to Zoe—longer going back than getting there. Too much time to think about things. None of it good.

"You know what I'm thinking?" Zoe asked after a while.

"Not a clue."

"The next time I get involved in a murder, would you please remind me to keep my nose to myself?"

"As if reminding you would do any good."

"I mean it, Jen. I'm supposed to be writing a deep and serious book and here I am running all over the state. Another dead end."

"Your career will be there. Cammy Otis is more important, right? You've been saying that. And, what I think is you're not getting any-where so you want to give up."

Zoe looked at Jenny's wide eyes. She opened her mouth then snapped it shut. She opened it again. "You're right. This brain better get working. I can't stand the idea of that kid out there—somewhere—for much longer. I can't take it. Never felt so useless."

Humility from Zoe Zola wasn't what Jenny expected. They drove for miles without another word between them.

* * *

Zoe stared ahead. A straight road, she told herself. That's all they needed—a straight road, without all the twists and turns and dead ends they'd been taking.

"Don't laugh, okay?" Zoe whispered, after a while, turning to face Jenny. "I swear to you, I know she's alive. It's not my nose smelling it out. And it's not the wind. She's there. I can almost hear her."

She nodded hard for emphasis, believing in the strength of her feelings.

Jenny's smile was almost loving. "I'm with you, Zoe. No matter how screwed up you seem, I still trust you."

Zoe watched the trees go by. She knew what she knew and would never doubt that she knew what she knew—not again. Not even if what she knew wasn't completely sane.

Chapter 32

Dora didn't dare look up at the kitchen clock for fear of telegraphing to her guests—again people from the mansion—that it was passed time for them to leave and, that over staying their welcome—as her mother taught her, was a sin against hospitality.

She sighed and pretended to listen to what they were talking and laughing about as she thought an afternoon call should not take up the *entire* afternoon. First there was Mary Smith, a plain name for this colorful—but not as young as she'd like people to think—peacock that Charles Bingman brought to the house with him. He introduced her as an old friend from Chicago. He said Mary had offered to help Fitz in any way she could.

"What a hell of a gift you're getting, eh?" Mary winked at Dora, who felt her skin bristle. If only Zoe'd been there. She'd put a quick end to this terrible woman—at least remove her from Dora's house.

They'd come to talk about the meeting, Charles had said. Then went on to ask how things would be handled: ideas and such, and if she thought they could come up with a worthy project.

"I'm happy Fitzwilliam's decided to stay." Dora tried to smile but couldn't.

"I never heard he was leaving," Charles said, raising his eyebrows at Dora.

Dora gave a slight laugh. Not the first time that day she'd been confused.

They'd been sitting around her table for more than an hour, already. Over an hour of witty remarks and jokes Mary laughed out loud over. Then curse word after curse word coming out of Mary's prettily red-painted mouth.

When Tony dropped by, awkward on his single crutch, she'd been relieved at first and then perturbed as the painted Mary teased him about being a carpenter, then mussed his hair and touched his cheek.

Tony pulled away from the hand on his cheek, but smiled. Charles didn't pay attention. The trollopy Mary was getting under Dora's skin.

Tony was being polite, Dora decided. Tony'd never been a man to flirt. That was one thing she admired about him. His steadfastness. Or maybe how much of life he missed, always something lodged in his head to think about.

She was sure that was something Jenny liked best about him. That is—if her flighty daughter liked anything about Tony any more. She hoped against hope that whatever was bothering Jenny would just go away. She wasn't being nice to anyone. Dora thought of her older daughter, Lisa, who might be there in a few weeks, with relief. Dora couldn't help herself. Her uncomplicated, sweet Lisa, home for a while would be a pleasure.

She stole a glance at the clock. Four. If her guests took the glance as being inhospitable—so be it. Jenny and Zoe were coming back empty-handed, and with more terrible news for Pamela.

If her guests got upset with her, or thought maybe she wished they'd leave—well—they'd be right.

Dora put the coffeepot back on the stove and sat down, exhausted. Talking for over an hour wore her out—even if she wasn't the one doing most of the talking. She'd had enough of people for one day, especially Mary. *Crazier than a bedbug*, Jim would have said, but at least the smell of her perfume had begun to wear off and Dora's eyes had stopped watering.

"You should have been there, Dora." Mary tossed her long, dark, and very curly hair back over her shoulder, then smiled with her red, red mouth. "I've never seen Delia so knocked back on her ass."

"Mary," Charles tried to hush her. "Delia is Fitz's friend."

"Why?" she said. "I will never understand. Nathan—well, he was Fitz's father's buddy. But Delia? For heaven's sakes! Have you ever seen such a nutcase?"

"Now, Mary . . . maybe it's time for us to go and leave this poor woman in peace."

A smile spread over Dora's face.

"Don't go on my account." Tony looked up, obviously not listening to much that had been going on. He leaned on his crutch and looked away from all of them.

"Delia's been around, like Nathan, since Fitz was a kid," Charles said.

"As I was saying." Mary turned back to Dora. "Delia asked Minnie Moon and her daughter, Dianna, over for dinner last night. I thought Fitz would blow an artery. Have you seen that Dianna? Slutty is as slutty dresses."

Charles shook his head at her. "Now you've done it. Dora's a friend of the Moons. Maybe you should watch what you say in this house, Mary."

Mary turned startled eyes to Dora. "Really? You're friends with those women? My, what a time you must have. But really, they are so funny. Minnie and that girl—in a skirt that didn't cover her ass, they came in like high society: Minnie mooing over how happy they were to be asked; Dianna scowling and asking if the gardener was around. My guess is that's who she's after."

"A very nice young man—the gardener. Though there's hardly any garden to see to." Dora snapped her lips shut. "Mostly, I think, he cleans the pool."

"Anyway, I can see Minnie's after bigger fish than a gardener." Mary took a deep breath. "Dianna kept asking me if I didn't think the gardener was quite a specimen. She had the nerve to warn me away from him, though she smiled when she said it—as if I'm not on to that particular tactic. So, what I did was tell her I hadn't had time to examine him yet but that I would put it on my to-do list. Which changed the look on *that* girl's face."

There was more laughter. Even Dora found herself amused.

"So, you know him, Dora? The gardener?" Mary leaned in, her drawn-on eyebrows rising to her hairline; remnants of that perfume tickling Dora's nose.

"Nice boy. His name is Jefferson Firestone. A fine family. It's Jeff's gap year, I believe. Between high school and college. He'll be going to Yale next fall."

Mary sat back in disbelief. "Well, that's a surprise. You mean Dianna's into brains instead of money?"

She laughed, turned to poke Tony, and laugh again.

Charles' interest was piqued. "Boys from Bear Falls go to Yale? That's amazing news. I wouldn't have imagined such a thing."

Dora nodded. "And girls, too. And to Harvard. Mostly the University of Michigan and Michigan State, though. Well, at least as many as can snag scholarships."

"Hmmm . . ." Charles thought hard. "That's good to know."

Mary grabbed her hair with one hand and held it up off her neck while smiling at Tony. "And you, Tony Ralenti. Does Fitz know you're a carpenter? He needs a carpenter at Rosings. Some things he wants changed. I'll have to pass the word about you."

"I don't have the time to take on more work, Mary." He gave her a regretful smile. "Not right now. Got a new business going."

Mary smiled a brilliant smile but had no interest in his start-up business. "Of course. I understand—this far north. So little summer for building. Fitz will understand."

Conversation finally dwindled to a few half-whispered comments between Mary and Charles. Dora no longer made any attempt to be hospitable; couldn't force herself to be polite. She was tired of talking and wanted to think.

Her company, including Tony, finally got up, stretching, preparing to leave, as the phone rang.

With the phone at her ear, and saying "Just a minute, dear" to Jenny, she waved a last goodbye to her guests.

"Charles Bingman brought over a terrible woman from Fitz's house," she said quickly into the phone. "Stayed forever . . . And Tony was here, which surprised me. He left. I think he wanted to talk to me about something . . . What? Oh yes, I'll call Jay Root. I'm going out there tomorrow, if it's okay.

"Oh . . . That's all right. I won't cook if you two won't be here. Anyway, I have a meeting. I hope Pamela's going to be all right. Another disappointment. Tell her we're all praying. And about her mother—I don't know what to say about that woman."

CAMILLE

She politely declined to wear a mask. It didn't cover her face anyway. It dug into her cheeks so she kept pushing it up, then pulling it down, then she took it off and handed it back to them, all the while keeping her eyes closed as she was told.

They got up and left as the terrible woman—it certainly was a woman—leaving a snaking path of perfume and the sound of moving silk behind her, said, "We won't do it today. We still have time."

They didn't take the teddy bear, but maybe they should have because when she hugged the bear his right eyeball fell out and she couldn't make it stay back in so he was a one-eyed bear. She loved him even more than before because in a way he was just the way she was. Not that she had one eye but sometimes she felt like there was something missing—especially when people looked at her funny like when she told them her ideas for building a big house in the woods and living there with the raccoons and skunks—which weren't as bad as people said when you didn't scare them, and with the bear, who once came around her sniffing, but went away without hurting her.

It seemed to her—she was thinking as she took the bowl of hard candies back to the bed with her, to eat them because they only brought her meatloaf again—that animals weren't as bad as most people said. The raccoons and skunks and bears were strangers to them and people were afraid of strangers, which made her think about the two people who kept her in this cold place and talked about her as if she wasn't there, and seemed to not like her because they didn't know her, and didn't know her real name.

She lay down, pulling the dirty dress over her two feet to keep them warm, and thought a big thought she'd been thinking for a while

195

now—*maybe for hours or maybe days—but that part didn't matter. It was still a very big thought.*

She thought that being an archeologist wasn't what she was meant for after all and that being a writer was a better thing. Like that little lady in town everybody said was famous, or would be soon if she kept writing books people wanted to buy. Once she went to the little lady's door when she was out selling candy to make money for the future nurses club at school even though she had no intention of being a nurse ever in her life. The lady—whose name was Zoe Zola, which was a very strange name when she stopped to think about it, which made her wonder if she would have to change her name to something like Camilla Camerado in order to get people to buy her books—bought a bunch of Snickers Bars and was very nice, giving her more than what the candy cost when she heard it was for future nurses.

This was the hour when she was going to begin to write her new book. It wasn't going to be a mystery book and she wasn't going to kill anybody or even lock anybody in a cellar. She thought and thought. The opening line had to grab people by the throat—that's what Mrs. Van Der Mollen, her English teacher said: "Grab them by the throat and don't let go until the last line of the story."

She thought and thought. She pulled the poor one-eyed teddy bear to her chest and rested her chin on his soft head.

She thought some more but what kept running through her head— and it kept her from coming up with a great line that would grab people by the throat—was what they'd said: "We won't do it today. We still have time."

Part 5

"Seldom, very seldom, does complete truth belong to any human disclosure; seldom can it happen that something is not a little disguised, or a little mistaken."

—Jane Austen, *Emma*

Chapter 33

The chief got up slowly when Zoe and Jenny came in. Deputy Flores stood at the high front desk, his hand on the shackled arm of a kid who looked at nobody, standing with his head down.

The deputy nodded to them, then turned back to the business at hand.

Ed already knew they hadn't found Camille but he seemed to still hope for something.

"You check the place out?" he asked, waving them to chairs, back in his office.

"Man's in a wheelchair. Pamela's mother is dead."

They all got quiet. Their hopes had been so high.

"Checked every registered sex offender in the area." He reported after a while. "Looks as though it's not going to be that easy."

Ed looked tired; his thin face was an off-gray color "Thought we had something this afternoon. I almost called you two."

"No service. Wouldn't have got us anyway. Not most of the way," Jenny said.

Zoe's eyebrows went up. "What was it?"

"On the kid's computer. The forensics guy got her emails. Messages to and from a guy in Alaska. Chief Sweitzer in Traverse thought for sure we had a predator."

"What kind of messages?" Jenny leaned forward, almost slipping off her chair, too tired to bend her body.

"You know, the kind of thing a pedophile starts with, pretending to be a kid himself. This guy was asking Camille all kinds of questions. Some about where she lived, where she went to school. Camille gave him her street address and described their house. Way too much.

Kids should be taught better. Don't think Pamela could have known about it."

"Did you follow up on the man?" Jenny asked.

Zoe sat at attention.

"Easy enough. It was the guy's real name. Abe Crosby. I called Fairbanks, got the chief there and he went out himself to talk to him."

"Did the chief know anything about him? Could the guy be involved?" Zoe wanted to know.

Ed sighed. He shook his head. "Just heard back. Only a kid. He's a kid in a wheelchair. Most of the time he's homebound. Charlie had to tell him why he came out there—that Camille was missing. Just about broke the guy's heart from what that chief told me. Sad. Really sad."

Ed looked from Zoe to Jenny. "Nothing new on Janice." He shook his head and fell into deep thought. When he looked up, it was with serious concern in his eyes. "I'm worried about Sally. Heard she's being really hard on Jay. Keeps bringing up an accident the kid had when she was a baby. Guess Jay was at fault. Maybe something happened again. You know—another accident. Maybe Jay hurt Janice worse this time."

"Why would she hide an accident?"

"Who knows? Just like they didn't report her missing until she was found dead. Odd. I was just wondering, is all." He pushed papers around on his desk, thinking.

"Sally's suffering." Jenny wasn't buying what Ed was saying. "My mom's going there to keep her company tomorrow. Mom's got a way with sad people."

Zoe put a hand on Jenny's arm and narrowed her eyes. "I've been thinking, too. Why does she hate Jay so much? If all that happened so long ago, why now, when they're sharing the loss?"

"Delayed anger," Jenny offered.

"Or maybe she knows more than she's telling us."

Zoe thought hard. "They had Janice pretty late in life. What if Janice wasn't the first child Jay hurt?'

"What's that mean?" Jenny asked.

"What I said. What if that wasn't the first time Jay hurt one of their children? How long have they lived here?"

Ed shrugged.

"How many years ago did they buy the orchard?"

"Maybe fifteen."

"Could you find out where they came from?"

Ed nodded. "I already checked back cases here. Nothing on Jay Root. I could get a copy of the bill of sale for the orchard. That would have their original address. I'll find out where they came from and start checking any past record he might have, wherever that was."

"We can check back newspapers where they lived." Zoe said. "If it became a police matter—that a child of theirs was found dead, or hurt, anything like that—we'd have a better idea who Jay Root is, and maybe what's really going on."

"Fifteen years." Ed Warner was thinking hard, too. "Janice was two when they moved here."

"Did you find anything more on Harold Roach?" Zoe asked him.

"Nothing I didn't know already."

"Tony told us. An old rape charge that didn't go anywhere . . ."

He nodded. "Guess word out was the father wanted to marry the girl off to just about anybody. Even the girl wouldn't testify against him though I heard she got a good beating."

Jenny had been listening, but thinking about something else.

"What's the connection between the girls? Driving me crazy."

"Cammy and Janice?" Ed Warner leaned back. He put his hands behind his head. "One big horrible coincidence."

He sat up to make notes on the yellow pad in front of him.

Zoe closed her eyes.

Jenny stared at a pulsing ceiling light above Ed's head.

Finally, Ed cleared his throat. "Guess we could use a good dose of that extra perception of yours, Miz Zola. How's it working?"

Zoe hoped he wasn't being rude. The whole crappy day had drained her of sarcasm. She couldn't even work up a biting remark.

"Feeling anything about Camille Otis?" He didn't let it drop and didn't seem to be making fun of her.

Zoe stared at him a long time. "I was just thinking. Janice was found on Saturday, the day after Cammy was taken. Could there be a connection that way? Like one girl was a replacement for the other?"

"Maybe," he said. "But *why*? Give me one connection between them."

He blew his lips out and settled down into himself. "Maybe we should go back to looking at the girls separately. Nobody's seen Cammy since last Friday. Nobody knows where she went. We find her clothes out in the woods, her cell smashed. Tell the truth—I just can't convince myself that she's still . . ."

"Don't say it." Jenny sat forward, a fist resting on his desk.

"Okay."

After a while Jenny asked when Pamela left.

"While ago. Think she's waiting for you at your mom's."

"Mom was going out. Probably about the meeting Friday. Flyers are all over town."

He shrugged. "That's what Miz Otis told me. Bet anything she'll be there whether your mom's home or not. Woman seems a little automatic. Can't blame her."

The silence was awkward until Jenny asked Ed if he'd seen Tony that evening.

"Might be with the group that went south of here a couple of hours ago. They're searching the swamps. But maybe not, with that ankle of his. He might be back to his workshop. Told me he's behind on orders for those Little Libraries. Not good for a new business."

Jenny remembered the package on the dining room table she should have taken to the post office on Monday. Here it was Wednesday. Most were bills for orders filled. Some were specs—following up what Tony sent by email. Nothing had gone out the way it should have.

She wanted to groan. She'd let him down. An unimportant job and she couldn't even get that right.

Zoe watched Jenny and Ed. They looked the way she felt: at sea, no place to turn. There was plenty she should be doing but it was as if she watched everything she'd built her life on since coming to Bear Falls fade off into background noise; slipping away behind the face of a sixteen-year-old girl in trouble.

Zoe hunkered down in the hard chair and concentrated, closing her eyes to visualize that very special, inquisitive, happy girl.

What more did she need to know in order to find Cammy? And, if her disappearance wasn't connected to Janice's death, why did it happen at the same time? A murderer and a kidnapper in Bear Falls? She shook her head. She sat up. Maybe the curious girl had been asking questions of the wrong people. Maybe she'd seen something she wasn't supposed to see as she dropped her flyers at houses along Shore Drive or just about anywhere in town.

Chapter 34

Pamela sat on the front steps of Jenny's house, waiting. She stood, when Jenny drove up, then raised a hand to wave.

Zoe tried not to notice the woman's face. Instead, she looked closely at Dora's lilies of the valley, growing thick in the flowerbeds on either side of the walk. Sadly she knew her own garden was flowering without her. *Too bad.* She turned her passion away from flowers and fairies.

It wasn't that Pamela looked thinner, it was more that her face had hollowed out, dark places under her eyes, sunken cheeks; her bottom lip was blood red from being chewed and, as she came down the front walk to meet them, her body trembled.

"Dora's out," Pamela said. "But I needed to see you."

She blurted, "Ed told me Cammy wasn't there. I'm grateful for that. But did you see my parents?"

She stopped abruptly.

"Saw your dad," Zoe said. "He's in a wheelchair."

She shook her head, not caring about him. "Were they worried when they heard Cammy was missing?"

Zoe looked away from the needy face. How many terrible things could they heap on this poor woman? "I don't think your father's got the capacity to worry about anybody but himself."

She took one of Pamela's hands in her small one, whether the woman wanted to be touched or not. "That man's going straight to hell. I don't think I've ever hoped to see the devil take anybody the way I want him to take your father."

Pamela almost smiled. "Guess you could call that a universal truth, Zoe. And I thank you for it."

"Did you meet my mother?" Pamela's look changed, something more like wistfulness to it. "She never stood up for me. Not once. Now that I'm a mother I know what she didn't give me. How could a mother . . . ?"

She stopped. "But since you met my dad, you know what a fierce hater he is. What could she have done? No education. No money. A kind of mental slavery." She looked from Zoe to Jenny. "Is there such a thing?"

Jenny tapped Zoe on her back, reminding her what else there was to say. "Zoe's got something to tell you, Pamela," Jenny said above Zoe's head.

Zoe shook off the poking finger.

"It's about your mom," Jenny said.

The woman's eyebrows shot up, as if expecting good news— something from a world other than the one where she lived now.

"She's gone," Zoe said.

"Gone?"

"Oh, for goodness sakes, Zoe." Jenny reached out to Pamela. "She's dead, Pamela. Your mom died a couple of months ago."

Pamela looked from Jenny to Zoe as if she was hearing a sick joke, or a new misery for the pit she lived in. She stepped back, her heel hitting the bottom step. She reached out to right herself, then took a deep breath. "He didn't call me," she said, as much from a sense of wonder as outrage.

"He didn't call to tell me my mother was dead. Not even to make me suffer more." She looked over Zoe's head and beyond Jenny. "I came from her body. That means something. It does. It means something." She looked hard at them before tears filled her eyes. The tears ran down her face. She didn't brush them away. She pointed to them: "This is all I've got to give my mother," she said.

Pamela took a breath. "Some women should never have children. It takes bravery."

After a while, she looked up at the women. "Ed said you're going to see Kent Miller. Please call me if he has anything we don't already know.

"And I want to tell you . . . you've been so kind." Her hand was on her car door. "You've helped me learn about myself, a thing I never imagined I would say out loud"

Zoe frowned. Jenny braced herself.

"I would kill for Cammy. When you went out there to see my parents, I knew it right then. If you'd come back and told me he'd taken Cammy, I was ready. I chose the knife I wanted to use, because it was the sharpest I've ever owned. I knew I could stick it in him and enjoy every second of my father dying in front of me. I wanted to watch his eyes . . ." She fumbled in her shoulder bag and drew out a long, and very sharp knife then pushed it back inside, closed her purse, and settled the strap on her shoulder. "But not my mother. I couldn't have hurt her. I had a dream of taking her and Cammy away somewhere . . ."

Zoe looked down. Something in the woman was changed.

"Maybe Kent remembered . . ." Zoe started to say.

"No matter what he tells you, I want to know. I'll be up. I always am—watching out the window."

* * *

Back in the car, Jenny, angry and hungry, called Dora at her meeting. She asked if she'd happened to notice the box and pile of envelopes on the dining room table.

"I took them to the post office," Dora said, her voice lowered, the sound of someone talking behind her. "You mentioned it earlier . . . hope that was all right."

Jenny hung up, relieved that she hadn't let Tony down after all— or someone hadn't let him down. She drove off thinking about mothers. Something special, and awful, about them. She couldn't imagine losing Dora. She couldn't imagine who she'd be now if Dora never loved her.

Chapter 35

"Myrtle's." Jenny said. "I think I've got low blood sugar. I can feel my stomach shriveling around my backbone."

Zoe made a noise. "What about getting over to see Kent?"

"Plenty of time." Jenny turned up Oak Street.

"You win. Myrtle's. Meatloaf night."

Jenny groaned. "It's always meatloaf night."

"Myrtle puts green peppers in hers. They're good for you. Only five dollars and ninety-five cents. With mashed potatoes. Green beans. And pie for dessert. Not the best pie. But at that price, you can't beat it. Better get there before the price goes up. I don't like paying eight ninety-five for the same thing that tastes okay at five dollars and ninety-five cents, but loses something at eight ninety-five. Especially that blueberry pie."

"So now we're in a hurry?" Jenny scoffed. "I'm having soup. I'm not eating that green meatloaf."

"And you'll pay through the nose for that soup, especially if she has to take it out of the freezer and heat it up. Myrtle hikes the prices on everything but meatloaf. Make sure we get two bills. I'm not paying for your excesses."

The usual early-bird special people were there, with both Delaware and Demeter Hopkins running between tables, trays of specials sitting atop their shoulders.

Answering greetings from most of the filled tables around the low-ceilinged room, Zoe and Jenny waved or nodded to everyone. Tiny Vera Wattles and her son Mike, six feet tall and built like a linebacker, were there. So was the Dyer family—all six children sitting quietly, circling their shy mother and taciturn father, who frowned but didn't wave back. There were the Sheratons, Sarah and Ralph. Very few strangers came for the special. It was more like a club you got to join if you lived in Bear Falls.

Except—Zoe couldn't believe her eyes. At a corner table, sitting upright and precisely half a foot apart, were Charles Bingman with a wildly painted woman she didn't know; then Delia Thurgood; Nathan Wickley; and Fitzwilliam Dillon—a miniature, out-of-place snob in the middle of an out-of-place, over-dressed set of snobs.

"Keep your head down and walk," she hissed at Jenny who turned to look around the room, caught sight of the mansion group, and waved cheerfully.

"Idiot." Zoe mumbled as she headed for a booth around the corner where she wouldn't have to look at Fitz, or any of his friends. Jenny caught her arm and pointed. "Look who's here, Zoe."

She headed to their table, dragging Zoe beside her, stopping in front of the group, grinning.

"Well, what do you know? Mr. Dillon." She nodded to Fitz, then pulled Zoe's arm. "Say 'hello' to Fitz Dillon, Zoe."

Jenny smirked as Zoe stood as tall as she could stand, looked from face to face, then stopped at Fitz.

"Hello, Zoe—you did want me to call you Zoe, didn't you?" His small, uneven face didn't light with a smile. It was more a pained look. "It's good to see you again."

"You, too, Fitz. See you're all here for the meatloaf. They don't have a dish like that in Chicago, I'll bet."

Fitz smiled.

"Nice seeing you in front of my house the other day. Stalking me, were you?" she asked.

He threw his head back and laughed. "Just looking over the town. Getting to know the streets and places."

"An hour at a time? Sit in front of every house? Going to take you a year or two at that rate."

Delia Thurgood spoke up, asking about plans for the meeting. Zoe was happy to say she knew nothing about it.

Jenny said she'd heard it was going well.

"And we'll see you there, Friday night?" Fitz stared pointedly at Zoe. She shrugged.

"But you must. We need our leading writer's input."

"I'll always vote for a public garden."

"Ah, yes," he shook his head slowly and looked around the table, smiling at his friends. "Always that. This woman is stuck on one idea . . ."

Zoe walked away, leaving Jenny to follow behind her.

Delaware, Demeter's daughter, in her short, brown uniform and white frilly apron, stood next to their booth, notepad in hand, bending her head so her long blonde hair (another new color for Delaware) covered half her face. "Better order before Myrtle's out of meatloaf," she said in a half whisper. "People've been ordering carryouts to take home and freeze. Those new people over there." She cocked her head toward Fitz and his friends. "They don't ever order anything else. That one little guy says he's never tasted anything better, which makes you wonder where they kept him all his life."

She bent down closer. "Myrtle doesn't like him. She's getting madder all the time. Doesn't like them in here. Shorts her on meatloaf. Doesn't like all their carryouts—especially that Mr. Dillon. His tab, you know."

"Why doesn't she just make more?" Jenny shook her head.

Delaware smirked. "Myrtle change her way of doing things? I don't think that's going to happen."

"I'll have a bowl of soup," Jenny said.

"Can't do it," Delaware flipped her long hair back over her shoulder. "A bowl of chili?"

Delaware shook her head again. "Good luck with that. Myrtle's got a new rule. It's meatloaf or nothing until six thirty."

"I don't like meatloaf."

Delaware made a face, then brightened. "I can get you a bag of chips. How about a plate of mashed potatoes and meatloaf gravy? I'll just leave the meatloaf off."

"Give me the damned meatloaf," Jenny growled.

"Good choice." Delaware bent down close, looking around the room, at the tables where people watched them. "You know they're all dying to ask you questions about Cammy Otis. Everybody in town is on edge. Most have been out looking, a lot of them, on their own. And there's Janice, too."

Zoe leaned out to look around Delaware. "Tell them we're still hunting." She leaned back. "I'm here to eat, not answer questions."

Delaware ignored Zoe and smiled down on Jenny. "So, Jenny, what's with you and Tony Ralenti? Don't see the two of you together any more. He just left. Surprised you didn't meet him in the parking lot."

Jenny shrugged, knowing better than to give Delaware, or Demeter, food for gossip. "We're busy people," she said and handed over her menu.

Delaware shrugged off Jenny's answer and turned to Zoe, determined to get something she could offer the expectant diners, who, after all, depended on Delaware for news.

"You find Margaret and Jeddah Otis? Everybody knows that's where you went today."

Zoe figured telling this much news wasn't going to hurt anything. "The father's in a wheelchair. The mother's dead."

"Really? Poor souls. I'll have to tell folks. Maybe they'll want to visit Pamela, give their condolences."

Zoe rolled her eyes and threw her hands up. "Delaware! Don't do that. Tell them—please. Pamela's in enough pain."

"Yeah. You're right. After all, nobody here liked Margaret and

Jeddah. And, what they did to Pamela—well—people called them devils, not Christians. First you take care of the life and people God gave you. Then you take care of your own soul."

She thought awhile, tapping her pencil against her nose. "So, they didn't have Cammy."

"No they didn't. Now could I get that meatloaf before Myrtle runs out?"

When the meatloaf came, Zoe wasn't hungry. She was thinking hard, staring down at her plate. She looked up at Jenny, putting her meatloaf away as fast as she could before she had to taste it.

"Green hamburger," Zoe said. "Where did we hear about green hamburger?"

Jenny put her fork down. "Like every week when Myrtle's cooking up her special."

"She doesn't call it green."

"All these green peppers?" Jenny stabbed one and held it up for Zoe to see.

Zoe shook her head. "Nope. I've got green hamburger on the . . ."

Jenny looked at her, understanding, then setting her fork down, coughing.

"The ME said hamburger with green in it. Something like that in Janice's stomach." Zoe poked at the meat on her plate.

Jenny nodded. "I remember." She put a hand to her throat. "Hamburger with green peppers."

"And a hard candy." Zoe said.

"What's it mean?" Jenny asked.

Zoe shrugged. "Maybe nothing."

Jenny looked around the room again. "Who in Bear Falls doesn't have hamburger with green peppers in them sometime during the week?"

"Nobody," Zoe said.

They were almost through eating when the door to the restaurant opened and Gladys Bonney, followed by Tammy, came in, looked around then zeroed in on Zoe and Jenny.

"Here she comes." Zoe slid down in the booth until her nose was just above the table edge. That left a pair of bushy blond eyebrows, and a voice warning Jenny. "Hold on to your hat."

Gladys bent to slap her hands on the table. "Saw your car outside, Jenny. I've been looking for you two. Been hearing things and wondering why I wasn't getting any calls about the meeting Friday. I offered to help, remember? Said: anything I can do."

"Meeting's set. That was Keith's job. Seven o'clock. Town offices."

Gladys moved to Zoe's side of the booth saying, "I know all that." She plunked her skinny bottom down, pushing until Zoe moved over, leaving Tammy standing awkwardly beside the table.

"Gladys, don't sit on her," Jenny warned.

Gladys looked down as if she didn't know Zoe was there. "You mean Zoe? Phooey. You're tougher than you look, aren't you, Shorty? You're the one I wanted to see. Heard something that's kind of disturbing. I mean, considering who me and Tammy are."

"What was it you heard?" Zoe squeaked, half-laughing, half-mad.

"I heard that Minnie Moon and that awful girl of hers got asked to dinner over at the mansion. Is that true? You know what that was about?"

"I heard they were going but I wasn't invited."

Gladys eyed Jenny. "What about you? That Nathan Wickley guy sure can't be interested in Dianna Moon, can he?" She threw her head back and hooted. "What a laugh that would be? Like a Kennedy marrying a stripper."

"Now, Gladys. That's not fair . . ."

Gladys hooted again. "Put that piece of trash next to my Tammy here. Like a skunk and an angel. Thing is the man didn't get to know Tammy well enough. If he'd invited us, he'd see." She blinked fast. "Think they'll be at the meeting?"

Jenny blinked back at her. "He's old enough to be Tammy's father." She shook her head, "And no, I don't know if he'll be there."

"Well, if he is, I'm going to make sure Tammy talks to him."

"What about Charles Bingman? I like him a whole lot more than that Nathan. How about you, Tammy?" Jenny looked up at the girl.

"I don't know about that one." Gladys answered. 'I saw him with some painted-up woman in town. He had that awful English woman with him the last time. Quite the playboy, you ask me. If that's the kind of wife he's looking for, I wouldn't want my daughter anywhere near that man."

"What do you think, Tammy?" Jenny turned to the silent woman again.

"Oh, me? Well, I like all the new people. I don't like that little man though. He wasn't nice to you, Zoe."

Tammy's smile was sweet, with a tiny hint of anger in it. The anger was for her, Zoe, because she'd been insulted by Fitzwilliam. She liked Tammy a whole lot more all of a sudden. The girl had real feelings. Nothing like her mother.

"I think you're better than all of those people, Tammy," Jenny said. "If I were you, I wouldn't waste my time trying to impress any of them."

Startled, Tammy shook her head, her pale eyes opening wide. "Oh, I'm not impressing anybody. I never do."

That wasn't what Gladys was looking for from her child. She clucked at the girl.

Tammy colored up. "I mean, I could never love a man who wasn't nice to other people."

"Quiet, Tammy," Gladys ordered. "Enough money can make up for whatever a man lacks in manners."

"Not everything," Zoe said under her breath.

Tammy's head dipped until she was looking at her shoes.

"Well, if you ask me, Charles is the catch of that group," Jenny said. "And what about you, Jenny Weston? Heard Tony Ralenti got hurt out searching for the girl. Hope he's okay. Good man. You don't snap him up soon . . ." Gladys warned, "Could be he gets a wandering eye. You know how men are. They move on when no one's looking after them. They move right on."

Jenny said nothing. Gladys, her hair like rows of bundled hay, her greedy eyes wide—got too much fun out of warning her.

With no one left to pump for information and no one left to insult, Gladys slid out of the booth, pulled her flowered dress out from where it stuck between her cheeks, and motioned to Tammy as she stalked off from the table, hissing as they left, "Get your head up, Tammy. Remember what I told you. Could be your last chance. Let's talk about Charles Bingman again. Maybe I've been looking at the wrong man. That Wickley's kind of small . . ." Her voice faded away.

Harold Roach, the newspaper deliveryman who'd found Janice's body, cornered them as they finished their pie.

He leaned down, resting both hands on the table, looking from Zoe to Jenny and back. He scanned the restaurant, then whispered, "Don't want to butt in; hear you two are working your tails off looking for Cammy Otis. You know she used to come around selling candy? Something about Future Nurses, I think. If I ever saw a girl who could take care of herself, that was the one. I wouldn't worry about the kid. She'll be back when she's ready." He nodded a couple of times then looked over at his wife Christina, who smiled back at him.

"She's pretty young, Mr. Roach," Jenny said quietly, watching the man's face and wondering what he was worried about.

"But sometimes it's in the girl, you know. That call of the wild. Can't do anything about it. You watch. Cammy Otis will come back when she wants to. If I was all of you, I'd just stop hunting."

They exchanged looks when he hurried off to where his young wife waited, an impatient smile on her face as she checked her watch and then the clock on the wall, then said something to Delaware as she finally brought them their food.

"What's he scared of?" Jenny asked.

"That old rape charge. He's scared to death somebody will find out."

"We already know. He didn't do anything. It was dismissed and Janice wasn't raped."

Zoe shrugged. "That's the thing about a secret. You don't know when it's going to leak out and get you all over again."

The mansion people left, Charles clutching their stack of carry-outs. Zoe didn't mean to watch them, but Fitz caught her turning back from the open doorway. He lifted his fingers in a V. The peace sign. She put her head down fast and then was mad that he made her act like she was afraid of him. She wished she'd waved back. She wished she'd laughed at him. She wished she'd done anything but act dumb.

The other early birds were clearing out. Zoe and Jenny finished their coffee. Myrtle, who rarely left her kitchen to talk to customers, finding them mostly annoying in person—scuttled through the swinging doors and over to their table as they were getting up to leave. She dipped her hairnet-covered head and spoke from the corner of her mouth.

"I've been figuring things out. Doing a lot of dishes gives you time for figuring. Think I can tell you where that poor girl got to. Know a lot about these woods going way back to when the Indians used to rule around here. There was a time when a little girl went missing. They never found her. It was said some evil spirit stole her away. That's what I was thinking. If there's evil spirits out there, maybe what you need to do is get yourself a witch doctor. Go over to the casino and ask 'em. Bet they'd know one or two in the area. Have him take off the spell and Cammy Otis will be back in a wink of your eye."

Jenny couldn't answer. Even Zoe was at a loss for words.

"Well, just wanted to put that out there. Give you something to think about."

The bell above the door rang. Myrtle ran as fast as her bent body could run for the safety of her kitchen.

Jenny and Zoe got out before another late group of diners arrived with more questions and advice.

Chapter 36

"I can't tell anybody." Kent Miller's head bent into his open hands. He sobbed between words. "Mom shouldn't've called you."

"Can't tell us what, Kent?" Jenny, on her knees in front of him, looked up into the half-hidden, sad face. "She's missing, Kent. Maybe she's hurt. Maybe she's just lost."

He sniffed and reached a hand toward his mother, motioning for a tissue. He blew his nose hard, wiped at his eyes, and stayed as he was, shuddering from time to time, not looking up at them.

Jenny got off her knees and nodded for Zoe to take over.

Not needing to get on her knees, Zoe rapped him hard on top of his head.

"Is Cammy your friend?" she demanded.

After cringing away from her, he gave her a dirty look as he sniffed, then sniffed again.

"Is this the way you treat a friend? Not do all you can to find her?"

He stopped sniffing and lifted his swollen face to look her straight in the eye.

"Is that what you think? You think you can't help us because you made a promise?"

He slowly, very slowly, nodded. "Cammy didn't want her mom to know until she was sure," he said.

"Sure about what?"

He reached for another tissue, blew his nose, and wiped his eyes until they were blood red. "About something she didn't want her mom to know."

"What? Come on, Kent. We want Cammy back, don't we? We're running out of time."

He drew in his breath and held it, then let it out. "I want Cammy back. We've got big plans for this summer. Mom's taking us to a farm . . ."

"So? She has to be here to go, doesn't she?"

He nodded. "Okay. Anyway, I've been thinking that maybe that man took her."

There was a startled intake of breath from Zoe.

"What man?" She asked.

"He wanted to give her a job. There was going to be a lot of people, that's why she trusted him. He was from a university. That's what he told her."

"Which university?"

He shrugged. "I don't know for sure. I remember, she said a man talked to her. He had one of her flyers, she said. She thanked me for making such a good flyer. She said it looked like she might get a really good job. The man said there would be other people working, too, and she was going to make a lot of money. Cammy was excited."

He looked into Zoe's face, so close to his. "Cammy was really happy. She was going to wait until she had her first paycheck and take it home and give the whole thing to her mom. Cammy said she wanted to make her mom happy. You know, Cammy's mom wasn't always happy. Cammy said her mom had a lot on her shoulders. And now she was going to help her."

"Who was this man? Did she give you a name?"

He shook his head. "I didn't ask her. At first I thought maybe she was going to work in one of the orchards. I hear they always need a lot of people. But they don't pay that good. Not the kind of thing Cammy would get all excited about."

"So, you don't know if it was somebody from Bear Falls or not?"

He shook his head again, growing sad, aware that he was letting them down. "I . . . I'm sorry . . . I just can't . . ."

"Can't what, Kent?"

He stopped talking. There were tears in his eyes when he looked from woman to woman.

"Kent. You said 'at first' you thought she was going to be working in an orchard. What was the second thing you thought?"

"I'm not supposed to say."

"But . . ."

"Can't say."

"Kent." His mother drew his face gently up toward her. "You mustn't keep secrets."

He nodded once, then looked from Zoe to Jenny, saying, "She might have got a job digging for dinosaurs."

"What?" Zoe took a step back, disappointed, not ready to deal with this wild stretch. The other two women said nothing.

He talked faster now. "Cammy really liked the idea of doing that. We put that on her list of jobs she was looking for because she said she was hoping to be an archeologist when she graduated from high school. That's why she was so excited. She was going to be an archeologist and help on a dig."

"Indian dig?" Zoe asked.

"No. Really. Dinosaurs."

It took a long time before Zoe could talk again.

"Dinosaurs? In Michigan?" Jenny asked.

He nodded. "That's why it was a secret. Nobody ever found dinosaurs in Michigan before. This was a really big thing.

"She said she was going out last Friday to look the job over. The man was supposed to pick her up after school. Then me and my dad left town and I didn't talk to her anymore."

"*Look the job over.*" Zoe thought a while. "What did she mean?"

He shrugged. "Going to some dinosaur place, is what she told me and then she wouldn't say another word about it."

"Did she say where this dinosaur place was?"

He shook his head slowly. "Maybe I should have asked her. I didn't think about it because she was so happy that she had a job and could surprise her mother with money."

"When was the job to start?"

"Maybe June. You think I should have told her not to go? Would Cammy be here now if I told her that?"

Zoe had other pressing questions. "So, this man was going to pick her up after school, you know what time exactly?"

"No."

"And she didn't tell you his name?"

"No."

"Was he picking her up at school or someplace else?"

"At her house, is what I think. He knew where she lived, so it would be okay because her mom was still at work."

"Didn't she know not to trust a strange man?"

Kent frowned. "But he wasn't a strange man. She knew him from meeting him to talk about the job."

They left the house with Kent still sniffling and asking his mother questions, needing desperately to know it wasn't his fault that Cammy didn't come home.

Chapter 37

"Archeology?" Jenny pulled out on to Maple Street.

"From Camille's flyer. She listed that as a job she was looking for." Zoe was still tucking herself in behind her seatbelt. "I found a book on dinosaurs under her mattress—remember?"

"So?"

"The kid got a job on a dig," Zoe said.

"You know there's no dig, don't you?"

Zoe settled herself, then pushed back against the seat. "Of course not. But . . . this is what we've got. This is it. We find the man and we find Cammy."

"Do we tell Pamela?" Jenny asked.

Zoe said she didn't know. "Seems almost cruel, doesn't it? The thought of her daughter out there somewhere with a killer."

"One thing . . ." she went on. "We know she's in the woods. That's where he was taking her. We've been on the right track all along."

Zoe stretched her neck, trying to see over the dashboard. "Getting dark."

"What has that got to do with anything?"

"Nothing. Absolutely nothing, except that it's getting dark, and Cammy is still gone, and we're only a little closer to her."

* * *

Jenny didn't turn toward Elderberry. She went in the other direction as she called the chief and told him what they'd learned from Kent. "She's got to be east of Shore Drive somewhere. If not the house Jenny and Tony found, then another one . . ."

"Or a hole in the ground."

He hesitated. "I'm not giving up."

"What about Cammy's phone? Those three unknown callers?.."

"All local. Turns out it was people who saw her flyer at Draper's Superette. They called but she didn't call them back.

"Say," he went on. "Could the two of you come over here, to my house? We've got a lot of things to talk about. Learned something about Jay Root."

Jenny agreed and told Zoe. "Give me fifteen minutes," she said to Ed. the deep funk she'd just slid into.

"Hey." Zoe sat up, noticing they weren't headed in the right direction as Jenny turned down a street Zoe didn't know well.

"I want to drive by Tony's house," Jenny said. "See if he's home yet. I'd like to run all of this by him."

"Really? That's what we're doing here?"

Jenny said nothing.

"You two still having troubles?"

"I think it's . . . better."

Zoe was still a while.

"I heard you ask Ed about Cammy's phone," she said.

"Three people called about the flyer. She didn't call them back. No call from the man who picked her up on Friday. Ed says we should talk. He found something on Jay Root."

Jenny drove by Tony's house, a small ranch on a street of small ranches. His truck wasn't there. She drove to the end of the block and turned around, checking a second time.

"Dinosaurs," she said as she drove toward Ed's house. "How strange."

Ed's wife, Lizzie, saw what was going on when Ed let the two women in. Having been a police officer's wife for many years, she knew to get her sweater and purse, lean over to kiss Ed on top of his head, and say she was going to see a late show.

The first thing Zoe mentioned was hamburger with green peppers.

The chief made a face. "Janice Root's stomach contents. I remember, but where's that going to get us?"

"You ever eat Myrtle's weekly special?"

"Her meatloaf?" Ed smiled. "Who hasn't?"

"Hamburger with green peppers."

He sat back and gave her an odd look. "You mean Janice could have had Myrtle's meatloaf before she died?"

Zoe rolled her eyes. "I'm just saying . . ."

"I'll get over to Myrtle's. See when they last saw Janice."

"I don't think that's it. What I'm thinking is it wasn't in the restaurant," she said. "Takeout. He had to feed her something those days she was missing. The trouble is, meatloaf takeout could be almost anybody in town, one time or another."

"Didn't Myrtle complain about the new people stocking their freezer with meatloaf?" Jenny asked.

Zoe shrugged. "Meatloaf is the plague of Bear Falls. Everybody's got it."

Ed then switched to something else bothering him. He wanted to talk about Cammy's flyer, worrying that he'd better get a safety class for the school going. "Teach 'em not to put out their address and phone number anywhere. Makes it easy for predators."

"You sure none of those three calls about the job were from this man?"

Ed shook his head. "People I know. All elderly, looking for help with their gardens."

"She was going out to the place where they were going to dig. That's what Kent told us," Jenny said.

"So the man knows the woods around here," Zoe said what she'd been trying to put together before, clearing new people in town who couldn't begin to know the woods in a few weeks.

Jenny shared a thought. "Tony and I met a woman in the woods when we were out there. She knew Cammy. Selma Grange. You know her?"

Ed nodded. "I know Selma Grange. She's been in with a couple of ideas, places to look. Her mother was kind of like the historian of the area. Spent her whole life learning the trees and the animals. Good woman—her mother. Selma, too. Not somebody I'd suspect of doing anything to the girl. Most out there wouldn't. Maybe I'd have to say none of them."

"So we've got this digging for dinosaurs. That's something." Ed leaned back, ignoring Zoe's dark face. He stared up at the popcorn ceiling and mentally noted a couple of cobwebs he'd better get to before Lizzie threw a fit and tried climbing up their creaky ladder and fell and broke a leg.

"No dinosaurs in Michigan. Think she knew that?" he asked.

It was one of those questions that lay where it fell.

"So somebody she knew, or met, when she was looking for a summer job. That's who we've got to concentrate on. Must have seen the flyer and went over to her house."

"Be exciting for a kid like Cammy."

"Excited about a job. Tell a kid they'll be hunting for dinosaurs and they'll follow anybody." Ed thought harder. "I'll check with Michigan State University, see if they've got any digs going on up here. Usually there're one or two a summer."

"I'll bet not looking for dinosaurs," Zoe said her voice quiet.

"There's no dig," Jenny said flatly. "If there was, Cammy would be home. It was all a lie."

For a reason Zoe couldn't explain, her eyes filled with tears. *Of course not—no dig. Just a very young, very happy girl, who was going to surprise her mother.*

Ed saw Zoe's tears and ignored them. "I think they need permits to dig on state land," he said, steering the conversation to plain facts. "Don't know about private land. Probably only permission from the owners. Can't imagine where this thing was supposed to take place. If we knew that much, we could talk to the property owner."

"Has to be in those same woods where her clothes were found," Jennie said.

"Yeah." Ed wandered off into deep thought.

Zoe rose up in her chair. "There is no dig. We have to concentrate not keep leaping all over the place. That man took her someplace out in the woods. But where? I've still got the feeling that the house with the birds in the chimney is somehow central to all this."

"How many times can we search out there?" Ed asked, his voice low because he saw the frustration on the little woman's face. "What I don't want to happen is for us to get mired down, going in circles."

Zoe lowered her chin to her chest. "There is something out there. Why can't I put my finger on it?"

"For a while I thought I had it nailed with that guy in Alaska," Ed said. "But that got shot out of the water."

"What about Jay Root? Jenny said you found something on him."

"Yeah." He leaned over and rummaged in a briefcase on the floor. He settled a folder on his knees, pulling out a yellowed sheet of paper, and then a newspaper article.

"Almost seventeen years ago." He looked up, then back down, as if hating to do what he was about to do. "I traced them, all right. They lived in Saginaw. There's a record on him. And a charge."

"Seventeen years ago—the time Janice was born." Zoe exchanged a look with Jenny.

He nodded. "Sally called the police about her baby. One of her legs had been broken. Child abuse was suspected."

"Whew!" Zoe leaned back, away from what he had to tell her

"They suspected Jay?" she asked.

Ed shrugged. "Here." He leaned forward to give Zoe the newspaper article. "I'm not sure if anything ever came of it. But . . ." he pointed to the article in her hand. "It said there were charges brought against the father—Jay Root. By his wife."

"Sally accused him of hurting the baby?" Jenny wrinkled her nose. "Then why is she still with him? Why did she put Janice in danger all of these years? I don't get it."

Zoe read over the article then handed it to Jenny "It says the charges were dropped. But nothing about Sally."

"That's all I could find."

"There's a doctor's name here. With social services."

He nodded.

"Did you call him?"

He nodded again.

"And?"

"He barely remembered the case. What he did say was he thought the father was cleared."

"Again—what about Sally?"

He shook his head.

"A baby with a broken leg?" Jenny listened but didn't quite understand.

Zoe put her fingers to her temples. She closed her eyes. When she spoke she only whispered, "What a tragedy."

Chapter 38

Spring. And light so late. Close to nine thirty and almost as bright as noon.

"I am exhausted," Zoe said when Jenny stopped in front of her house. "I want to go to bed. Or work in the garden. Anything to stop thinking about Cammy Otis. My brain's going to explode. I've got the girl in here." She tapped the top of her blond and very fuzzy head. "But she's not giving me enough to find her and time is passing while I twiddle my thumbs."

"Go work on your book. We're doing the best we can do, Zoe. Writing seems to focus you. Maybe the concentration will help."

"Focus me?" Zoe frowned at Jenny. "You have no idea what it takes to write a book. To have all those pathetic characters running around inside my head. I'm trapped for life with a bunch of Jane Austen's terrible women. I'm even thinking Dora should be pushing Tony for a proposal before it's too late and you're condemned to a life of abject spinsterhood. That's how bad this Jane Austen thing has gotten. Nothing in my life seems real. Not my work. Not this hunt for a dear child who needs all of our help."

"Zoe! You are a . . ." Jenny couldn't find the words.

Zoe ignored her. "And then I look at me and think I'd never make an Austen woman—not a single wile to save my life. And no skills. If I tried to bat my eyes at a man I'd get my lashes stuck together. Being coy turns my stomach. Imagine me flattering that awful Fitz . . ."

Jenny couldn't help laughing, and then couldn't stop.

Zoe shouted over her, "Imagine me decked out in man-catching clothes . . ."

With Zoe pleased that she'd made Jenny laugh, she was about to slam the car door shut when Jenny held up a finger, wiggling it at her.

"Forgot to tell you. Mom's going out to see the Roots in the morning,"

"I hope Sally talks to her." Zoe started up her walk then turned. "Are you going to tell Dora about Jay?"

Jenny shrugged. "Have to."

She started to pull away from the curb, then stopped again. "Don't call me too early. No. Forget that. Call me whenever you need me. I don't mean to be cranky. It's just so much . . ."

Zoe waved at her. "Me too. I want it over with. I want Cammy back home with Pamela. I want to know who murdered Janice. I want this damn book finished. I want you and Tony settled. Then I'm going to do something different. I want to work on Agatha Christie—that's who. Now there's a writer I can get my teeth into."

"You forget that Agatha Christie had a nervous breakdown when her husband left her? Talk about a weird woman . . ."

Zoe's eyebrows went up. "You think that was it? You think that's all her disappearance was about? Just watch. Can't wait to send Jane Austen back to her dirty little English town and let the real Agatha Christie come out from behind her curtain."

* * *

As soon as Zoe put the key in the front door lock she heard paws scratching on the other side. There was a lot of wild barking and when she pushed the door open, into a distraught Fida, the dog knocked Zoe off her feet to the floor. With Fida on her chest whining and barking, Zoe lay like a bug, arms and legs flailing as the dog licked her face letting Zoe know in dog language that she was mad but also happy and telling Zoe she'd better never leave her alone that long again.

When Fida was pushed far enough away so Zoe could get up, she made a circuit of the house looking for puddles of pee and piles of poop but found none.

Had to be Dora's doing. She'd probably kept Fida most of the day or she'd come over and cleaned up. She was supremely grateful to her friend.

Back in the kitchen, she pushed the dog out the back door, on the happenstance her excitement at seeing her housemate also excited her kidneys.

Alone, in the kitchen, she dug her phone from her pocket and sat down heavily at the kitchen table. She took a few minutes to think out what to say to Pamela and what parts to keep under wraps, then decided to tell her about the dinosaurs and the job and the man—which was just about everything. Her whole body ached at the thought of the pain she would cause.

Pamela answered at the first ring, as if the phone had been in her hands. Her voice was breathless. Zoe knew she was hearing what terror felt like.

"It's Zoe Zola. Couldn't call until now."

"That's all right, Zoe. What did Kent say?"

"He said Cammy had been looking for a summer job."

"But I thought she stopped . . ."

"No, she didn't. What she wanted was to surprise you with her first paycheck."

The sound that came over the phone held too many things for Zoe to think about.

When she could talk, Pamela asked, very slowly, "Did anything come of it?"

"Somebody contacted her."

"About gardening?

"About a job on an archeological dig." Zoe frowned down at her hands even as she said the words.

Silence.

Finally, "Was that a joke?"

Zoe explained what she knew.

"Then this man took her." Pamela's voice was unemotional. Not her voice at all.

To Zoe's surprise, Pamela hung up.

* * *

Only ten o'clock. The day was never going to end. No use trying to sleep, not with Pamela's voice in her head. It wasn't despair. It wasn't acceptance. Nothing she knew. Nothing she wanted to guess at.

Zoe couldn't write. Couldn't watch television. She was exhausted, but couldn't sleep.

She peeked through the side curtains to see if the lights were on at Dora's. They weren't.

With nothing left her, she sat down with Fida in her lap, and tried to think very hard about a missing girl and why she would imagine dinosaurs ever lived in Michigan.

Because she wanted so badly to surprise her mother.

Because she thought she was in on something that would make big news around the world.

Because . . .

And Janice Root?

What was there about the two of them that attracted the attention of a predator? How were they the same?

She pictured Janice, when she came to her house selling peaches. Pictured the pleasant face, a little acne, a little awkward—not really much of a door-to-door salesman. Then pictured her walking away. The girl's limp made Zoe's cement steps a little hard to manage.

A slight limp . . .

And Cammy. A slight mental difference. She'd been selling candy.

Did either of these things mean anything?

At a thump on the front porch, Fida went into a frenzy, throwing her body against the door, woofing until Zoe struggled up from the sofa and peeked out behind the curtain.

Nothing. She looked as far as the window let her, up and down the street. She searched for a car at the curb.

Then there was knocking at her door and Zoe flattened her body back against the wall.

More knocking. This time harder.

She stood behind the door and yelled as loudly as she could, "Get away from my door or I'm calling the police."

A voice on the other side. "Miss Zola?"

That was all. She thought about getting a butcher knife from the kitchen but figured she wasn't the kind of woman to stab anyone through the heart for knocking on her door.

"Yes?" she called.

"It's Fitzwilliam Dillon. I'm sorry it's so late but I'd like to speak to you."

She unlocked the door, then unlocked the screened door, and pushed it open, hitting Fitzwilliam in the shoulder. He gripped his shoulder with one hand and pulled the door open with the other.

"I called your number but you didn't answer." He said, as if to himself.

She shrugged. "I've been busy."

She led back into the living room, pointing to a chair while she sat on the sofa, holding a still muttering Fida in her arms.

"Your dog needs training. If it were my dog, I'd see she went to school."

He struggled into the chair and sat, smoothing his suit pants then pulling his jacket neatly around him.

"If she were your dog, she'd have bitten you to death by now."

"What a dumb thing to say." He rolled his eyes, then looked around the room. "How ever do you live in so small a place?"

"Better than that pile of stone you live in."

"Must be what poor people are like, making do with any old thing."

"You are one big piece of . . ."

Fitz held up his very square and very small hand, pointing one short finger at her face. "This is not what I came for."

She raised her eyebrows.

"I came here because I understand you don't like me." His outsized nose went up in the air.

"An understatement."

"In that case, I've come to say I'm sorry for any way in which I made you angry. It was purely unintentional."

"Baloney!" she exploded, causing Fida to growl and nervously burrow under her arm.

"Please shut that awful little dog up," he said.

"This is her home. She has a right to her opinion."

"Really? A dog? And you are supposed to write books of deep discernment? Books that see into the places between words, down into the truth of literature?"

"You've been reading my reviews." She calmed a little, amused that he'd taken the time to check her bona fides.

"Did you write them? The reviews."

"Please, stop being a jerk. Say what you came to say so you can leave."

He sat up very straight and cleared his throat. "I came to tell you I'm sorry for any discomfort I gave you the other day."

"You said that already."

"I don't know what came over me. I'd been looking forward to meeting you. I knew you were like me—a Little Person—and I thought that surely you and I would be friends."

"You mean because we have our size in common?"

"That, and because I really have read one of your books and liked it. The Emily Dickinson book. I liked the digging you did— inside that great mind. Imagine, if anyone knows eternity—certainly

Dickinson did, and tried to tell us. I like to think my mind works that way, too."

"You were a miserable bastard to me." She wasn't going to be distracted.

"But I didn't expect to meet a beautiful woman."

Zoe blushed, then frowned at him. She was totally without words.

"I truly think you intimidated me," he said.

"So then you insulted me at every turn. Been reading *How to Make and Keep Friends* have you?"

"I'm telling the truth."

"And then you sent Nathan and that Delia women to fix things. A fine pair those two. I heard you sent Charles and some coarse woman named Mary to Dora's."

"Really? I don't remember." He thought a while. "I truly am a moral coward." The stiffness melted out of him. He smiled a genuine smile. "I'm a terrible man."

"I agree."

He shook his head. "And I'm still hoping you will be involved with the gift to Bear Falls and with the party we'll throw later."

"Why?"

"Because despite what a tremendous boor I was the other day I want us to be friends."

She took a deep breath and stuck her chin out. "I was coming to the meeting anyway, you know, though I don't know why you need my help. And I have a right to my own idea for a splendid gift to our town. If that's what it is—a gift, and not a bribe to get people to like you."

"Not that garden again." He ignored her insult.

"Yes. That 'garden.' A lovely garden in the park. An arboretum. We could train master gardeners here. They'd come from all over the North to learn, and we'd get tourists. Gardens draw families."

"Two million dollars for a garden?"

"Are you attacking me?"

His hands were in the air. "A large garden would be very nice. I, well, had in mind something that would benefit everybody in town, not just flower lovers."

"Such as . . ."

"Maybe we'll learn Friday night."

She thought a while.

"I could pick you up," he said.

"In that black car of yours?"

"Yes. That's the car I drive."

"Ever been near the missing girl's house? Parked, the way you were here?"

"And where is that? The girl's house?"

"Never mind. You'd know the street.'"

"My friends take my car from time to time. Charles. Nathan. Even Lady Cynthia. They don't like to, because of the extensions but mine are removable. And I have other cars I like to drive."

"Why would any of them be parked on Cammy's street?"

"Cammy is the missing girl?" he asked.

She nodded.

"I have no idea."

"Are they going to be living here with you? All those people?"

He made a face. "Not on your life. Nathan's looking for a place of his own. Maybe Delia, too. Nathan used to live in Michigan and wants to come back to his roots. Lady Cynthia claims she's enamored with Northern Michigan and might decide to move here, but I doubt it."

Zoe tried to take in what he was saying. "Are Nathan and Delia related?"

Fitz laughed. "That pair? They don't really even like each other, if you ask me. It's just that they've been friends for such a long time. Both date back to when my father was living. And, anyway, I think Delia has a husband somewhere. Maybe back in New York. Or maybe he's dead. I don't really know. Or, for that matter, care."

"Really close to your friends, I see."

"Don't be snide, Zoe Zola. Remember, I inherited them. It's like any old uncle—you don't ask questions, do you? He just is. And that makes Delia my old aunt."

He slid from the sofa to the floor, adjusted his jacket again, and headed back toward the door. "If you're sure I can't pick you up on Friday . . ."

He gave her a smile—an almost shy smile, warming his eyes and his face.

"But you'll be there? That's all I'd hoped. Whatever you can do to help this along, I'll be very grateful." He smiled again. "And whatever I can do to make up for my earlier boorishness . . ."

The man wasn't so bad looking when he didn't sneer. She waved a hand at him. "I like that word: boorish. Apt, I think. Yes. Apt."

"Ah." When he smiled at her, his eyes lighted. "Apt. A lovely word. Apt to be boorish . . . Imagine what the two of us could wrought, or write, together."

She stifled a laugh and waved him toward the door.

He turned in the doorway. "Give me a chance, Zoe. I will really try to make you like me."

"Then don't stalk me the way you did the other day."

"I wasn't stalking. Just trying to get my nerve up."

"And don't come calling at ten o'clock, giving my dog the shakes."

How could she not laugh at this man's indignant face? "But you weren't home when I came earlier. That part is entirely your own fault."

After he'd finally taken himself to the porch, she stepped outside to watch him go, hurrying along the walk to a car parked down the street.

She smiled, thinking how maybe they could be friends. Until he drove off, passing under the streetlight across the way.

That car was certainly black. It didn't belong in her neighborhood, It was very shiny.

Chapter 39

It wasn't that Jenny got up early on purpose but more that she barely slept. Too many events from the day before refused to leave her in peace.

By seven, she was ready to stop thinking about Cammy and get out of bed, going into the kitchen to surprise Dora, who was scrubbing the kitchen sink with even more than the usual zeal she brought to tasks she didn't like to do.

"You scared me!" Dora jumped when Jenny, barefooted, black hair standing electrically up around her head, pattered into the kitchen, saying, "Good morning."

"Are you going to see Sally Root today?" Jenny poured herself a cup of coffee then went to the table, her bare feet up on Zoe's chair.

"Anything I can do to help. Poor Sally. She'll never have another child. She didn't have Janice until she was in her late thirties, from what I understand. When a woman has to wait so long . . . Can you just imagine that kind of loss?"

"And poor Pamela. Both of them with a child who was the very center of why they're living."

Slowly, examining every bit of what she was saying, Jenny told her what Kent had said: about the summer job, about the dinosaurs, the man who picked her up at her house on Friday.

"The poor kid was in agony, telling on his friend. But how I wish he hadn't kept it a secret."

"Dinosaurs? Is he sure? Really?"

Dora sat down across from Jenny, rubbing hard at her eyes for a minute. "That's a crazy truth, if he's right. A dinosaur dig."

They sat without talking until Jenny couldn't hold in the thing about Jay Root.

"Charged?" Dora listened, then leaned back and looked hard at Jenny. "What was it exactly they charged him with?"

"Child abuse. Sally made the complaint."

"Sally? I don't believe this. Janice's leg was broken?"

"She was dropped. Sally said he did it on purpose."

"Did he go to jail?"

Jenny shook her head. "Ed talked to the doctor who oversaw the case. He remembered everything was kind of hushed up. I guess Jay wasn't guilty of anything."

"Then who was?"

Jenny had nothing to add.

After a while, Jenny asked, dreading the answer. "Did Tony call last night?"

"No. Not a word."

"Was he here yesterday?"

Dora nodded. "He was here, along with Charles Bingman and his friend, Mary somebody or other. He got on pretty well with Charles Bingman and with that awful girlfriend. I'd say that one's a handful. Quite the flirt, though Charles didn't seem to mind. That woman seemed to take a liking to Tony but he barely paid her any attention."

Dora pretended to be the bearer of good news.

"I get it, Mom."

"As I said, Tony didn't seem to notice."

"I don't have a job yet, Mom."

"I'll miss you, if you go back to Chicago. I'm used to you being here. And Lisa's coming soon. That would be so . . . complete. To have the two of you home. Without you the house will seem . . ."

"I'll miss you, too."

"And Tony?" Dora shook her head. "But, that's none of my business, is it? You're my daughter. You'll always come first. I'd rather you never married again than be unhappy."

* * *

Later, on the way to Draper's to pick up cheese and bread for lunch, Jenny's phone rang beside her. If it was Tony what did she say to him? Something like: *What's going on? I thought we were okay?*

The number wasn't his. It was local—but it wasn't Tony's.

"Miss Weston?" The voice on the other end of the phone was male, young, hesitating as if he might hang up if she didn't talk fast.

"Who's this?" she demanded, in a level voice, handling her disappointment along with her curiosity.

"I'm . . . eh . . . It's Kent Miller. You remember? You and that other lady were here last night?"

"What can I do for you, Kent?"

"There's one more thing. I didn't think anything about it, but Mom said maybe I should tell you anyway. I went with Cammy out to her place in the woods one time. Mom got mad when I told her. But after the other secrets . . . well, I figured I shouldn't keep anything to myself. You see, usually I didn't want to go with her because I don't like the woods the way Cammy likes the woods. Always made me feel . . . I don't know how to say it . . . scared. Too quiet out there but Cammy said that's what she liked most about it. You know, quiet."

"Okay. Maybe you . . ."

"Did her mom tell you about the time she was just walking and didn't come home all night?"

"I heard something like that. I thought it was out looking at owls."

"Well, Cammy lied. I didn't want her to do that but she didn't want her mom mad at her and maybe not let us be friends anymore."

"What did Cammy lie about, Kent?"

"This won't be trouble for her, will it? I mean, when she comes home."

"We have to find her first, Kent."

"Okay, then I'm going to tell you about the place I went with her." She let him gather his nerve.

"I can take you there. I'm pretty sure I remember where it is."

"What kind of place is it? A house?"

"No. Not a house. But it was Cammy's house. That's what she called it. Her house in the woods."

"But not a real house."

"No ma'am. It's like a tent; only it's made out of sticks. Just sticks and branches. It's at the bottom of a sinkhole. That's what Cammy called it: a sinkhole. That's a place where the earth just sinks down a long way and leaves a big hole behind."

"You two were there? And she lied to her mom about it? Can we go out there today?" she asked.

"My mom said it would be okay, if you wanted to go. And . . ." He seemed to be holding his breath.

"Yes?"

"It's just that when we find her I'm going to ask Cammy to be my girlfriend. Soon as I see her. I'm going to ask first thing. I really miss her."

"I know you do. So does her mom. I'll be right over. I'll pick up Miss Zola. No more than half an hour."

He turned away from the phone, his voice muddled. When he turned back he said, "It's okay, Miss Jenny. I'll be ready."

No time for cheese and bread. No lunch again.

Jenny called Zoe, then turned her car around.

Chapter 40

It seemed strange to Dora, as she drove in, how dilapidated the Root's house was now. It had been so . . . happy . . . when she'd come out in fall to buy apples and peaches; when cars had been lined down the road; and when Jay held a piece of fruit between his hands, polishing it, showing a customer the blush of a peach, the deep red of a Delicious apple. Such pride in what he did. Both of them. Sally at his side. Cammy filling bags and handing over receipts, her smile the best thing about the fruit stand.

Dora knew about things dying. After Jim was killed she let everything go. No painting over the paint he'd last put on the place. No changing anything in the house—she expected him back at any minute. She wanted him to know that it was still his home.

And then the long months of depression when she couldn't bring herself to care about anything as ordinary as how her house looked, or even how she looked. All of that lasted for months when there didn't seem to be a reason to keep on caring about anything. Jim had always been the center of her life—along with Lisa and Jenny.

Then one day she realized that Lisa and Jenny were still with her and there was reason, after all, to go on living. Like Sally Root would learn—if she and Jay made it through this terrible time.

She parked in their drive and got out. Still a nice house though a little neglected. The orchard led off behind a large barn, trees in straight rows and, at this time of year, growing nodes of leaves along the gnarly branches. She hoped Jay Root wasn't going to let the orchard go.

And Sally, a little shy, but friendly, her eyes always so wide open. What would become of her?

Papers blew across the yard. Last year's leaves, gusting up from the orchard, skittered toward the front ditch. The yellow brick house, with white-trimmed front windows and the red barn beyond, had an empty, abandoned look, not the way she remembered at all. Their black car was parked up close to the door of the barn.

She walked toward the house. Old leaves squished underfoot. Probably a useless trip. If Sally was the way Zoe and Jenny said, the woman needed more help than she could give. Maybe a minister. Maybe some time away . . .

Death took hold in different ways, she knew. The one kind of death Dora had never let herself imagine was the death of a child. And here was a woman just beginning this trip through hell.

On the porch, Dora told herself again not to expect anything. Not of Sally and not of herself. Maybe, she thought, she'd go in and sit with her. Not say a word unless Sally wanted to talk.

A very different Jay Root from the man she'd known for the last few years, opened the door and held it for her to enter.

"Thanks so much for coming, Mrs. Weston." Jay's eyes, when he briefly glanced at her, held nothing. No emotion. No attempt to go through the usual routine of greeting a friend or neighbor.

He pointed toward the kitchen and led the way, then pointed to a chair but Dora didn't sit.

"I'm here to stay a while with Sally," Dora said. "Where is she?"

He motioned back the way they'd come. "In our bedroom. Won't come out. Even hates when I open the door, like she's in some kind of trance and I break it. Once in a while I hear her talking to herself."

"Could I . . . try?"

With a shiver moving over his bare arms, he led back through the house to a closed door. He stood aside and nodded.

Dora knocked softly at the bedroom door, Jay beside her, his head down, hair falling over his forehead.

"Sally," he called softly when there was no answer.

He turned the knob and opened the door a crack.

"Somebody's here to see you, honey."

There was no sound from the room.

"Honey?" he said and waited.

"Not now, Jay. Please thank whoever it is. Just tell 'em I'm not feeling very well right . . ."

"Sally?" Dora called around Jay. "It's me, Dora Weston. I'm the lady with the Little Libraries. I see you coming to get books lots of times."

"Oh, yes. Dora Weston." The voice was a little stronger.

"I brought you a book. It's the new Mary Alice Monroe." She listened, ear to the crack of the door. "May I come in?"

"Well, I'm not feeling up to company. Can't read right now. Hope you understand but . . ."

Dora pushed the door.

The air in the room was thick with the smell of sleep and unchanged bedding. It was overheated, and dark. The shades were pulled to the windowsill so very little light got in. The room was a mess. Clothes were tossed at the foot of the bed, over a ladder back chair in one corner, and over another chair beside the bed.

The woman lay curled on her side, her hands clutching a pillow to her.

"I came to sit with you. I don't need to talk, unless you want to."

She closed the door quietly behind her, leaving Jay alone in the hall.

Sally groaned and turned away. She pulled the crumpled sheet and blanket up to her chin but didn't open her eyes.

After removing jeans and blouses from the chair beside the bed, folding them into neat piles she set on top of the dresser, Dora sat, her purse, and book, on the floor. She folded her hands in her lap and said nothing.

She stayed like that for a long time. An hour passed before Sally Root finally sat up a little and turned her head around. "I thought you were gone."

"I'm right here."

"You can't help me, Dora. Nobody can help me."

"I know that," Dora said matter-of-factly. "I'm not here to help you. And I'm not here because I can make your pain go away. I'm just here to sit in case you need somebody to talk to."

The woman in the bed curved one arm up over her eyes.

Another hour passed. Dora could tell Sally had fallen asleep by the change in her breathing and the soft hesitations as her chest rose and fell.

At one point Jay pushed the door open and looked in. She only stared until he backed out, pulling the door behind him.

Maybe sensing the air moving in the room, or unable to make herself sleep any longer, Sally opened her eyes. She looked at the ceiling.

Dora said nothing.

Sally sighed finally. "You know, Mrs. Weston," she talked toward the ceiling. "I put my whole life into Janice. When I had her—well, she was so little at birth. I was afraid then I was going to lose her and I promised myself I'd never take my eyes off her until she was grown up. Then I took my eyes off her and Jay dropped her. He broke her leg. Course he didn't mean to do it. No parent wants to hurt their child. Surely not me. I'd never do a thing to hurt Janice. I loved her more than any mother could love a child and I'd never hurt her."

She shook her head fiercely.

"Then she grew up and there came this night when she didn't come home. We'd been having a few troubles with her. Well, again, mostly Jay. She wanted to get a job and he said no, we needed her right here in the orchard. Like we couldn't give her a little freedom once in a while. She got mad at him. She really did. And then she stayed away from home. Jay said it was okay. Jay said she was like all teenagers—rebellious. But he was wrong. I shouldn't have listened to him. He was so very wrong. We should have called the police right away, the way I wanted to do."

Dora said nothing, waiting to see if Sally had more to tell her. She didn't.

"Not Jay's fault, Sally. Nobody's fault but the person who did this to Janice."

Sally was quiet for the next half an hour.

She finally rolled over, put a fist under her head, and looked straight at Dora. "I can't help blaming him. I know it's awful but I do."

"He's suffering the same as you are, Sally."

Sally made a face and threw her head back, groaning until she stopped groaning.

"There's no sense to this, Sally. Your God didn't put this on you. No fate brought what happened to Janice. Jay didn't want this to happen. There are monsters among us. Always have been. Always will be, I suppose, until we fix whatever it is that makes monsters. They are out there and we pray every day that we don't meet one. Or maybe we pray, most of all, that our children don't meet one. We make magical wishes to keep them away. I know I always promised God that if he spared my girls I'd be a better person. But once in a while it happens. Nothing to do with you or Jay, or anybody, for that matter. Once in a while a monster shows up and nobody knows until a terrible thing is done."

"What do I do now?" Sally pulled herself up to sit with her back against the headboard, her shoulders down, her small breasts barely pushing up the front of her woolen nightgown "Tell me, Mrs. Weston, what do I do to stop all this hate I've got in me?"

Dora reached over and pulled the woman's hand to her, holding it.

"Could be you're stuck with that hate for a while. But time will sap it away. That's what happened to me, after my Jim was killed."

"I know about that. Heard when we first moved here."

"A lot of pain and a lot of hate so I know what you're feeling. Maybe not as much as you're carrying, but enough to make me sick for a while. Made me not want to talk to people for a while. And not care about much of anything for a while."

The woman reached for a tissue on the nightstand. She blew her nose.

"You still had your girls."

"You've got Jay."

"How?" Sally sat up. "Tell me how to be kind to him?"

Dora held her breath. She recognized the shadow-life that could overtake Sally if she let it.

"I'm not the one to say, Sally. Maybe just get out of bed. Maybe if you hug Jay, you can cry together instead of separately. Maybe you can hold on to him and he can hold on to you. Right now, he's got nobody."

Sally listened.

"You know Cammy Otis is missing?" Dora said.

Sally drew in a long breath, letting it out in slow small puffs.

"I forgot all about Cammy Otis. Oh, my Lord, how is her mother doing?" She turned tired eyes up to Dora.

"Not well. But she is trying to help everybody find her girl."

"Wish I could help."

"You can."

Sally pushed her feet around to the side of the bed and sat there with her head down, long, dirty hair hanging to her shoulders "How? Show me."

"There's a question . . ."

Sally looked up, startled. She ran a hand through her hair and slid her bare feet to the floor.

"What kind of question?" she asked.

"About a summer job Cammy wanted. She put a flyer up at Draper's, put some in mailboxes. She asked around town. Somehow the summer job she got is connected to her disappearance."

Sally's eyes got big. "A summer job? You mean like . . . if Janice got a summer job and was keeping it from her dad—like that?"

"Yes, just like that."

Sally took a breath in and held it until it came shuddering out.

"She didn't want Jay to know,' she said. "Jay might get mad, you see. We need all the help we can get right here, in the orchard."

"What kind of work?"

"Gardening. She said she was going to be gardening for some nice people who lived a ways out of town. They told her she could come whenever we didn't need her."

"Did she say who they were?"

Sally shook her head. "She said it wasn't for sure yet. She was going to tell me more about it but then she didn't come home."

"And you never mentioned it to Jay?"

She shook her head again. "Janice didn't want me to. Her dad was strict with her. Now me . . ." She gave a small laugh. "With me she could get away with things. My girl and me often had our secrets. But I protected her. Ever since that bad mistake when she was little. I watched extra careful over her."

Sally stopped talking.

Dora listened hard for what should come next: maybe the truth.

There was a knock. Jay came in and stood just inside the door saying nothing.

Sally got out of bed and stood with her back to him. She found her slippers under the bed and was tying the sash on her robe when Dora put a hand on Jay's arm, then left, with Jay following behind her, trying to thank her for coming, stumbling over his words.

At the front door, Dora said, "She's fragile again, like she was that long time ago when your baby got hurt."

She turned to leave but couldn't help herself. The man's face was so needy.

"You didn't hurt her, did you, Jay? No matter what was said, it wasn't you who dropped the baby."

He looked frightened. He moved his arm away from holding the door. He stepped back, letting the door close on Dora.

She hurried to her car.

As she pulled out on to Shore Drive, she took a last look at the Root's house and yard. The sun had come out from behind the clouds, drawing long, gray shadows through the bare trees. The wind had died so nothing blew across the grass.

She wasn't any happier than when she'd arrived. Maybe worse. There was no guarantee that the Roots were going to make it. The secret they'd kept between them could still tear them apart.

Chapter 41

The layer of last year's leaves, slick and soft from that afternoon's rain, made walking through the thick woods difficult. Leaves and broken branches kept shifting underfoot, like something alive instead of dead.

Zoe, climbing over a fallen log, got her sneaker caught, sending her down flat on her face and coming up with a lot of swearing and damning anything that moved around her.

Jenny, ahead, couldn't help but laugh as Zoe untangled herself and stood, covered with dirt and leaves; a mushroom in her wild hair. "Great camouflage," she said, then was shamed by Kent helping, picking leaves off Zoe's blue sweater until she pushed his hand away.

"I can do it myself," she growled and gave him, and then Jenny, a look that normally stopped people from laughing at her—except people who knew her.

Once they were deeper into the woods, Kent wasn't sure which way to go. He made wrong turn after wrong turn, getting mad at himself until he finally stopped in the middle of a clearing, looking around in complete frustration.

"I know we're close," he said.

"Don't worry," Jenny assured him. He'd been certain they'd find Cammy's house beyond the last thick windfall.

"But that was it." He stood still, refusing to move. "Right there. I know that's where it was."

"Come on, Kent," Zoe urged. "We're probably close. Watch the ground. It'll start to slope if we're near a sinkhole."

He walked slower, searching left to right, talking under his breath.

Jenny considered giving up the hunt since nothing seemed to be coming of it. She exchanged a defeated glance with Zoe, who shook her head, knowing what Jenny was saying but not ready to stop.

"There!" Kent ran off ahead of them, going through the trees as fast as he could run, disappearing.

Jenny, the closest one behind him, was quickly out of breath. Zoe huffed and struggled behind her until they came to an edge where the ground slipped into a wild tangle of bushes, and then dropped out of sight.

Kent ran down through the thick brush, quickly disappearing then coming back into view, waving his arms at them. He leaped around, then pointed, to a kind of shelter, or lean-to made from dead branches.

"See?" He smiled broadly when they stood beside him. "I told you I'd find it."

Jenny stared at the lean-to. Thick leafless branches closely entwined to form a roof and walls.

Kent dropped to his knees and crawled inside, then yelled at them, "I told you so."

Zoe crawled in behind Kent. Jenny tried to follow, but wasn't as little as Zoe. She didn't fit.

"See?" Kent pulled wet comic book pages from the bare ground. "I brought this with me. It was a house present for Cammy. Spider-Man. I like Spider-Man. Cammy said she didn't like him so much but was happy to have the present."

It was dappled dark inside. Little light came in, except from places barren of leaves. Some of the roof branches had come loose and hung low, touching their heads. Brown and black leaves littered the bare earth beneath their feet.

At the back, where the branches were still thickest, there was a gray blanket—now filthy and wet—in a corner. Zoe picked up an empty Snickers wrapping. And, in a place dug into the hill behind them, Zoe pulled out a picture of a dinosaur, probably from Cammy's book—slick paper. Someone had written "tyrannosaur" in pen across the bottom.

"Could this be the dinosaur Cammy thought she'd be looking for?" She held the picture out to Kent, who shrugged his shoulders.

"Maybe. Looks like something she'd really like to find. Not the whole thing, just the bones. She would really like to find some of those old bones."

Zoe wasn't sure where to take her questions from there. What more could the kid know?

Rain came down hard for a brief period. Zoe shivered. Jenny, outside the lean-to, kicked at the leaves, overturning them, uncovering a brown paper bag, like a grocery bag—large—turned almost black from the rain.

Something more of Cammy's, Jenny thought as she poked the wet bag with her toe. She bent to pull it open since there seemed to be something inside. Maybe an animal had pulled it from the lean-to. Maybe it was nothing but garbage.

Jenny bent, wiped rain from her eyes, and opened the bag to pull out a dirty pink and white striped shirt. There was a pair of black tights in with the shirt. She pulled out a black skirt. Then a black jacket with a hood.

Jenny knew what she'd found. The clothes taken from Janice when she was forced to wear that old dress.

Zoe was beside her as she pulled each item from the bag and dropped them to the ground.

Jenny looked at Zoe. She asked, in a whisper, "Janice Otis?"

Zoe nodded, then shook her head. She moved close to Jenny's ear. "Don't say a word. Kent brought us here. Nobody else knew about this place . . ."

Jenny drew in a long, cold breath. "I can't just leave them . . ."

Kent was behind them. Jenny was on her knees, gathering the clothes into the torn bag while keeping her back hunched away from him. She wrapped them as best she could, then got up, turning from Kent.

"Whatcha got there?" he asked, when he saw Jenny clutching the wet paper bag to her chest. "You find a bag? What's in there?"

"Clothes."

"Oh, good. Must be Cammy's. She's going to need them when she gets back."

They walked up the side of the sinkhole the way they'd walked down, only it was much harder going.

Zoe considered the girls. Cammy—who wanted to dig for dinosaur bones. Janice—what would have brought her out here? Maybe it should be *who brought her here*?

A man. A friendly man who needed kids to dig for dinosaurs.

She looked over at Kent. Not this boy. He loved Cammy. Didn't seem to know Janice.

But the clothes . . . In Cammy's 'tent' in the woods . . .

The connection was there now.

A dinosaur dig where Cammy felt comfortable going with a stranger. And Janice?

Zoe looked around at the silent woods, quickly darkening, shimmering in the last light.

Everything had happened among these trees.

The girls were connected.

CAMILLE

She shivered because the blanket never did warm her completely and she was getting worn out from being cold. She wondered if they would ever let her go home, or maybe back to her house in the woods—she told him about that place and how she could stay there and never tell a single soul in the world that he'd put her down in this awful place.

She was lying. She would tell as soon as she could.

The man kept saying he wasn't going to keep her forever but she knew days were passing—at least she thought it had to be days. Maybe a week already. She couldn't keep count. When the sun didn't come up and didn't go down where you could see it, there was no way to say for sure if a whole day had passed or if it only seemed that long.

She just wouldn't play games and didn't pretend that she ever would play games with the lady. The lady was the one who said she disappointed them and told her to be nice. She didn't want to do any of the baby things they wanted her to do because she wasn't a baby and didn't like the awful lady although she sometimes acted like she wanted to be nice. Still, she called her Mandy. That wasn't her name.

Cammy tried to sleep, not knowing if it was night or day. She wondered if the sun was still coming up every morning, and what Mom did without a daughter to feed breakfast to. But that led her to think about how Mom was missing her, and that made her think how much she missed Mom and that made her cry.

Tears didn't come as fast as they did when she was first put down in this place that smelled like dirt. She thought maybe her tears were all drying up and she wouldn't have enough left for the rest of her life.

Only a few hours a day. That's what the man said when he called her *about the job. He would pick her up in the morning and take her home at night. And she would make a lot of money. That was how it was supposed to be in June, when her job was going to start, but she had to go with him the first day to check out the "job site" in the woods.*

She waited for the sound of that door to be pulled open because it meant they were bringing her food to eat and water to drink and she was always hungry and thirsty now because they only came once a day.

When the lady was with him, they stayed and talked and tried to get her to play games though she wouldn't, not even when they told her she was supposed to play, and not even when he got mad and hit her.

If she had a clock maybe she could tell if it was almost mealtime. Instead she thought about other things. Her toilet can was almost overflowing and smelled. The man would empty it when he came but he didn't wipe it out unless the other one told him to do it.

"She doesn't play anything," the woman complained. "She won't do anything right." And then the man said, "No more. Let's not get another one." And the woman would say, "You owe me that much. After what you did, they would put you in the electric chair, you know. If I told, they would take you away and kill you. Shoot electricity all through your body until you're dead. Is that what you want?"

And the man said, "No."

"Then leave us alone for a while. I want to talk to her in private."

He left them alone and the lady started talking to her in a very low voice, talking about when she grew up what friends they were going to be and maybe then they could get rid of HIM and go away where they could be happy.

She never answered the woman, only sat at the table, when she told her to sit there, with her face in her hands, one time moving the blindfold.

"You don't deserve my sister's teddy bear. I think I'm going to take him away this time."

She almost looked at her. She almost asked the woman not to take him. She would have nobody if she took the one-eyed teddy bear but she still wouldn't say a word,

When he came back down the lady said in a sad voice. "She's not right at all."

And then the lady went up the steps with him hurrying behind her. But she didn't take the teddy bear.

Part 6

"Let other pens dwell on guilt and misery."

—Jane Austen, *Mansfield Park*

Chapter 42

Friday morning. Jenny and Zoe were at the police station early but Ed Warner was gone.

"Went to Traverse after Jay Root identified the clothes you brought in. The medical examiner's going over them now. See if there's anything that could help find the . . ."

Deputy Flores bit at his lower lip. "Mr. Root got here early but the chief had to drive him back home after he saw the bag of clothes. Ed had to break the news to Sally. Ed said she took it better than he expected. Jay even had his arm around her when the chief left."

"Got to be those woods for sure." Zoe looked around the empty station. "We'll need a lot of people."

Flores nodded. "Chief's pretty upset. He said he didn't know which direction to go in next. Every inch out there has been covered again and again. Woods. Swamps."

He looked from Zoe to Jenny. "Both a you been out there. You know what it is. Every house's been searched. Wrecks and ruins and places people live."

"That doesn't mean she's not there," Zoe insisted. "We just haven't found her."

He nodded. "Chief's hoping something on the clothes might identify the man. Like a hair or a fingerprint on one of the shoes. Anything."

"Have to find him first," Zoe grumbled under her breath as Flores turned to take a phone call, then assure a woman at the other end he'd be out as soon as possible to get her cat out of a tree.

"Chief's got another search party lined up first thing in the morning. People coming in from Traverse City and Charlevoix. Even

Petoskey. They'll cover the whole territory. Best we can do. He's working as hard as he can and you know that meeting's tonight. Expecting a lot of people."

*　*　*

Back in Jenny's car, Zoe sat with her arms folded, mumbling from time to time, then frowning at Jenny. "What are we going to do?" she said.

"Think. You've got that big brain you're always bragging about. Come up with something." Jenny's voice held her frustration. "Can't ask Tony to help. That ankle's still bad. He pretends it doesn't hurt but I've see him wince."

"We need something else." Zoe shook her head. "My brain hurts."

Silence after Jenny started the car.

"I'm thinking we should go see Selma Grange again."

Jenny made a face at her. "You think Selma's got something to do with this?"

Zoe's "No" was short. "But she's lives out there. At least I'm calling."

Selma Grange answered on the second ring. Zoe told her about the discovery of Janice's clothes in Cammy's handmade house, at the bottom of a sinkhole not far from where Selma lived.

"Think I know the place." She didn't say anything for a while. "I'll keep looking . . ."

"Big search party out there tomorrow morning."

"Stop by my house and get me," she said. "I'll go with you." She was quiet. "I keep thinking there's something I should remember . . ."

Zoe slumped in the front set of Jenny's car. "We've got nothing. Smoke and mirrors, is all. There's Cammy's handmade house. There's her love of everything to do with those woods. There's the sense that dinosaur thing was a big moment for her. Then there's where the clothes were found. Looks like somebody could be trying to make us think the girls were together, or were friends—when we know they weren't. Like somebody's playing with us."

Eventually she shook her head, looking more depressed than she'd been earlier. "She's out there." Zoe pointed off in what could have been the direction of Cammy's woods. "I know it."

Chapter 43

Pamela came to the door in her robe, face gray, mottled red around her eyes.

"I don't know what it means." She went inside to sit in a chair, her back straight. "It puts the girls together, doesn't it? He knew about Cammy's hiding place and Janice's clothes were there—like a trail of breadcrumbs."

She looked up at them. "And there's no one out in the woods searching?"

"Ed took the clothes to Traverse. He's hoping something in them will tell us about the man who took her. Plenty of people are going out in the morning."

"That meeting's tonight." Her voice was bitter. "That's why nobody's looking for Cammy. I should go alone."

"And then we'll be out hunting for you instead of your daughter."

"It's the fucking money."

Terrible eyes looked from Jenny to Zoe. "Sorry," she said. "Didn't know I could say that word. I've been such a good girl all my life . . ."

Jenny put her hand out to take one of Pamela's.

"You fucking well deserve to say it," Jenny whispered, "And any other fucking word you can think of."

Chapter 44

The downtown streets were double parked by six thirty. Ed Warner stood in the middle of Oak, whistle blowing, arms waving people on.

Jenny stopped her car beside him.

"Got everything ready for morning?" Zoe called over to him.

"Seven o'clock. Nothing much on the clothes. ME found a couple of hairs. Got to check, see if they're Janice's or not. We're collecting evidence. Now all we need is the man."

He hurried off, blowing his whistle as one car triple parked.

Jenny went up one side street then down another, then around the block again, but still found not a single place she could squeeze her car into.

She tried Evergreen. She tried Maple. She headed for Walnut. It would be a little walk from there, but it was their only hope.

"There's Fitz's car." Zoe leaned up, nose to the window. She pointed to the shiny black Cadillac parked in front of the movie theater.

"You knew he was going to be here, didn't you?" Jenny asked. "It's his money we're fighting over."

She turned to Zoe. "You ever think, it's this two million dollars that's keeping all of us distracted from what we should be worrying about?"

She shrugged. "Makes you wonder, doesn't it? About all of us."

Zoe looked out at the sidewalk and the road filled with people. She slid back in the seat, shaking her head at the crowd of familiar faces.

Jenny got back into the line of traffic on Oak. The traffic jam was far worse around the town office building. People stood on the grass and some wove their way in through the big double doors.

Jenny stopped beside a double-parked car. "Nothing," she said.

"Phooey!" Zoe shook her head and pointed ahead. "Turn at the corner."

"We did that al . . ."

"Just turn."

Jenny turned.

Zoe pointed. "There, park up there."

"Says 'no parking.'"

"Don't pay any attention. That's Jim Sweet's place, isn't it? He sells porn flicks out of his garage; you think he's going to call the police? And if he did, who would come?"

"On your head." Jenny parked directly under the no parking sign. They half-ran back to the meeting, pushing through the crush of people standing outside the door, then confronting a bigger crowd in the lobby. Zoe yelled "Emergency!" People looked around to see where the voice was coming from then smiled down at her.

Once inside the larger office, filled tight to the door with chairs and all the chairs filled with townspeople, Jenny looked for Dora or Tony.

Dora sat up against a sidewall, holding on to two chairs next to Minnie, Dianna, then Gladys and Tammy—all in a row. Beside Tammy was Nathan Wickley, then Delia Thurgood, done up for the occasion with her hair dyed a brilliant white and set in curls piled on top of her head. She looked back and forth, over the heads of others, her patrician face saying she smelled something she'd never smelled before and wasn't liking it.

In the row behind them, Charles sat between Mary and Lady Cynthia Barnabus, with Tony next to Mary, deep in conversation.

"Come on." Zoe pulled Jenny between the rows of people, stepping on a few toes, leaving Jenny, behind her, to say: "Sorry" again and again.

Zoe pushed Minnie to move over so she could fit in. Jenny squeezed next to Dora, sitting halfway on the extra chair.

"Anything happen yet?" Jenny looked around at Minnie, who pulled her wide red skirt from under Zoe.

"Nope. But did you ever see a crowd like this for anything in Bear Falls? They're passing a box around for people's ideas. Looks to me like we'll be here all night."

Minnie sighed and pushed Zoe so she could claim more of the chair before dipping close to Zoe's ear. "You hear that Nathan Wickley invited me and Dianna over for dinner the other night?"

Zoe kept her eyes wide and innocent. "How'd it go?"

"Oh." Minnie waved a hand at her. "That man's crazy about Dianna. Bet he asks her out."

"How's Dianna feel about him?"

Minnie shook her head. "Not great, but wait until he starts showering her with presents. Then she'll see which side of her bread has butter on it."

"And how was the food?"

Minnie put a finger to her lips. "Don't say anything to anybody but I was expecting a lot more than meatloaf."

"Meatloaf? You're kidding."

She shook her head. "Tasted like Myrtle's, you ask me. Nathan said it was the cook's night off." She sniffed. "Guess when it's the cook's night off you eat anything you can get your hands on. What I did though, was tell Nathan that he would never have to eat meatloaf again if Dianna was around. Said she was a great cook."

Zoe laughed along with Minnie. "Dianna doesn't cook, Minnie. You lied."

Minnie's eyes went wide. "Now, don't you tell Nathan that. Really doesn't matter. You know as well as I do what men are interested in. And it's not meatloaf, I can tell you."

Dianna, who'd been half listening, leaned forward and snapped at Minnie. "*I'm* never marrying some puke like that guy." She shot her middle finger toward Nathan. "I'm marrying whoever I want to marry. It might be sooner than you think, Ma."

She turned away from them, leaving Minnie to explain under her breath that the girl wasn't thinking straight. "She's after the gardener. Can you beat that?"

"Heard about it. Jefferson Firestone. Wouldn't be a bad catch, but I think he's got maybe six years of college ahead of him."

Minnie leaned close. "Would you tell her that? I'd consider it a favor and I don't forget people I owe favors to."

Jenny scanned the room, watching from the corner of her eye as that woman in back of her hung on to Tony. Laughing up at him. Touching his cheek. Had to be that 'Mary' Dora talked about. Or warned about.

There was a stir at the front of the room. Keith Robbins walked in and raised his hands for quiet. Ladies in the front row turned around and shushed people behind them until the room was almost silent, except for a chair squeaking, a baby mewling, a whispering voice.

For the next five minutes Keith, looking much more harried than usual, explained why they were all there. When he mentioned that they sought ideas, or at least one grand idea they could all agree on for a wonderful, new addition to Bear Falls, everybody in the room clapped and whistled.

"Two million dollars, folks. Thanks to Mr. Dillon, our new neighbor out on Shore Drive." Keith shouted above the noise and pointed to a chair in the first row.

"And here he is, Fitzwilliam Dillon. Let's give him a hand."

People clapped as a head rose from among those in the front row. Fitz Dillon was helped to stand on a chair until, with Keith holding him by the arm, he was as high as he could get. He raised his arms.

Behind her, Zoe heard a man snicker. "Stand up," the man said under his breath. He and his friends laughed until Zoe looked around, shooting daggers their way.

At the front, Fitz turned his head from one side of the room to the other, giving a long whistle. "You all have ideas?" he asked, meeting with another round of applause. "Never saw anything like this."

"We're here for you, Fitz," Charles called from the audience.

Mary, next to him, whistled with two fingers between her lips.

"Why don't we get started? There's a microphone back there somewhere. People outside are sending in their ideas. We'll read them when we've exhausted this room. And if we don't get to all of you tonight, your ideas will be collected and considered until we put it to a final vote, what you want for this great little town."

Cheers and whistles and then the screech of a microphone.

"My name is Harold Roach," a deep male voice was first though Jenny could barely make out the man for all the people around him. "You know me from delivering your newspapers. What me and my wife were thinking was we could sure use a fine museum around here. With all the history we've got. I mean, from the Indians to the logging days and up 'til today, I think we need to . . ."

"Lots of museums around, Harold," someone at the back of the room shouted. "Don't need another one."

Harold turned to see who was yelling and hollered back, "Yeah, all little ones. They're here, there, and everywhere. Let's collect the stuff in one place. Show off who we are."

Another man called out, "Hey, Harold, we don't need no mummies. Need something that doesn't collect dust. How about a speedway? You know, so we can bring car races to town?"

Harold stepped, or was pushed, and a woman bent to the microphone. "My name is Angel Arlen and I can tell all of you . . ." Angel's voice was aggrieved. "I can tell you, Bear Falls needs a lot of things." Angel pushed her long blond hair back from her face and looked around the room. "But what it needs most is a new jail for all the hoodlums we're letting take over our town. A good big jail would keep all of us safe."

"Hey, Angel. Be big enough for that husband of yours?"

Angel turned toward the voice. "It's your boy that's the most trouble, Mason Folger." She shouted back at the man. "All we really need is a jail big enough for you and your other boys. Then we'd be safe. Saw Richard over in the park this week and . . ."

She was eased out of line by the town dowager, Abigail Cane, who stepped up to the microphone, causing the room to fall into a respectful hush.

The tall, imposing woman, whose family had, itself, given at least a million dollars to town charities—for good or bad, as she said often enough—cleared her throat. "Personally, though my family has also endowed the town from time to time, I would like to see Mr. Dillon's generous offer go toward infrastructure."

People around her looked at each other and shrugged, though no one dared catcall or complain.

"What I mean by 'infrastructure' is having our pot-holed roads repaired, our sidewalks repaved, our park re-sodded. I suggest we plant lovely maples along all of our streets until we are a veritable forest of trees. I suggest tubs of petunias by each and every downtown store, and new canopies—of a hundred different colors. We need charming streetlamps."

Trixie Donaldson of Trixie's House of Beauty, only slightly elbowing Abigail out of the way, leaned over the microphone and crooned in her best seductive voice, "What we all need is a dance club . . ."

Keith was on his feet, hands in the air. "This isn't for a single business. That's not what we're about. Please folks," he patted the air to quiet the grumblers. "Something for everybody. And not just for today, but for the future, for our children and our children's children."

Clyde Harrington of Harrington's Drugstore reached around Trixie, his bald head catching the overhead light as he stepped up to the mike. "Abigail's right. What we need are new sewers," which made the room erupt in boos. "Get the slightest rain and I've got water in my basement." He shouted over the noise. "New sewers is what we need."

Again Keith called for order. His face red, his stiff body screaming his frustration with how the process wasn't working. "Now, folks, let's give everybody their say, okay? We all want to get our two cents in so let's keep everything orderly. Okay? Can we do that? Keep it orderly?"

Dianna Moon came next, to a lot of whistles and mumbled threats from the mothers of the town. She stood very straight, in her almost nonexistent skirt and shrunken-down sweater, turning to where the remarks were coming from behind her, to eye the boys at the back of the room. "You guys just get your nerve up? Glad to see you can get something up. Hey, Richie. Yeah, you. I'm talking to you."

She flounced her body back around, which moved the tight sweater in ways a tight sweater didn't usually move. Leaning down to the mike, she said only, "Beauty school. That's it. We need a beauty school."

The Reverend Robert Senise, his wife, and seven children crowding around him, suggested a contemplation center. "Not Buddhist, mind you," the man, jostled by his little ones, looked out at the crowd with obvious wistfulness. "A lovely center where we can all go to sit in silence . . ."

Priscilla Manus of the Bear Falls Historical Society echoed the need for a local museum, followed by three women in a row who wanted a childcare center. Others stood to ask for a new playground. The coach at the high school said what Bear Falls needed was a stadium where their teams could play. Men around the room called out things about the Bearcats losing ways, which started a loud argument with parents of the boys who lost those games.

The room quieted when Dora stepped up to say how much the town needed a library. Heads bobbed agreement around the room. Others stood to second her idea until the fragile order in the room fell apart. Zoe crawled around and over people to pull the microphone down to say what the town needed was a big garden in the park, which brought hoots and hollers. Everybody in the room began yelling at each other, some not willing to wait to express their idea and some, in the back, just tired of standing so long and needing to get a little movement going.

As order in the room broke down, people took to grabbing the mike and shouting their ideas into it.

"New gym!" That was from the only body builder in town.

"Playhouse for our actors!"

"Grist mill down in the park. Let's use our falls for something."

"Waste disposal. That dump of ours draws bears."

Keith, mike in hand again, yelled for order though no one listened. People headed for the doors, pushing to get out before the riot started.

Ed Warner, in the back of the room, whistled over the yelling and arguing and pushing. A volunteer, right behind him, grabbed at arms and led people out the door and directly into another brouhaha going on outside.

Zoe, her head caught between somebody's belt buckle and somebody's wide hips, yelled at the top of her voice until a man reached down and grabbed her around the waist, pulling her up as high as he could.

Rather than kicking to be set free, she looked around into Tony's stormy face as he, still limping, moved her through the thinning crowd to a safe place outside, on the other side of the street, where he dropped her and told her to stay put. He headed back to join Ed moving people along, then putting two into the patrol car: Angel Arlen's son and a friend nobody knew but was later said to be a hooligan from out of town.

The building, and then the street, were cleared of the last hangers-on. Jenny ran to Zoe, out of breath. "I've been looking all over for you," she complained, bending toward her.

"Should've looked here."

"Dora went home."

"Good. I hope nobody got injured. What a mess!"

"Hmm.

"Your Tony saved my life . . ."

"You weren't in danger. I just talked to him."

"Really? Well, that's all you know. Anyway he told me to stay put until he came back."

"We're going . . ." Jenny look around then pulled keys from her jacket pocket, dangling them toward Zoe. "Want to take my car?"

"How am I supposed to see out the front window? You know I can't drive that thing."

"I forgot. Okay, I'll run you home."

"And where are you going after that?"

Jenny leaned down to whisper into Zoe's ear. "I had to get that awful woman off Tony. She kept yelling for someone to save her so I kind of dragged her to safety. Kind of. Now Tony wants to take me out for a drink to thank me."

Zoe made a noise. "Yeah. 'Thank you.' Sure. And I'm dumped."

"Not dumped. I said I'd take you home . . ."

"Yeah. Charity ride. No thanks. I'd rather walk."

"Don't be a . . ." Jenny's eyes were almost shut. Her hands were on her hips. "You're just a . . ."

"I'll take you to your home, Zoe," someone behind them said.

Fitz Dillon stepped from a dark place among the trees, and soon offered, again, to drive Zoe home.

"Sorry about all . . ." Jenny stretched her arm out, trying to apologize. "I've never seen our neighbors act like this before."

Fitz sighed. "Money. Money turns people into beasts. I should have known better."

"The last I saw of Keith he was tearing his hair out," Zoe said. "He's scared we've lost the two million."

Fitz, his out-sized face breaking into a smile, shook his head. "No way. Not for showing a little passion. I'm not giving up because the town needs so many different things. We'll think harder."

"No garden?" Zoe's eyebrows shot up.

"No swimming pool?" Jenny asked.

"I didn't hear that one asked for." Fitz tipped his head.

"I didn't have time," Jenny said.

After Jenny hurried to catch up with Tony, Fitz took Zoe's arm, drawing her along beside him.

She went without complaint, following as he led to a red sports car parked down a side street. He opened the door for her.

"Didn't you come in your Cadillac?" She hiked her body up and into the tiny seat.

"Charles took it. We've switched."

The ride to her home was quiet. Zoe was tired. Tomorrow they had to get back into the woods. Waiting chafed at her. She felt as if she should know where the girl was. *Which woods? A dinosaur dig?* It was a terrible, even a cruel, joke—that dinosaur thing. The man had picked any kid's dream.

Her hands closed. She beat them once on her knees. She'd never, in all of her life—despite some awful things she'd been through—been so unhappy with who she was. Incompetent. Inept. Devoid of ideas.

When Fitz pulled up her drive, she got out with only a grudging "Thanks."

She hurried inside to pick up a barking and leaping Fida and bury her face in the squirming dog's curly, smelly, hair.

* * *

At six thirty the next morning Zoe called Jenny.

"She's not home, Zoe," Dora said.

"Not home?"

"No. She and Tony had things to talk about."

"Really? Talk, eh?"

"Now, Zoe."

"Okay. I'll call over there and get them moving." She left Dora clucking and making other noises Zoe didn't have time for.

Tony's phone rang four times before he answered with a gruff, "Yeah?"

"Tell Jenny to get home. I'll meet her there."

Zoe called Pamela, praying she would answer.

"I'll pick you up at eight," she said, relieved Pamela wasn't out in the woods.

By seven thirty she was hurrying across to Dora's with Fida in her arms.

Chapter 45

Selma Grange led them directly to the ruined house with stone chimney, a lot of birds, and a Michigan basement. Since it was a familiar place to everyone but Pamela, it would be the start of their search.

"My mother knew the woods better than I did," Selma explained herself to Pamela as they stepped into the clearing. Pamela said little. She watched faces, and went where she was told to go. "Mother felt it was up to her to keep the history before it was ruined by summer people and strip malls," Selma went on.

As the four of them stepped into the clearing, everyone was quiet until Selma rubbed her hands up and down her arms. "There's nothing good about a house left like this."

Pamela stepped away from the others. She looked at the terrible, shattered house in front of her. She put a hand to her throat, took a deep breath, and screamed, "Cammy. Cammy! Cammy!"

To Jenny the ruined house seemed even more ominous than the last time she'd been there.

Small birds flew upward in flocks, but they didn't sing.

It was darker than before—the day, the sky, the clearing. There seemed to be a scrim of permanent shadow over everything.

Zoe shivered. First at Pamela's plaintive calling, then at the broken dollhouse in front of them. She turned to the others, hoping they didn't see and think what she was thinking: that Cammy couldn't be alive in that place.

Jenny grabbed on to Pamela, who staggered as she called her daughter's name.

Nothing but a single shred of curtain on the back wall moved, and a blue jay in the chimney—watching them.

With a compass in her hand, Selma went through the trees to the south, to the burned over clearing. Nothing but open space and overgrown weeds. Among the dead weeds were the same piles of charred boards.

Pamela stood in this clearing, as she had the last, crying out, "Cammy!" again and again.

"There's nothing here," Jenny took her arm and gently pulled. "Not even a house to search."

Pamela's eyes were wild. "How do we know where to look? Cammy could be anywhere. She's a roamer."

She darted past Jenny, who tried but couldn't grab her. She cried out Cammy's name then fell hard to the ground, sitting still until Jenny and Zoe got to her.

Her clothes were covered with soot. Her face was bleeding. Blood ran from a cut over her eye and another cut on her cheek. Pamela looked up at them, blinking as Zoe pointed to where her slacks were caught on a nail sticking from a board, blood running out around the nail.

Selma poked down into the tall grass, getting a hold under the board. With Jenny's help she lifted Pamela's leg from the nail as Zoe held her.

"You've got to go back." Zoe said to Pamela. "That leg should be seen to right away."

"I can't," Pamela whispered. "I feel her."

Jenny was on her phone "No signal. I better get her to town. Want to call it a day?"

Zoe shook her head. "Not me. What about you, Selma?"

"Me either. I'll stay with you. I know the woods."

With only the two of them left once Jenny and Pamela were gone the empty clearing looked larger. Nothing but grass, blackened boards, and a pile of dead tree limbs at the other end of the clearing.

They made their way out to H Road.

Tall, thorny branches formed thick walls along the road where they walked. Then mounds of raspberry bushes. They startled a doe that leaped in front of them and ran off down the road until she bounded back into the woods.

Zoe stopped, her feet hurting, her back aching, her breath coming harder.

Selma pointed to the other side of the road.

"There's a place through there," she said.

"How many after this one?" Zoe asked, her feet hurting. She wished for the first time in years that she was five feet ten with long legs and big feet and a sturdy body.

"You can't take much more, can you?" Selma said.

Zoe shrugged, not admitting to weakness.

"One more." Selma pointed ahead. "I haven't been here in years."

They climbed over large tree trunks in their way. They maneuvered around stumps. Selma forged ahead, walking slower and slower, waiting each time for Zoe to catch up.

The clearing was studded with circles of young maples. It led out to where fields of dead grass rolled away in front of them. The remains of a small cabin stood near the edge of the forest. The roof had fallen in on one side; on the other side lay a heap of rock—remains of a chimney.

Weathered logs outside the building lay at angles in places, one on top of the other, listing badly, about to give way.

"Cammy!" Zoe yelled though her throat hurt. She was calling in Pamela's place and didn't want to stop. She was thirsty. She was weak. She yelled again and again, until Selma put her hand on her arm, stopping her. Selma, in her dignified way, took over calling out Cammy's name.

Back on H Road, there wasn't anything left to say.

"Maybe one of the other groups found her." Zoe tried to sound hopeful. "Bet anything."

Selma Grange used to being alone and very still, said nothing. When they got to her house, Zoe called Jenny to ask about Pamela.

"The hospital wants to keep her," Jenny said. "Those nails were old and rusty. She didn't remember when she had her last tetanus shot."

"Anything new on Cammy from the others?"

"No," Jenny said and soon hung up.

CAMILLE

"Cammy!"

She heard her name and sat up on the bed and answered back, but then there was nothing. She answered back one more time just in case it was real and somebody was calling her.

After she answered she lay down and hugged the bear up near her chin. She went on listening because, when the people weren't there, she didn't have much to do or much to think about anyway. Sometimes she thought about the stories she would write when she was older. Then she thought about Kent and wondered if he would want to marry her so she could have a baby.

She took a deep breath, then coughed, then squeezed her eyes shut against the light that burned on the far wall, burned forever, even though sometimes it went out. It always blinked back on. When the light went out it scared her because it was the only light where she was and when the light went out she heard things scraping at the places the air came in, and she heard sniffing and sometimes, on one day, she heard rain or something like rain, but faraway.

The light always came back on.

When she thought she heard her name again, she crawled off the bed, pulling that awful, smelly dress around her body so she didn't trip on it, and went to the place where cold air came in above her head and listened as hard as a person could listen. Maybe a person could call back and be heard here, like when she was in the woods and she answered the crows. She knew their calls and felt safe because it was almost like having someone to talk to. But not down here. The crows didn't hear her or they just didn't answer.

Part 7

"What is right to be done cannot be done too soon."

—Jane Austen, *Emma*

Chapter 46

When the doorbell rang, Zoe could barely move her legs from the sofa. Her feet hurt, swollen into lumps of flesh with little bumps for toes.

Selma Grange stood on Zoe's porch with what looked like a stack of notebooks clutched to her chest.

"I found something," she said immediately, pulling the screen door toward her, entering the house.

"Aren't you tired?"

"Of course." Selma looked surprised. "What has that got to do with anything?"

Zoe shook her head. "Nothing," she groused. "Nothing at all."

She pointed to a chair, inviting Selma to sit. "I'd ask if you want coffee but I'm staying off my feet."

Selma shook her head. "I don't need anything."

Selma held out the pile of notebooks to Zoe.

"My mother's diaries. She wrote in her diary every day. What I didn't realize until I found them in her closet, was how many years she'd kept them. Way back before I was born. A lot of history."

Zoe couldn't help the yawn she had to stifle. She'd passed being tired a long time ago. All she wanted to do was sleep and not think. And especially not talk. But the woman had come to help.

"This might not be the right moment for a history lesson, Selma. I appreciate your coming back but . . ."

Selma slapped her hands on the notebooks.

"There's something in here. My mother wrote about a tragedy that happened back fifty years ago. There was a child, a little girl, found dead in her bed. She was found with a blanket wrapped around her head. Asphyxiated." She pulled a folded newspaper sheet from the pages of the top diary, opened it, flattened it against the notebooks in her lap; then handed it to Zoe.

"Read this. I don't know if it has anything to do with the missing girl, but the family is from out here. The article says H Road, that's where we were most of today. Just H Road. No address."

She went on, jabbing her finger at the diary. "I thought . . . what they said about Janice Otis. Asphyxiated, you know. When I read that . . ." She nodded toward the paper in Zoe's hands. "Such a strange word, don't you think?"

The newspaper was soft, almost skin-like, against Zoe's fingers. The date on the page was August 3, 1967.

A grainy photograph showed a man and a woman standing beside a girl who looked about eleven or twelve. Behind the girl, a boy of about nine or ten half-hid his face.

The man was identified as Thomas J. Whitsome, a hefty man in overalls with a cap pulled down over his eyes. His face was in shadow. Standing beside Thomas J. Whitsome was Mrs. Whitsome in slacks and a nondescript blouse. The children weren't named but the girl had curls reaching to her shoulders. She stood taller than her brother.

Zoe smoothed the old article between her hands and bent to look closer, and then to read that Mandy Whitsome, the five-year-old daughter of Mr. and Mrs. James J. Whitsome of H Road, had been found dead the day before in her bed. The ministering doctor, Andrew Lorde, said the child died of asphyxia from getting tangled in her blanket as she slept.

The article went on to give the family's history in the area. From Chicago, Illinois. Came in the early fifties, due to Mr. Whitsome's desire to bring the cause of Survivalism to Michigan's back woods. James Whitsome taught classes in the Survivalist Philosophy at the local library in Petoskey, talking about not only the enemies of the United States of America and what the world would be like after the bomb dropped, but the practicalities of survival, keeping a family alive—with instructions on building a workable bomb shelter to protect loved ones until the radiation was gone.

And then the writer went on, how Mr. Whitsome talked about beginning the world again . . .

Zoe looked up at Selma with her mouth open.

Selma nodded. "The man was a survivalist. He taught people how to build bomb shelters. There must be a bomb shelter out where that house is."

Zoe nodded. "No address. How will we find it?"

Selma lifted her head, sticking her narrow nose in the air. "Let me read you what my mother wrote after that."

Selma opened the top notebook, turning to where a bookmark rested between the lined pages.

Such a dark day. That dear little girl with a sunny face and curls and her little twisted arm. I can't bear to think of what's being whispered through the houses in the woods. Dear God. They're saying that it was her brother who killed her. Marty Tollis saw bruises on the poor child. That's what I heard said today. And that the mother said to Marty it was just her kids playing rough, nothing else. But everyone knew about the brother. They said he tortured the little girl. I can't bear to think he killed her. What will his life become, knowing what he's done? And how will his sister ever forgive him?

"You see what I'm saying? Something wasn't right about . . ."

Zoe's mind raced, setting square pegs into round holes, then mixing up the pegs and starting over.

"You don't know exactly where these people lived?" she asked.

Selma shook her head. "Mother knew them, or at least heard the gossip. I went through all of her journals. She never mentions them again."

Zoe looked at Selma and closed one eye. "How do we find that house?"

"The Register of Deeds in Charlevoix," Selma said, then nodded.

"We can go first thing in the morning. Find which house on H Road belonged to the Whitsomes." Selma tipped her head back and smiled a calming smile.

Zoe slipped from the sofa to her feet, which didn't hurt as much as before. She found her phone and called next door. Zoe explained to Dora that Selma Grange was in her living room, they needed help again, in the morning, and could Jenny come over about eight to go to the Register of Deeds in Charlevoix with them?

Dora didn't ask a thing. She said that Jenny was at Tony's but she would call right then and have her at the county offices when they opened.

"Tony's again?"

"They seem to have a lot to talk about."

"Phooey."

"It's her life, Zoe."

"Of course."

"What she wants to do with it is up to her, not us."

"I know, Dora. But . . ."

"No 'buts' about it," Dora said. "Let's keep our minds on Cammy Otis. One calamity at a time."

When Zoe hung up, she didn't know whether to laugh or cry. But Dora was right. One calamity at a time.

Selma left, though Zoe urged her to stay the night.

"I'm up early. I'll be waiting at the Register's office when they open." She hurried down the steps, diaries back under her arm.

Zoe sat in her living room until after midnight. Fida snored in her lap while Zoe thought again and again about a bomb shelter. Probably fallen in years ago. Probably nothing but a hole in the ground by now.

Then why hadn't any one of them—out searching day after day—fallen into it? Why hadn't someone mentioned a big hole in the ground?

She grabbed up Fida, who gave her a sleepy, one-eyed look, hugged her again and again and kissed the top of her hairy little head.

Cammy Otis, hidden in a terrible hole in the ground.

Zoe shuddered.

She went to bed, Fida under her arm, hoping to hurry the morning.

Chapter 47

A uniformed man unlocked the door of the Charlevoix County offices on State Street promptly at eight.

Selma, Jenny, and Zoe were waiting in the hall, Jenny going over the diary entries. They filed inside, and asked for the Register of Deeds, to be directed down a narrow hall to a chest-high counter, waiting until a pleasant woman in her late sixties came from her desk to ask if she could help.

Zoe, who couldn't see a thing, stood on her toes but could only wiggle her fingers until the woman looked over the edge. She gave a surprised, "Oh" then frowned at Selma and then at Jenny as if they were playing a trick on her. She asked Jenny what she could do for them.

"We're looking for the owners of a piece of property on H Road."

"If you could give me an address . . ." The woman said, standing on her tiptoes to look over the counter's edge again.

Zoe, being more patient than usual, smiled up at the woman. "We don't have an address," she said nicely then pulled in a deep breath.

"May I have your name, please? I like to know who I'm working with."

When Zoe gave her name, the woman's face went through a series of transformations, ending with a big smile. "You're the writer. Of course, my sister lives in Bear Falls. Grace Prather? She loves your work. And so do I. Very exciting to have you living nearby. I have to tell you, Grace drove me passed your house when I was down last time. I'm coming back in June. I can't imagine what your gardens will look like then. I hear you've got fairies."

She would have gone on but Jenny broke it up. When Zoe was

flattered, the talk of flowers and fairies might go on for hours. "Ma'am. I don't mean to interrupt but you see we need to find the owners of this property. There's been a murder and a kidnapping . . .'

"Oh, yes, I read about it. Terrible thing. Grace was telling me the whole town is on edge, thinking they've got a killer right there in their midst."

"We don't know exactly where this property is but it's important." Jenny did her best to keep the woman on track.

"Well, certainly. If you could give me a name, or property description . . ."

"James Whitsome. On H road."

The woman wrote down the name and the road and walked away. They waited.

A half an hour passed before the woman was back, paper in her hand.

She laid out a plat map on the counter with Zoe jumping, trying to see until the woman invited them in back, laying the map on a table and leaning forward, her finger on the map.

She smiled at Zoe. "You know the house burned down?"

Zoe only looked at her.

They all gathered close, Selma placing her finger on her house—at the corner of Orrin and H Road, and then back up the map.

"Tollis. That's the house with birds in the chimney. I remember that name now," Selma said.

The woman assured them that the Tollis family still owned the property though they only paid taxes on the land since the house had no value.

The woman moved her finger along the road, then in. "This next piece . . . ? That's where the Whitsome home was. I didn't know the name. Something happened there. I was in my teens. A terrible tragedy. In was in all the papers. We lived down Road G then, pretty close by."

"About a little girl?" Jenny asked.

The woman nodded. "A very sad event. I've never forgotten it. The child died with a blanket wrapped around her face.

"If I remember . . ." Her face wrinkled as she thought. "The fire was not long after the little girl died. The family moved away. Nothing left. With the death of that little girl, well, you wouldn't expect them to stay and rebuild."

"Do you remember the other children in the family?"

The woman thought, then nodded. "I think so. I didn't know them. They weren't in kindergarten with me. Maybe taught at home. A lot more of that now—homeschooling. Truthfully, I worry about kids who don't get out of their houses and . . ."

"The house burned down." Zoe looked from Jenny to Selma, memories of charred beams and soot working through her head. And boards with nails sticking out.

"Were there any other structures on the property?" she asked the woman.

"You mean like a barn?"

Zoe shook her head. "I mean like a bomb shelter."

The woman smiled, then shrugged. "Really? That's what you're looking for? Seems odd. But I can tell you, back then, if a man who lived in the woods wanted a bomb shelter he didn't come in for a permit. Doubt we even had such a thing."

"Was the property ever sold?" Zoe asked.

"Not that I could find. It looks as if somebody in the family still owns it. Taxes are in the Whitsome name."

She looked down at her paper again. "People live in Chicago. The names are . . . let me see here." She turned the small piece of paper around to show them. "Whitsome. Yes. Same family. Probably the kids. Says Nathan and Delia Whitsome."

Chapter 48

Jenny drove.

They barely spoke.

Zoe slumped in her seat. She stared at the dashboard

It had to be there: somewhere on that property—a father's bomb shelter.

Brothers and sisters—not old friends. Both from Michigan.

A little girl dead of asphyxia. Blanket over her face . . .

Zoe shook her head, hoping it would reorder her thoughts.

The killer had narrowed it down for them, where Cammy's clothes were found, Cammy's favorite places—the stick house in a sinkhole. Janice's clothes found there.

There were the notes from a mother's diary:

They're saying it was her brother who killed her . . .

What will his life become, knowing what he's done?

. . . how will his family forgive him?

She shook her head hard—holding on to pictures and words:

A twisted arm . . . Mandy Whitsome.

A crooked leg . . . Janice Root.

A crooked . . . What? Zoe asked herself. Because Cammy was different?

Was that all she could come up with?

And a house that burned.

A girl in the newspaper photo—all those curls.

A short boy in the shadows . . .

Zoe put her fingers to her forehead, massaging thoughts into place. No motive. Nothing to say *this* is why their little sister, Mandy, died and the family went to pieces.

Who was this man and this woman that they would come back to Michigan to kill two girls they didn't know? How was it connected to the long ago death of another girl?

Nathan was looking for property—as if he didn't own any up here. As if he didn't have a history . . .

And *Whitsome*, not Wickley, not Thurgood.

Delia said she'd never been to Michigan before.

Everything a lie. Even their names.

"Call Tony?" Zoe turned to Jenny.

"Better do that." Jenny slowed as a raccoon waddled across the road.

"Damn!" she said, eyeing the rearview mirror, making sure Selma saw her brake.

"What about his ankle?"

Jenny made a face. "It won't be only his ankle hurting if we leave him out of this."

Zoe dialed, worrying: *An old bomb shelter. Where would they look? After all these years . . . What if those two were out there already? What if it was time for Cammy to die the way Janice did?"*

Jenny drove faster, turning from U.S. 31 on to Orrin, heading deep into the woods.

Tony answered. He listened, then said he was on his way. "Give me about twenty-five minutes, okay? And don't go down to that place by yourselves."

"We'll be at Selma's. Orrin and H Road."

"You sure about all of this? I can't imagine those two . . . We're talking murder and kidnapping. Liars—yeah, I can see that but we're talking murder."

Zoe stopped him. "There's so much more."

"Okay. I'll call Ed."

"I'm calling him now. He's got to stop those two from coming out here."

The phone went dead. No signal. She couldn't make another call.

Jenny pulled into Selma's yard and parked in front of the lilacs, now in tight, purple clusters. Selma parked behind them.

In the house, Zoe barked into Selma's phone, "Ed. Glad I got you. Me and Jenny are at Selma Grange's house. Orrin and H Road. Tony's on his way. You've got to get over to Fitzwilliam's place and arrest Nathan Wickley and Delia Thurgood."

"What am I arresting them for?" Ed Warner's voice was slow.

"Murder. And kidnapping."

"You sure about this? That's a lot to put on that nice couple." Ed's voice slowed even more.

"I do." She told him what they'd found in Charlevoix. "They must have Cammy. Or, at least, they had her."

"Bomb shelter, eh? Haven't heard about one of those in years."

"We're going to find it."

"Can't arrest them on nothing."

"I told you—they lived out here. Delia Thurgood and Nathan Wickley. Both of them. They're brother and sister."

"Can't arrest them for that."

"Chief. Please, stop them. Hold them on anything you can think of until we find Cammy."

"Okay. I'll head over to the Dillon place, see what I can come up with. But don't you ladies go out there alone. I'm tellin' you, Miss Zola . . ."

She hung up. Her head was pounding.

Another phone call. This time to Fitz.

"Zoe Zola? I was going to call you this morning. What's going on? Have you found the girl yet?"

There were noises from the other end of the phone, along with a slipping away of sound. Fitz was back. "My breakfast just arrived. Do you know it's only nine o'clock?"

"Most people are out of bed by now. Look, Fitz, I have to ask you something. It's important."

"I hope you don't mind if I chew my toast in your ear."

"Did you know that Nathan and Delia own property up here, together?"

There was a very brief pause. "Really? No, I didn't know, but I suppose they could. Old friends, you know. They never spoke of investing together, but I've shared investments with people I didn't know at all. It's the sort of thing one does, you know, when you have the money. But . . . just a minute . . . didn't Nathan say he was out looking for a piece of property."

"This property is deep in the woods."

He hesitated, thinking. "I knew Nathan was from Michigan, but Delia's from New York. I find that odd that they wouldn't say anything. I'm sure she told me she'd never been to Michigan before. Yes, I'm sure that's what she said."

"On this deed she's listed as Delia Whitsome."

"That can't be right. Whitsome? Maybe from a previous marriage though I don't remember her ever being called Whitsome." He thought awhile. "No. I'm sure I've never heard the name before."

"Nathan's listed as Whitsome, too."

"What? Not Wickley?"

"Could you do me a favor, Fitz? Could you see if they're still in your house? We're going out to that property and . . ."

"But I'm not dressed, Zoe. Anyway, I never see them before eleven."

"Just go, okay? Trust me. I need to know."

"Oh, well," he said.

He was gone.

And gone a long time.

When the phone was picked up again, there was an odd hesitation, a long breath.

"They're not here. This is very early for the two of them to be up and out. I can't imagine . . ."

"That's all I need to know."

"No, wait. You said they share the same last name."

"Whitsome," she said.

Fitz took a while to think. "I checked his room. It's empty. His bed hasn't been slept in. I checked her room. It looks as if two people slept there. I mean, two pillows with identical head dents. Do you think that's strange? My father knew them so long ago. He was their attorney. He should have known if they were married."

"Maybe he didn't know them well enough."

"Zoe. Do you mean the two are man and wife? Why . . . ?"

"Not man and wife, Fitz. They're brother and sister."

"Oh dear. Maybe that's more than I wanted to know."

"Ed Warner is on his way to your house. Tell him those people are gone. He should call Tony Ralenti and then get out here as fast as he can. Selma Grange's house. H Road and Orrin. Please remember . . ."

"Can't you tell me what this is about? I mean, other than the awful thing it looks like?"

She hung up.

CAMILLE

The light went out. Like the sun going down—but a lot faster. She could see and then there was nothing to see, only what she could feel—the blanket, the teddy bear, her skin.

The light had gone out before but it always came back on so all she had to do was wait.

She wondered why her throat hurt. Maybe she was coming down with something though she hardly ever got sick. Anyway, if she just went to sleep everything would be okay when she woke up.

Or never okay again. And nobody would let her out. But she wouldn't have to see them—not ever.

Something inside her was sure. Sure enough. They weren't ever coming back. They didn't like her and she didn't play her part the way they wanted. But she wasn't anybody called Mandy, who the woman said had a crippled arm. She couldn't be somebody else just because that man hurt the little girl and the lady didn't like that and she said she would never forgive him.

She was closed up in this big cement box, and it hurt to breathe. She couldn't hear things outside the way she used to be able to hear things out there. And used to feeling air coming in.

She couldn't think about death because she didn't know exactly what it was, but it had to be a lot like sleep.

Better to let it all go and sing to the teddy bear.

Rock-a-bye baby . . .

Part 8

"How little of permanent happiness could belong to a couple who were only brought together because their passions were stronger than their virtue."

—Jane Austen, *Pride and Prejudice*

Chapter 49

Zoe couldn't tolerate Selma's house. She paced, but there was no room, too much polished furniture, and even though she was small she couldn't pace far enough in one direction before she had to turn and begin again.

And other things in the way—throw rugs, and magazine holders, and wastebaskets. Every breath she drew, every step she took, diminished her. Every minute she wasn't running down the road to look for a bomb shelter was too long a minute to waste.

"I'm going out," she yelled at the women in the kitchen, then left before they could tell her to stay where she was.

Outside, under the arbor—the rose bush filled with tiny red buds—she could at least breathe in and fill her lungs. She was in the midst of flowerbeds and new blooms and greening grass. She took steps toward H Road.

Once on the road, she paced one way and then the other along the verge, stopping to hold her breath and listen for a siren or the motor of a truck.

She paced again, stopped, listened, but heard nothing. A slight breeze came up. The leaves shook. A bird cried far off. Another answered.

This was why she didn't live in the country, she told herself. Nothing and nobody. All kinds of terrible things could be going on and there wasn't anyone near to see or hear. One big, blank canvas where awful things could be written.

She stood at the corner of H Road and Orrin. Damned trees. Damned bushes in every direction. She put a hand to her chest, feeling for her heartbeat. It was too much to have to wait for other people to do what they were supposed to do. *Too much.*

She closed her fists and pushed them into her thighs.

Asphyxia. The word pounded through her head. *Asphyxia.* An old bomb shelter, from back when everybody was afraid of nuclear war.

She stood still, thinking. How did they get air into one of those things? They were afraid of fallout. But it couldn't be all closed up. What about filters? What about generators? She turned to walk along Orrin Road, her eyes straining to see if anything moved down that way. She hoped for a police car, She took a few more steps.

Asphyxia . . .

She went back to H Road.

She started to run on her little short legs.

If Nathan and Delia were gone, so was Cammy. One way or another.

The thought made Zoe run faster. She knew exactly where she was going.

Chapter 50

Not a branch moved as Zoe passed. There was an eerie stillness around her, as if the trees watched. She could hear the sound of her sneakers tapping along the packed dirt as she moved, still much slower than she wanted to move for fear of toppling into the hardened mud.

One foot up, the other down. She ran and breathed but didn't dare think of what she was running toward. It could be too late. Maybe Cammy Otis was already dressed in an old white dress and about to be dropped beside U.S. 31.

She thought of a bomb shelter again. Of course there had to be a way to get air in and a way to get used air out. And a way to stop the air all together.

Janice Root's air was cut off. She'd died a horrible choking death in a dark, underground grave.

Then why not leave her there, where she died? Who would have found her?

Because there was another girl to take her place. And that girl had to breathe, until they didn't want her to breathe any longer.

Tears ran down her face when she burst through the trees into the burned over clearing. Her legs were on fire. She bent to catch her breath.

The clearing was empty. Zoe lifted her head and looked around, harder than she had before. Piles of timbers pushed up hillocks of grass. Everywhere, there were boards blackened with soot. In some places the ground had buckled, cracked and broken open. But which hillock could hide a bomb shelter?

Taking deep breaths, she stepped forward. Her foot hit a board and, when she turned it over, long nails stuck out. That could be the whole clearing—a landmine of nails and burned boards. She could be hurt the way Pamela had been hurt.

She skirted the place where the house must have been, nothing but a depression in the ground where timbers lay or stood on end, covered over with tall, dead grass. Heading around toward the place where the woods opened and empty fields moved up and down small hills, she walked slower, even more carefully, though her brain screamed at her to hurry. She stopped every few feet to lift boards and look beneath, to see if there was anything buried. She moved on until her arms ached and her hands and clothes were filthy with soot.

She looked around her. There was nothing. Or maybe she was too short to see. Or not smart enough to figure it out.

She stood in place, among the yellow grass growing to above her head. She looked one way and then another, and then again,

In one direction, back toward H Road, she could see that the grass was disturbed, partially beaten down. Maybe when they'd come through—not knowing there was anything to be careful of.

She turned in the other direction, toward the very back of the clearing, where the woods began again. The grasses were disturbed in that direction, too, even more than toward H Road.

She walked along the line of flattened grasses. They formed a path. The path led—as far as she could see—to nothing but a pile of old, dead brush.

She stood in front of the brush pile looking over the dead trees limbs.

No vines wove themselves through the branches. No grasses filled the spaces between limbs. Zoe picked up a branch and dragged it off to the side. And then another. They weren't twisted together or stuck to one another. They weren't too large for her to move. The branches had been laid out as if in a pattern—one branch carefully set atop the next. Easy to pull aside, and easy to re-pile, especially if someone wanted to hide something.

She pulled the last of the tree limbs away. A large, very wet cardboard lay beneath, a cardboard with an indentation in it—as if it had molded itself around something below.

She tugged the cardboard out of the way, wiping her hands along the sides of her khaki pants. A large, metal square lay buried in moss-covered concrete. A set of handles lay folded within the square. An opening to something. Maybe a well beneath. Maybe a root cellar. Maybe . . .

She tugged at the handles but they didn't move.

She stepped back to see how whatever lay beneath the handles was configured under the ground. She pushed her fingers through the dirt and moss, down to something hard. Concrete. She knelt and crept along feeling the cement as it continued until she was at an edge. She turned a corner—still on her knees, hand over hand—until she came to a place where the ground dipped down, as if deliberately cut away. She moved her small hand into the depression in the earth, dug her fingers through wet leaves, then ran her fingers over a cold steel rectangle before laying on her stomach, coming nose to nose with a metal grate screwed into a cement wall. When she explored the surface of the metal she felt holes. When she poked a finger into one of the holes, she hit more metal. If this had been a metal window, or an air duct— it was closed.

She bent as close as she could get to the grate. "Cammy Otis!" she called.

"Cammy Otis!" she called again, then turned her head, expecting a reply but hearing nothing.

Zoe scrambled back to her knees. She needed to know how big the shelter was so she walked along, bending every few feet, feeling for cement.

She turned corners. There were three more metal grates. They all should have been rusted shut. They shouldn't have felt oily. Zoe estimated that whatever was beneath her ran to about fourteen feet long and twelve feet wide.

Down on her knees again, she called into another closed grate: "Cammy!"

Wiping her hands along the sides of her jeans, Zoe sat back to think.

She could wait for the others to arrive—but if the girl was down there with no air, she could be dying, or dead. The grates, the metal door—they seemed used enough. The pile of boards and branches, over the top, hadn't fallen naturally but were collected, laid in sequence to hide the entrance.

And the trail leading through the grass from the road . . . of course people had been out here.

Zoe ran back to the metal door, and put her hands around one handle. She pulled. She pushed. It wouldn't budge. She was too small for a job like that.

Too small . . .

Too small . . .

She tried again. Pulling until the handle lifted a little.

She couldn't hold it. She hunted for a slim board, a thin branch. Something she would use as a wedge.

The perfect thing—solid branch, but split in half. She tugged at the handle until she could push the branch beneath the door—just a little.

More flat boards and broken branches. She pulled again, and pushed a board beneath. Another. Another. Until the handle was up and the door beneath halfway open.

Bigger branches to open it farther. And then a final tug bringing the door up and over, with a clank to the cement behind it.

She sat at the edge, dangling into the opening until she felt a ladder or set of metal stairs underfoot.

She was through the opening. Her shadow lay across the floor below, hazy sun reflecting down around her.

She held on to the ladder and bent to see what she could see. Below, at the foot of the ladder, a body lay on the floor.

"Cammy. Cammy Otis," she called out only to hear her own words come back at her. She started down the ladder, one foot at a time.

"Cammy." Near the middle of the ladder she bent forward to see if the body moved. It was still. She could see it was a young girl, a young girl in a long white dress.

Zoe hung on to the ladder, feeling for the next rung when her foot slipped and her leg went off into space. She fell, bumping from rung to rung until she hit the cement floor and lay there, beside Cammy Otis. Her left leg was caught up around the ladder; her right leg lay crumpled beneath her.

Chapter 51

Jenny ran along the side of the road, fear driving her faster than she imagined she could run. Her feet pounded the uneven surface—deep holes and ridges from car tires. Over and over again she stumbled, thought she was going down, then righted herself—arms wheeling.

She should have seen Zoe by now: puffing and struggling along, short arms pushing back and forth. How fast could she run, after all? *How fast?* She hoped to hell it was fast enough—no matter who was out there.

She was in her head. Panic drove her blindly; she almost didn't hear a car coming down the road behind her. She stopped, animal caution kicking in, jumping out of the road to blend with the trees.

Tony. Or Ed Warner. One of them. But no siren. No urgency.

She planned to run out and stop the car but caution made her stay where she was; a shadow among shadows.

A black car stopped ahead, pulling to the side of the road. Nothing happened for a while and then car doors opened and slammed shut.

She heard a woman's voice.

Not Selma Grange's voice but a high-pitched, affected voice.

Jenny slid to the ground, using an oak tree as a shield.

"I told you she wasn't right to begin with. If only you listened . . ."

Delia Thurgood's voice filled with disgust. "If only you were a real man. Instead of a weak brother."

"She's dead by now," Nathan was saying.

The pair passed within a few feet of where Jenny lay.

"So unnecessary," Delia said. "If only you could fix what you did to Mandy. How many times . . . My poor Mandy. What you did to

302

her! The least you can do is make *me* happy. You promised you'd give her back. And look at all of this. You burned it down. No wonder Mother and Father hated you. Stupid. Cruel. You always promise but . . ."

They were in the clearing.

Jenny watched as they moved out of the trees, avoiding half-burned boards. They walked to the other side of the clearing, along a barely visible path.

Jenny tried to see ahead of them, to where they were going. But there was nothing but branches. Where would a bomb shelter be?

At the far end of the clearing, something dark stuck up from the ground. She got on her knees to see better, then fell back as Delia and Nathan turned, their eyes searching the woods.

They might have caught her. She had choices—get up and run like hell or confront them, knowing that Tony or Chief Warner would be there soon.

Or stay where she was.

She lay on her back. Zoe must have heard them and was hiding, as she was. Or maybe she was in the bomb shelter. Where they were headed.

Jenny was watching when the Whitsomes began to run. Nathan led then stopped abruptly, pointing at the ground then motioning for Delia to come see what he'd found. As they stood side by side, their voices came back to Jenny in high, angry words she couldn't understand. They were arguing. Delia's voice was louder than his, escalating to a scream. "Your fault! Jealous! That's what you've always been. Jealous. Jealous. Jealous. You . . . you ugly . . . Now look. Somebody's down there."

Jenny held her breath. She realized that the bomb shelter was real, and it was open, there, at the Whitsomes' feet.

If she could calm down she'd know what to do . . .

They'd gone directly to the shelter. They'd lived here once—until a little girl died and the house went up in flames. They knew the place well. They knew where to hide the girls he kidnapped.

Delia's words were clanging inside her head: *Jealous. Jealous. Jealous.*

Jenny rubbed her forehead trying to get her thoughts in a row— put one thing she knew after another. A line of truth.

Delia was the force here, not Nathan. He supplied little Mandys for her. How many others had there been?

She put her head up to look again. They were both busy at the bomb shelter, bending forward. She heard the clank of the door and then Nathan screamed, "Leave it! There's someone with her. We've got to get away."

"No! No! No. Idiot. We can't leave it for another person to find."

"We'll come back later. They'll both be dead. We can leave them."

"No. No. No. They'll rot. It'll be ruined and we'll never find another place like this to keep them. We have plans."

Nathan grabbed her arm and pulled. He talked softly now, but Delia, arms filled with branches, wanted to cover the door to the shelter. She screamed at Nathan and began running back and forth: pulling branches into place to hide the door below.

Nathan watched her.

Chapter 52

When the overhead doors crashed down behind the man and the concrete shelter went dark, Zoe crawled from the corner where she'd hidden. He knew she was down there. He'd cursed her. The door was shut.

She couldn't move her leg, only drag it. The pain was terrible. She would never get back up the ladder. Soon there would be no air. She would be gasping for breath and then her brain would die.

Others might never find the bomb shelter.

Asphyxiation.

"Are you still here?" A small voice called.

It came from behind the stairs.

Zoe sat up, but that brought a groan.

"Cammy?" Zoe said softly, then heard a gasp. "Are you all right?"

"Who are you?"

"Zoe Zola. Remember me? I bought candy from you last fall. You were making money for the future nurse's club."

The girl was quiet a long time. She coughed. "I remember. You were very nice. And I wasn't even in the future nurses club, you know."

She coughed again.

"Are you okay?"

"It's so cold in here now. My chest hurts and sometimes I need to cough."

Zoe heard shuffling and the next time she spoke the girl was very close. Zoe reached out and touched a cool arm, then ran her hand down to take the girl's hand in hers.

"Someone will be here soon, Cammy. I came to take you home."

Cammy's voice came back as a whisper. "But those people won't let us leave. I think the air's turned off. Or it can't blow in anymore. They're awful people. I hope the police catch them. I'll go to court against them. I promise I will."

"We've been looking for you. So many friends and neighbors. Your mother was in this very clearing yesterday."

"I heard her voice. But then I hear her voice a lot and I didn't believe it was really her."

Zoe heard a snuffling beside her and squeezed the hand again.

"How will they know where we are? The man saw you and he saw me and he closed the door."

"They'll know. I found it, didn't I? They will, too."

"I've got a teddy bear. I was afraid they were going to take him away from me so I hid him. I've got him with me now. He helps me. He'll help you. I know your leg was hurt."

Cammy took Zoe's arm and laid something soft and furry in it. She didn't say anything. Then she began to hum, and then to sing a lullaby.

Chapter 53

"That person down there saw you," Delia said.

"Won't matter. They'll be dead by morning." He put a hand out to push Delia to go faster up the path.

"I like that Tammy, you know," she said as she tripped in the grass, righted herself, then stopped to catch her breath. "She's a little old, but I'll bet she'd be happy to be away from that awful mother of hers. I'll bet she could be fun, too—if she wanted to be." She gave a loud laugh. "Imagine that mother wanting her girl to marry you. That's almost funny. You!"

"How can I marry? You keep me . . ."

"As it should be!" She was loud. She screamed at him, her body bent into a stiff angle, her head stuck out. "A horrible murderous creature like you."

Jenny held her breath. There was a break in the normal sounds around her. A holding of breath as the earth shivered with their footsteps. She pushed up to watch them as Nathan began to run. With no hesitation, he ran into Delia, knocking her to the ground. She fell on her face. She stuck her head up, astonished. She turned to look over her shoulder at him.

"Don't you ever . . ." Delia's face drained of color. She tried to rise. "I will call the police as soon as we get back to Chicago. I swear I will, Nathan. And leaving that girl beside the road . . . Why? With all these woods? It's time you paid for what you do and I will see that I'm the one who tells."

"Shut up!" He screamed and kicked her in the head, a sound that came to Jenny with a sickening cracking noise. And Delia wailed. She lay on the ground and held her bleeding head in her hands. She screamed at him.

And screamed at him.

With blood inching down the side of her face, Delia tried to sit up, cursing him. "Now you'll die in the electric chair. I'll make sure."

She tried to get to her feet.

Nathan stepped back, watching as if mesmerized. She put a hand out, ordering him to help her, waving at him again and again.

He didn't move. He watched. When she was almost to her feet, he ran at her, hitting her with all his force, pushing her to the ground, then standing above her, looking down.

"If I only had a knife, I'd cut your throat," he screamed above her, then fell to his knees, put his hands around her neck and squeezed until his face was bright red, his eyes were closed. He squeezed.

Chapter 54

Jenny watched as Nathan got back to his feet but didn't stand erect. He bent forward, his back arched. He turned his head one way and then the other, searching for an escape.

When Nathan heard the cars out in the road, he hunched farther until he was bent in half. For a moment he stayed absolutely still and listened, then took off running, back beyond the bomb shelter, into the woods.

Tony, the first to burst through the brush, saw Jenny standing with her hands out to him. He hobbled as fast as his legs would let him to put his arms around her, then lean back, asking, "Where is she, Jenny? Where's Zoe? That black Cadillac is out on the road. Where are they? Did they hurt her? Is Cammy alive?"

She pointed to the clearing. "She's dead, Tony." Was all she got out. "He killed her!"

"Oh, Christ!" His dark eyes got darker. "Not Zoe."

She shook her head, then pointed. "Delia. He left her there."

She was pointing as Chief Warner ran up from the road, gun in hand. He heard what she said and ran where Jenny pointed, calling over his shoulder. "Fitz called me. He told me they'd left his house."

Selma Grange was there, saying nothing, her eyes on where Chief Warner was standing over Delia Whitsome.

He knelt beside the body on the ground. "He did this, huh? Where'd he go?"

Jenny nodded toward the place where Nathan disappeared.

Ed was off his knees. He ran where Jenny pointed, disappearing into the woods.

* * *

The three of them pulled branches away from the bomb shelter. Jenny kept her eyes toward the ground, so she didn't fall. Selma and Tony worked beside her.

The metal handles were uncovered. Tony fell on his knees, groaned, and grabbed at both handles until the door gave way, the two metal sides came up, and fell to the concrete. All they could see, as they gathered around, was a green metal ladder going down. Beyond that everything was in shadowed darkness.

Jenny fell to her knees, calling into the darkness, "Zoe?"

The air coming from the hole was stale. Jenny screamed as loud as she could scream, "Zoe! Zoe! Are you down there?"

Nothing.

"Zoe!"

"I think she's sleeping, ma'am." The voice echoed. Then the voice yelled, "Can you hear me? I said the lady is down here. She fell off the ladder and hurt herself. Maybe bad."

"Cammy?" Jenny stuck her head further into the opening, trying again to see. Tony turned on a flashlight behind her, aiming it into the darkness, shining it down on a young girl's face. She sat on the bottom step, looking at them.

"Yes, ma'am. It's me. I don't know how you're going to get Miss Zola out of here. Maybe a rope or maybe you . . ." She covered her eyes against the light and pointed at Tony. "Maybe you can carry her. She's pretty small, for a fully grown woman."

There was another voice, but unintelligible. The girl looked over to one side of the empty space around them. "Somebody's here," she said. "There's a big man who can carry you."

"Zoe!" Jenny called again but was pushed aside by Tony who shoved the flashlight into her hands as he jumped down through the hole, swearing as he got down the ladder and hit bottom. He blocked the light while he talked to someone in the dark.

"About time!" A weak voice complained from below. "Where the hell have you people been? I'm down here with a broken leg . . ."

"Tell Selma to call an ambulance from Ed's car," Tony shouted up, over his shoulder. "And more cops."

There was an echo around his words.

Cammy called up at Jenny, coughing, "I hope you brought us a sandwich! Me and Miss Zoe are really, really hungry. Can I go home and see my mother now?"

Chapter 55

In the spirit of ecumenism, both of the Reverend's Senise officiated at Janice's funeral: Everett, with his loving wife, Elizabeth, beaming up at him, tears in her eyes throughout; and his twin, Robert, beside him. His wife and their seven children lined down a pew and a half, behind Sally and Jay Root, then Pamela Otis and Cammy.

Jay and Sally huddled together. Sally kept her head on Jay's shoulder throughout the ceremony, her eyes closed. She looked at no one afterward, not any of the neighbors coming up to give them a healing word; not anyone wishing them well, not anyone who said how much they'd loved Janice. Jay nodded to everyone, tears in his eyes throughout. He was gracious, holding his wife until she seemed to be sleeping against his shoulder.

Zoe, in a cast and on child's crutches, was helped into a pew by Fitzwilliam Dillon. He sat beside her, leaning to ask, in a whisper, if she was comfortable. Zoe frowned at him, bit her lip, and only whispered back: "Fine, thank you."

Dora Weston and Jenny, with Tony behind her, followed the others into the pew. Dora relaxed back with a huge sigh. So much unhappiness and yet, underneath, she was happy. Lisa sat near the back of the church. Both of her girls were home.

Myrtle, who closed the restaurant for the day—a thing unheard of in town history—sat between her waitresses: Delaware and Demeter. She wore a green floppy hat that half-hid her eyes as she nervously glanced back and forth at the crowd around her, and once reached out to take Delaware's arm for support.

Near the back the whole Roach family took a pew: Harold, his wife, their boys, the boys' wives, and a couple of granddaughters. Harold said to neighbors that he felt compelled to be there. He was the one who found her, after all. Harold looked down the pew at his children and was thankful for every one of them—no matter how they got there.

In another pew, seated next to Kent Miller and his mother, Charles Bingman settled in beside a friend of his, a good-looking man introduced around as Archie Nicely. Gladys Bonney tried to put Tammy between the two men but Charles steered Tammy down to where the town druggist, Clyde Harrington, sat. Clyde graciously moved over to make room for one of his favorite people. She smiled at him, grateful to be saved another moment close to those men from the mansion.

When the celebration of Janice Root's life was over, the two ministers turned to the assembled crowd and, holding hands, raised them above their heads, saying only, "Go in peace."

One by one the people filed out around the open casket, standing in the middle aisle. The people blew kisses to the dead child in her pretty blue dress. Last to come up, because they'd been waiting for the crowd to clear, were Pamela and Cammy Otis.

Looking down at Janice, Cammy pulled a one-eyed teddy bear from under her jacket, and slipped it into the casket, into Janice's hand. She smiled at both of them.

Mother and daughter joined the others, walking out of the church holding hands.

On the lawn, waiting for the casket to be rolled out, Jenny reached to take Tony's arm, helping him where the grass sloped down to the street. He squeezed her hand and pulled her close.

Just that morning, Jenny'd heard she'd gotten a job in Traverse City. A very good law firm. She would stay in Bear Falls.

When she looked at him—the rough and gentle man—he grinned at her.

She would tell him about the job later, when they were alone, though he already seemed to know.

Epilogue

June twenty-fourth was glorious, with sunshine and a spotless blue sky. Lake Michigan was spread out in front of Rosings—a wide sheet of ruffled water. The mansion was at its best, the grounds changed from sand sculptures to sinuous flower beds with a stately fairy placed here and there among the flowering trees and rhododendrons.

People flowed back and forth through the downstairs rooms of the mansion, exclaiming as they found something wonderful in each of the twelve rooms. In the long great hall eight tables, with pretty maids in a row behind them, offered shrimp and salmon, lunch meats and cheeses with crusty rolls to put them on, and lobster spreads and pates—each with a tiny silver knife. There were surprises wrapped in pastry that everyone tasted then argued over the ingredients, especially Myrtle, Demeter, and Delaware after Myrtle said she might add things like those to her menu and both women told her to stick to meatloaf.

A few of the rooms were filled with nothing but local wines and craft beers, pop, and waters. There were bottles of something called "Liquors" and, of course, tea—not mimosa, and coffee.

In other rooms there were hams, studded with cloves and baked in Vernor's Ginger Ale, huge roast beefs, and platters of sausages.

There was what everyone called The U.P. Room with turkiettas from Elmer's Market in Escanaba; and pasties from Lehtos; Trenary toast from Trenary; and Cudighi from Vangos Pizzas in Marquette.

Three rooms held desserts. One with pies. One with cakes. And one—very cold to walk into—with tiny pastries and ice creams, molded into princesses and superheroes, for the children. And, of course, there was a special, small table for Gladys Bonney's blueberry cobbler, where Gladys hovered, taking note of who did and who did not want a piece of her renowned dessert.

Jenny, her black hair cut neatly to her shoulders, took Tony's arm as they walked through the rooms, admiring the feast, but too full after the Great Hall to eat any more. They strolled from the house down to the beach where they stood off alone, away from the swimming children and the six-foot tall lifeguard in a Spider-Man bathing suit and cape.

Being engaged was new to both of them. His answer to her news was to propose. "Let's get married," he'd said as if it was all settled.

Jenny said yes, adding, "I love you, but I still need time to get used to who I am now."

He agreed. "But not too long, Jenny. Not too long."

On the front law, a huge white tent with a proper stage at its center, was erected and filled with folding chairs. At six everyone was to gather there for a special announcement so, of course, there was much speculation as to what this announcement could be, with the women betting there would soon be a wedding between Zoe Zola and Fitzwilliam Dillon, though others, who had watched the two arguing in Myrtle's, didn't think that would happen.

Zoe, whose leg was healed well enough to walk around the house and grounds on Fitz's arm, wouldn't give even a hint of what Fitz's special announcement was, though asked again and again by Dora and Jenny.

* * *

Tony and Jenny, in lawn chairs set in front of the house, leaned in to suggest the secret was that Dianna Moon was engaged to Jefferson Firestone, Fitz's gardener. Minnie, in a chair behind then, wearing an oddly muted blue dress, tapped Tony's back to say Dianna had already eloped. "I'm going to be a grandmother. Can you believe it?" Her wide smile was genuine.

Candace Moon, Minnie's youngest, said she bet Charles Bing-man was getting married to one or the other of those girlfriends of his. Either to that Lady Barnabus, the one who looked like she just ate a canary, or worse, to Mary Smith, who wore a perfume that could make your nose wrinkle up and was a bigger flirt than Dianna Moon.

Which, Candace added, nose in the air, would serve him right for passing on Dianna, who would have loved living in the mansion and being rich, and being very nice to her little sister, which is what Candace and Minnie both thought she deserved.

Tammy Bonney and Clyde Harrington, his drugstore closed for the day, walked arm in arm along the beach discussing Tammy's painted tiles and how they would sell well in his pharmacy. He suggested that she give classes at the back of the store. Tammy smiled up at him, batted her eyelashes, and said she just loved his ideas.

When Chief Ed Warner arrived in his dress uniform, along with his wife, Lizzie, everyone had questions.

"Her body was sent to Chicago for burial, ma'am." He politely answered Vera Wattles question about Delia Thurgood.

"Charged with murder and kidnapping." He turned to Johnny Arlen, who asked what that crazy murderer was facing.

"Yup." He nodded to Selma Grange. "Fingerprint on the button belonged to Delia. Guess she's the one ought to be charged, but she's dead. We got him on two murders. Probably killed his little sister, too, but I don't think we'll ever know for sure."

He turned to Priscilla Manus. "Those dresses went back to something Delia's little sister used to wear. Guess Delia had them made in Chicago. Nathan said their mother dressed Mandy in 'em,"

"Should give 'im the electric chair," Dianna called from where she stood with her arm linked through Jefferson Firestone's.

Minnie leaned back to assure Jefferson, with a wide smile, that her daughter didn't mean it. "Don't know what's got into her. Dianna's usually such a quiet thing."

She lowered her head and mumbled toward Dianna, "We don't electrocute in Michigan. Jefferson's going to think you're dumb. Better watch your Ps and Qs. You're going to New Haven, you know."

"Well, anyway, they should do something awful to him." Dianna smiled big at Jefferson, wiggling her bottom closer to his.

* * *

There was a stir when word spread that Pamela and Cammy were there, along with Cammy's friend Kent Miller. Then came a push to be the first to hug Cammy. When Cammy got tired of being hugged, she headed for Jenny giving her a kiss on the cheek and showing her that the blue pendant was back in place. Kent stood beside her, holding her hand.

* * *

Most of the food was gone by six. Kids were tired of swimming and were wrapped in towels, sitting beside Spider-Man, who told them stories of saving kids in far off places where he would take a gun and kill the bad guys who tried to blow his head off . . .

Which brought the mothers running to reclaim their kids and take them off to quieter pursuits like playing video games.

At six o'clock an announcement was made that the meeting in the white tent was about to begin. The announcement was preceded by a chorus of bells to attract the attention of everyone, finishing the last of the food, or on the beach playing volleyball, or on the terraces where most of the ladies sat talking about how summer was predicted to be a hot one, and how last year the Thompson's lawn burned right up, and how the Evangelical Church was sponsoring a potluck supper next Friday.

At six thirty, with everyone crowded into the tent, Keith Robbins took the stage and raised his hands for attention. He introduced Fitzwilliam Dillon, who took Zoe Zola's arm, bringing her up from her chair to stand beside him on the stage.

Fitz raised his short arms to stop the applause. When the crowd was properly quieted, he began by saying things from his heart—how sorry he was he'd ever brought those people to Bear Falls; how his dad thought he owed them something, he never knew what. And . . .

But Johnny Caulfield, in the last row, yelled, "Stand up, Fitz. Can't see you."

There was nervous laughter. Fitz looked down into the faces of his neighbors—one after the other—and said to all of them. "Just want you to know I'm staying in Bear Falls, despite idiots like Johnny back there."

More laughter.

"Now let's get going on the really big news." He looked around then motioned Zoe closer. A few people exchanged satisfied looks. They'd been right after all.

With Zoe next to Fitz, he raised a glass of champagne that had been handed to him.

"To Zoe Zola," he said, smiling at her. "To my new friend. And to her completed book: *Caged: Jane Austen and Marriage.* Written under difficult circumstances, she assures me, but soon, I hope, to be a best seller."

Fitz next called for Charles Bingman to come up on stage. Charles was all smiles as he jumped to the stage, energetically waving to people in the crowd.

"Got more happy news," Fitz leaned in to say into the microphone. "Charles let me know only this morning that he's getting married in the fall."

Applause all around and a few cheers.

Women in the know looked back to where Lady Barnabus stood with Mary Smith, each giving the other false smiles and dagger eyes. Some looked to Tammy Bonney. They no longer bothered with Dianna Moon.

Men in the back of the room put down quick bets on which of the lot had snagged Charlie.

"I'd like to introduce you all to my partner, who's agreed to make me the happiest man in the world." Charles, still all smiles, towered over Fitz as he waved to the front row.

"Come on up." he called again, encouraging his friend, Archie Nicely, to stand, turn to wave, then bound on to the stage to take his place beside Charles, who leaned close and gave him a kiss on the cheek.

"He's just returned from Rwanda," Charles yelled. "My dear love feeds the masses."

Charles beamed at his intended.

The crowd went wild.

Fitz was back, clapping and beaming. "And now a decision on the two million dollars set aside to improve Bear Falls," he said into the microphone.

There was a gasp. People, who didn't remember voting, looked around to see who could possibly have made the decision for them. Fitz motioned Jay and Sally Root up to one side of the microphone. They came up the steps reluctantly, standing beside Pamela, Cammy, and Kent Miller

A gentleman from the local Rotary Club was introduced first. He stood looking around at the huge audience, then around at Sally and Jay Root. His message was that in Janice's name a new recipient was chosen to receive the Rotary Scholarship for the year. He turned to Kent Miller, calling him over to receive the official envelope. Again, great applause.

Fitz, smiling, but very serious now, was back.

"Ladies and gentlemen," he began. "It's been decided that the best thing for Bear Falls, now and in the future, would be a program to guarantee scholarships for every child of Bear Falls, to any school they wish to attend, in any profession. The program will be self-sustaining through investments."

He cleared his throat. "We are calling it: The Janice Root Guaranteed Scholarship Program."

Now there was wild applause. Sally and Jay Root held each other and smiled out at the people.

Fitz raised his arms again. "I take great pleasure in introducing to you our first awarded scholarship recipient. Camille Otis. She's chosen Michigan State University. Her degree will be in forestry."

* * *

It was a satisfying day. At the end everyone was overfull and overexcited, and pleased with how the gift to their town had worked out.

Women, especially, gathered around Zoe and her friends, leaning in to congratulate her on her latest book.

A little drunk, and a lot happy, and then a lot sad—all at the same time, Zoe looked up at her circle of friends. To thank them.

"How'd you ever handle a book like that?" Minnie looked around at the other ladies. "From what I hear, that Jane Austen wrote about terrible women, all they want to do is marry off their daughters for a lot of money. Can you imagine a mother acting like that? Why me— I'm completely happy with the man Dianna picked out, all by herself. Never catch me trying to fix my daughter up with a rich man. What woman does that in these modern times?"

"Nobody," said Gladys Bonney, turning to smile at Tammy, who was holding Clyde Harrington's hand.

"Why, that's not even civilized," Gladys went on. "Like giving a precious daughter to the highest bidder."

"Sure glad we don't live in those times," Dianna rolled her eyes up to Jefferson and smiled.

"That Jane Austen would never recognize a place as advanced as Bear Falls, Michigan," Minnie Moon laughed along with the others.

Zoe turned to Dora, and then to Jenny. They kept their faces straight as, around them, women laughed, congratulating themselves on being nothing like the women of *Pride and Prejudice*.